THE DEADLINE
IS MURDER

◼

Dragan unrolled a small segment of the tape and held it up for Suzanne. She leaned forward, hands on her thighs, and Dragan stepped back again. "Put your hands behind your back."

"Don't be ridiculous," she replied in a nervous voice. Instead of complying, she folded her arms across her chest. Dragan stepped forward, holding part of the yellow paper tape unrolled so that she could see it. She squinted.

"Okay," Dragan announced, "tell me what you see. You see your number, don't you? Sixteen. You set this story, didn't you? You set it the night Blasingame was killed didn't you?"

She was silent.

Dragan softened his voice. Dangling the tape from one hand, he placed his other hand on Suzanne's shoulder. "Miss Quering," he said, "this is your tape isn't it? You set it very early Tuesday morning, October 4—the Tuesday morning Ralph Blasingame fell into the presses. In fact, you set it after he fell into the presses, didn't you? That same evening, you lost your silk scarf—the scarf that Blasingame had given you. Admit it," he encouraged.

"It's my number," she answered softly. "It's number sixteen. But I didn't set that story. I didn't punch that tape."

DIRTY PROOF

BARBARA GREGORICH

PAGEANT BOOKS

PAGEANT BOOKS
225 Park Avenue South
New York, New York 10003

Cover artwork by Franco Accornero

Printed in the U.S.A.

First Pageant Books printing: September, 1988

10 9 8 7 6 5 4 3 2 1

For my mother and father,
and in memory of
my brother, Mark

DIRTY PROOF

Chapter One

■

Chicago,   October 1978

SHE WRENCHED THE door open as if doorknobs were disposable, nuisances rather than aids. I flinched, scattering a handful of index cards across my desk. Of course, I didn't know it was a she when the doorknob clattered, so I'm not telling the story in its proper sequence. But what burst in was a she, very definitely.

"Are you Frank Dragovic?" she asked before I could say hello, yell for help, or retrieve my scattered cards. Then she gave the room a slow once-over. Perhaps she was expecting a better-looking office, with a more successful-looking detective in it.

"Yes, I am," I replied, admiring her mass of dark red hair.

"I'm Suzanne Quering," she said, striding up to

1

the desk and extending her hand. She had beat me to the punch twice now. As I stood, I pushed back my old oak desk chair, which would never roll smoothly when I wanted it to. Her hand was warm and her grip strong.

"I need help." Her next words tumbled out before I'd even had a chance to offer her a seat or sit back down. "Have a chair," I offered, waving my hand at one of the two extra chairs in my office as I sat back down.

Instead of taking the chair, she continued to stare at me.

"Help with what?" I asked.

She hesitated, then finally sat. "I think somebody's trying to frame me." She gripped the arms of the old oak chair with such force that her knuckles turned white.

"For what?" I asked after a pause.

She swallowed. "Murder . . . is there anything else people get framed for?"

I shrugged. "Embezzlement. Theft. Bribery . . . Whose murder?"

She swallowed again. "Ralph Blasingame. Do you know about it?"

Everybody in Chicago who read the papers knew about it. Ralph Blasingame was one of thousands of young business executives in the Windy City—which is another way of saying that before last week, hardly anyone had heard of him. Blasingame might have been well on the way to becoming, someday, a gray-haired editor of the *Chicago Truth-Examiner,* a newspaper whose mergered past had coined an interesting name. In Chicago we called it simply the *Truth*—some of us more seriously than others. But now Blasingame would never become its editor. All I knew about his death was what had appeared in the papers. Late one night—Monday night (or rather Tuesday morning), exactly a week ago—Blasingame had been at the *Truth,* up on the fourth-floor catwalk, watching the presses run the 2 A.M. Tuesday release. Blasingame came out with his edition—fell over the railing and was mangled by the presses. Not a pretty death.

"The papers say it was an accident."

"I *know* what the papers say," Suzanne Quering replied in an annoyed tone. "I *set* what the papers say. The fact is that whatever the papers say, the police think it was . . . murder." This was the second time she had trouble getting that particular word out. "They keep asking me questions."

"The police always ask questions. It makes them feel good. You still haven't explained what makes you think somebody is trying to frame you." I watched her as I talked. The case, or potential case, was looking interesting already. The average person involved in a murder case doesn't think somebody is out to frame him, or her. And this wasn't a murder case. At least not yet.

But it was more interesting than that, even. Despite what you see in movies, the clients of private detectives seldom live up to their glamorous image. Don't get me wrong. Suzanne Quering wasn't glamorous. That would have been the wrong word to describe her. She was beautiful. Her face had strength, character. Her red hair was thick and glossy, long and wavy. Her eyes were gray. And from where I was sitting, the rest of her looked just as perfect. I readjusted myself in the chair.

She was scraping a thumb along the arm of the chair, as if concentrating hard. Pulling a sliver of wood out of the arm, she twirled it in her fingers. Then she looked up at me and began to talk.

"There are two reasons. I work in the composing room. I typeset the articles that appear in the paper. On the night that . . . on that night, I was working the nine o'clock shift. Somebody—not me —set a story that came out dirty. The proof was dirty, all full of errors. I'm a very good typesetter. I make *mistakes*, but I don't set dirty proofs. My slug was at the top of the galley." She stopped and sighed, toying with the old oak chair. There was no point in interrupting her: I had the feeling she would tell me what I had to know.

"I did not set that story. I don't know who did, and I don't know how my slug got on it; but I did not set it. But . . . the police think it means I . . . pushed Ralph into the presses, and it upset me so much that I wasn't myself and so I set a dirty proof," she finished in a rush.

The name had said it all. She didn't have to go on. But she did.

"I . . . I mean *we,* had been lovers. No, that's wrong. We had had an affair. While he was married. He still is. I mean was. I guess the police think I killed him out of jealousy, or spite, or something, who knows what they think," she finished in another rush. She looked at me, her head tilted back and her chin defiant. She hadn't been in the room for five minutes and had already caused me to scatter my case index cards and emotions everywhere. I never knew Blasingame, and here I was already not liking him. Pushing aside my index cards (whose cases were looking less and less interesting), I pulled open the center drawer of my desk, grabbed a handful of paperclips, and began to arrange them in even rows along the desktop.

"So you think that somebody deliberately put your slug—what is that, a name?—"

"A number."

"—on a story full of mistakes?"

"Yes. But with a purpose."

"I was getting there. For the purpose of calling attention to you."

"Yes."

"The police keep asking you about this dirty copy?"

"Dirty proof, it's called. The copy is what comes down from the reporters. The proof is the typeset story. The *Truth* was supposed to convert to floppy disks a year ago, but still hasn't. None of this would have happened, then. Yes. They ask me every day. And they're asking everybody I work with. I'm a sub, and I work only when a regular hires me. All of a sudden, here comes a weekend, and I don't get a single hire. Am I supposed to believe that it's just a coincidence that I didn't get a hire Friday, Saturday, or Sunday?" Her clenched fist pounded the arm of the chair.

I wondered what a floppy disk was. I wondered whether she was more indignant about losing work or about losing her reputation. I also wondered whether my chair would survive her visit. As I watched her, she pulled a splinter out of her finger, then sucked on the finger. "You should sand down this chair," she advised. "It could look really—" Her face turned red. Possibly she thought she had committed a gaffe. She looked beyond me, out the window, until her flush subsided.

"Did you have any motive for killing Blasingame?"

"*No! I'm* the one who broke it off. What reason could I have? My god, I couldn't *kill* somebody.

Not in cold blood. I mean," she explained, "I couldn't *murder* anybody!" She shuddered. "I didn't hate him."

"You still loved him?"

She gasped—certainly a strange reaction to my question. "No. I didn't. I didn't love him, and I didn't hate him," she replied evenly. "I didn't like him, either. I don't know what that leaves. It's kind of hard, you know, to find a word for feelings that used to be, that you thought were one thing, but then . . . then. . . ." Her words trailed off. She simply stopped and looked at me.

It was also hard to find a word for feelings that yet weren't. I certainly couldn't put a name to them. I wanted to believe her. You always want to believe your clients. That's part of the problem, separating the wanting-to from the believing. Her denial of wanting to kill Blasingame had been vehement. Was it the vehemence of innocence, guilt, or simply fear?

"Blasingame had been your lover. He fell, or was pushed, into the presses. You think that somebody put your slug on a dirty proof that same evening. What's the second reason you think that somebody's trying to frame you?"

"He . . . they . . . I . . . ." She shook her head in anger. "Somebody . . . some*how,* I mean, a silk scarf was found with . . . Ralph's body."

I stared at her, knowing what was coming, wondering by what strange quirk of thinking she saw it fit to list the dirty proof and the silk scarf as equal reasons. "The scarf is yours," I stated.

Suzanne Quering sighed. "I don't know. It's all covered with ink. And blood. It could have been a brand new scarf that Ralph bought. To give to somebody."

"But you had one like it?"

She nodded.

"And Blasingame had given it to you."

She grimaced. "Yes."

"And where is your scarf?"

She shrugged. "That's the thing. I don't know. You see, what if somebody took mine?"

I saw, all right. I saw that what she needed was a lawyer, not a detective. But when I told her so, she shook her head.

"No. I can't afford both a lawyer and a detective. If I hire a lawyer, the lawyer will hire a detective, right?"

I nodded my head.

She continued. "Then I'd have to pay for both the lawyer and the detective. Why can't I just pay you?"

I tried to explain why it was important for her to have a lawyer, but she was adamant. Stymied, I told her my terms. "The fee is two hundred dollars a day, plus expenses."

She gulped, but that was all.

I took it as acceptance. Studying her, I asked, "Did you do it?"

She looked astonished. "No! I didn't. I told you— somebody is trying to frame me."

Sweeping the paperclips off the desk and into the drawer, I made up my mind. I gathered the index cards and stacked them. "Okay. All right. I can go to the police and see what they have. I'll see what I can find out."

"That's all?"

"That's all for the time being," I replied. What was she expecting, some Mike Hammer threats or Nero Wolfe ponderings? "I can't clear you of a frameup unless you're charged with murder. And I don't think you want that, do you?" I could have bit my tongue, it sounded so patronizing.

If she recognized it, she ignored it. "I don't want you to clear me. That's negative. I want something positive. I want you to find out who killed Ralph—if he was killed. That way, I'll automatically be cleared."

I stared at her. She merely wanted me to discover who had killed Ralph. That's all. A mere nothing.

I probably mumbled something indicating I would try my best. Then I took a retainer fee, as well as her address and phone number. She shook my hand and left.

I sat in my chair a long time, rubbing the finish and wondering about Suzanne Quering.

Chapter Two

■

I KEPT WONDERING about Suzanne Quering. What would she look like when she smiled? She had a small gap between her two front teeth. I wanted to see her smile. I also, of course, wanted to know more about her.

She had come to see me at 9:30 Tuesday morning. The earliness of the visit was unusual. People who have need of private detectives seldom seem to pay morning visits. A morning case was as good as an evening case, however, so I wrote "Quering" on a new index card and alphabetized it into my card stack. The crisp new card fell right behind the dog-eared Petkovich card—the oldest case in my file. Still unsolved. Pushing aside thoughts of the old case, I sat and thought. And thought. I even examined the splintered arm of the oak chair. Maybe, I thought, I should sand it down. Later.

I said I wanted to believe her. Totally. One hundred percent. So far, I believed her, say, fifty percent. That was because I hadn't checked her out yet. But I wanted to believe her without having to run a check. That's the dilemma a detective is always in. Does he believe because his instincts are keenly honed and finely tuned? Does he believe simply because he wants to? Or does he believe because all the facts make him believe? If it was desire that was making me want to believe, my fifty percent might be worth, say, ten percent.

Standing, I shook my head, as if trying to clear it. Walking to the window, I looked down on Rush Street. It had been a long time since anybody had aroused so many thoughts and emotions in me so suddenly. That's the problem with lonely jobs: they're conducive to fantasizing—a grave mistake in the detective business. Turning away from the window, I grabbed my tweed sport coat and walked down the two flights of stairs.

What did I know about her? Nothing. I shouldered my way past two male homosexuals who gave me the once-over. It used to annoy me. At one time I even thought of having a special T-shirt printed: DON'T LOOK AT ME, MAN. Clever, I thought. But what if they didn't get it? Besides, what would clients think? I dropped the thought and put up with the occasional stares.

The fall day was crisp. Somewhere there were

crackling leaves of red, brown, and yellow to
crunch underfoot. Not in the Loop, though. The
Hawk, as we in Chicago call the wind, cut through
the streets and made people clutch their coats
more closely. The Hawk could make a ten-degree
difference between the picture world of thermom-
eters and the real world of feelings. Maybe Suzanne Quering could have the same effect, only in
reverse.

A few minutes after eleven o'clock, I entered the
revolving doors of the *Truth-Examiner*. Somehow
it didn't seem fitting to have to pass through revolving doors to get to the truth. A straight swinging door without doorknobs seemed the best bet.
Three blue-coated security guards—with badges,
billyclubs, and guns—patrolled the spotless hallways. I went up to the guard who sat behind an
imposing circular desk. "Could you tell Marcia
Paxton that Frank Dragovic would like to see her?
The extension is 2201."

Marcia would be in. She always was. Food writ-
ers seldom got to go out and cover a hot story.
When was the last time a muffin mugged somebody in Lincoln Park?

The guard motioned me up, and I took the stairs
instead of the elevators or escalators. There were
many approaches to the *Truth*.

Marcia was waiting for me at the top of the
stairs, a tray of pastries in her hand. I smiled. Marcia hadn't changed.

"Hi, Frank. Try some. Fresh out of the oven. Coconut turnovers."

"No, thanks. I hate coconut."

"I forgot." She looked at the pastries and
frowned, then looked at me and smiled. "What
brings you here, Frank?"

I didn't love Marcia, and I didn't hate her. But I did like her. She held no grudges.

We walked back toward her desk. Yes, she had a desk and a typewriter, not just a stove with a number on it. Through the glass wall of the test kitchens, I looked out at the news room. Marcia wore a pale blue dress that swished as she walked. Around her neck was a string of pearls. I thought she looked like the perfect hostess. Not answering her question, I leaned against the top of her desk and crossed my legs at the ankles, every inch nonchalance. "Why don't you grab your coat and we can grab lunch? It's early, but we can have a drink anyway."

Off she went to check with her editor. Apparently nothing big was cooking because she came back with her coat. We took the elevator down.

We had often gone to a nearby Polynesian restaurant, and it seemed natural to keep things the same even though everything was different. Some food critics call Polynesian food a pseudo-cuisine. Marcia wasn't one of those; and me, I draw the line at pseudo-foods, not pseudo-cuisines.

We sat in wicker chairs at a small wicker table. An outrigger hung above our heads. Amid the dripping water fountains, the Japanese fishing bubbles, and the puffer fish, we ordered our drinks. As we exchanged small talk, I looked for an opening to steer the conversation around to Blasingame. It came and I did.

According to Marcia, Blasingame was about what I had surmised from the newspapers. Already second vice president and director of sales and marketing, he could have been, given another ten years, head honcho—president and publisher.

"He wanted to be, you could tell that," com-

mented Marcia, sipping something orangish-pink
from a wide-mouthed, tall-stemmed glass. I could
smell the coconut in the drink.

"Power hungry?"

"I guess so. Everybody thought he was arro-
gant."

"Hmmm. Still, it's an awful way to go. What's
the safety record at the *Truth?*"

"Golly, Frank, I don't know. What do you mean?
Accidents and that?"

Maybe she thought I meant burns in the kitchen.
"Sure. It seems unsafe to have an easily accessible
catwalk. What was he doing up there anyway?"

"I don't know. Visitors take tours of the presses
all the time. We have tours twice a day. But the
only time I've ever seen the presses is from behind
the glass walls. Maybe that's where the editors
watch from, those catwalks."

I doubted it. The walks were probably for the
mechanics. "Oh yeah? You never took me on a
tour," I jested.

"That's not true! I showed you the test kitchens
many times."

"Marcia, Marcia. A newspaper is a lot more than
test kitchens." It might have developed into another one of our old arguments, the news versus
the features, but I stopped myself. "Who'll take
Blasingame's place?"

She stopped sipping and looked at me. "Why do
you want to know?"

"Just curious. You know how detectives are."

"You don't think he was . . . killed, do you?"
she asked, her eyes widening.

"Golly," I mocked, "do *you* think he was killed?"

"Gosh, I don't know. I've heard some talk about

it. The police keep coming around and asking questions."

I leaned forward. "Oh yeah? Have they asked you any?"

"No, but I heard they've been in Gayle's office almost every day, and Ted's, too."

"Who are they?"

"Don't you read the papers?" she admonished. "Gayle Blasingame is Ralph's wife. Widow, I mean. Either she or Ted Haapala—they're both associate editors—will probably be promoted to take Ralph's place. Or maybe they'll bring in somebody from the outside."

I didn't remember the names. Most certainly the name of the widow must have been mentioned, but it meant nothing to me at the time.

"Are you working on a case?" Marcia asked. She leaned over the table and inquired in a confidential whisper, "Did Gayle hire you? Are you working for Ted? Is anybody under suspicion?"

"Marcia, how can I be working on a case? The papers said it was an accident."

"Oh. I thought maybe you were."

Sometimes I hated myself. Evasions were so easy to use, so difficult to spot. That's what I hated. What I wanted was someone who would spot the evasion for what it was. "So," I continued, "you think maybe the police suspect the widow or this Haapala, the successors?"

"Only one of them could be the successor, Frank."

The waiter arrived to take the order, and after perfunctory studies of the menu, we ordered the special platters, same as usual.

"Marcia," I coaxed, "imagine yourself a detective. That's kind of what you might be, sitting there, watching the police parade past, into the offices of the would-be successors. If you were a detective, what question would you ask yourself?"

She gave me a superior smile, indicating that she knew I was leading her on. "Motive, of course. What would be the motive, if it was murder."

I smiled. "Well?"

"Well," she said, dropping her voice, "Ted *really* wanted Ralph's job. He thought he had been unfairly passed over anyway. Actually, he probably was. Ted knows a lot more about newspapers than Ralph ever did. Ralph used to be in banking. Ted's been around newspapers all his life. Ted gets along with people better, too. He should have been promoted. How's that so far?" she asked as the waiter brought our orders.

"Did he ever threaten Blasingame?" I asked, digging into the sweet and sour chicken.

"Don't be ridiculous, Frank."

"It's not ridiculous. People have been known to threaten others."

"Men, you mean, not people."

"Women make threats, too. What motive would his wife have had?"

Marcia opened her mouth to speak, then stopped. Instead of speaking, she took a bite of food. Then another.

"Well?"

"This is silly. I'm not a detective. I'm a feature writer—even though that's what women are pushed into writing about. Features: human interest, food, culture. And Gayle Blasingame wouldn't have killed Ralph. She's—"

I stared at Marcia as if a new person had just materialized inside her. "Marcia—are you . . . discontent with writing food articles?"

She laughed nervously. "I know it sounds strange, doesn't it? But, well, yes, I am. That's why Gayle—" Again she stopped.

"Yes?" I encouraged. "What about Gayle Blasingame?"

"She's helping me, Frank. I've asked the city editor many times to be transferred to news—to straight reporting. But he always finds an excuse to not do it. So . . . well, I kind of went over his head, to Gayle. She's helping me."

"That's great," I replied. "I'll look for your name in the front section." Finishing my chicken, I thought about how happy Marcia must feel. "What are you covering?" I asked.

When she didn't answer, I looked up.

"I can't tell you, Frank. In fact, I shouldn't have told you as much as I did. But I had to let you know that Gayle . . . well, she wouldn't do anything like kill her husband."

I tried to sidle up to the topic of motives in other ways, but it was no use. Marcia had clammed up as sure as a clam bisque, bake, burgoo, or whatever other clam concoction would have come out of the test kitchens.

Still, I reflected after I paid the bill and we walked back to the *Truth*, I now knew the police were visiting the offices of Gayle Blasingame and Ted Haapala "almost every day" according to Marcia. That might be a good sign for my client—who may or may not have owned the silk scarf that was found with Blasingame in the presses. It seemed unlikely, though, that the police believed Blasingame's fall was accidental. *That* made it bad for my client.

I escorted Marcia back to the *Truth*'s kitchens. There hospitable food testers offered me a fool (I was told that was a dessert, not a person), a dowdy (likewise not a person), and a nine-layer crepe dessert—each layer filled with a different sweet. Refusing them all, I reflected that the *Truth*'s sugar bill must be enormous.

Back downstairs with the three blue-coated guardians, I asked for the schedule of the *Truth* tours. Since the next one started in half an hour, I decided to wait.

Chapter Three

THE TOUR BEGAN in the public relations office. It seemed strange to me that, having close to a hundred pages of newspaper available every day, the *Truth* still needed a special department for public relations. There were only eleven of us in the group: four who looked like teenagers, six who looked like the sixty-plus generation, and me. First we were shown a twenty-minute movie history of the *Truth-Examiner*. The paper traced its pulpy roots back to the 1870s, when it was the *Chicago Call*. In the 1880s a rival newspaper, the *Herald*, was started. In the late 1890s both the *Truth* and the *Examiner* were born, gracing Chicago with four major dailies. By the late 1930s the *Truth* had purchased the *Herald*, and in 1947 the *Examiner* bought out the *Call*. So we had the *Truth-Herald* and the *Examiner-Call*. I'm sure you're with me so far. These historic mergers were easy to understand because each of the newspapers had its own building (all still standing), and the camera zoomed in on the nameplate of each building. Heavy stuff.

By the late 1950s the *Examiner-Call* was in deep financial trouble, so the *Truth-Herald* bought it out. That meant presses, reporters, typesetters, everything. Each merger must have put people from both papers out of work, but the movie didn't mention that. The *Truth-Examiner* was presented as the culmination of a particular historical process. What remained was new and, therefore, good.

Snapping the overhead lights back on, the tour director talked about the things we would see as she took us through the building.

"Will we get to see the area where type is set?" I asked, still blinking from the sudden glare of lights.

"I'm sorry," she replied, "but we don't take tours through the composing room. It would be too distracting. We will get to see the area where the *new* composing room is being built, though."

So. I wouldn't get to see the area where Suzanne Quering worked.

As I thought about that, the guide took us through the newsroom and editorial offices, pointing out something called the city desk. She smiled at the reporters, many of them with typewriters and tv-like screens (terminals, the guide called them), on their desks. Apparently it was okay to distract reporters by tramping through their domain.

When we walked through the test kitchens, Marcia stared at me, her mouth slightly open. I gave a sheepish grin and a perfunctory, I hoped unnoticeable, wave of my hand. But at my back, I felt Marcia frowning at me.

I knew that particular frown well. It wasn't her frown of incomprehension, nor was it her frown of anger. It was *the* frown, the one of disapproval.

After the newsroom and test kitchens, we viewed a large area that would house the new typesetting department. With the aid of wall posters, the guide showed us what the new typewriterlike machines would look like and do. I learned that a floppy disk was the same medium I would use to store information using my home computer, if I had one. By 1980, predicted the guide, Americans would be buying small computers for home use. By 1985, she projected, tens of millions of computers would be sold; and by 1990, nearly every home would have one. I wondered briefly whether a home computer would help me solve my cases. Perhaps I could throw away my index cards altogether. Dismissing the thought, I listened to more facts about the soon-to-be typesetting department.

The culmination of the tour was the presses, and they were what I was most interested in. Up to the fourth floor we went, following the guide up one of the escalators. She zigzagged down several hallways and brought us out before thick glass walls. Below us we could see the giant printing presses, certainly no different from the kind you see in every clichéd opening of every movie about the newspaper industry. (And, I might add, the very presses that had provided the opening of the *Truth-Examiner*'s public relations film.) Proudly, the guide explained that these were web-fed rotary presses, capable of printing thousands of feet of paper per minute, with on-the-run splicing from one roll to another. The *Truth* never stopped. But the powerful presses we stared at were silent and harmless, not yet bidden to spin their giant webs of truth.

The *Truth* timed its tours impeccably: the 2:00 P.M. edition was about to run. As the guide pointed out the last of the molded plates being fitted on the presses, we waited with anticipation. At least I did. Below us the pressmen were foreshortened figures wearing newspaper hats. The unfailing guide pointed out the hats, telling us that they protected the pressmen from getting ink in their hair. In addition, she promised that when we left the vantage point of the glass walls and descended to the press floor, each of us would be given just such a hat, made by the pressmen especially for the tours.

A grayhaired pressman, hatless, ambled over to a wall and pressed a button. I caught my breath as the presses started up—slowly at first, then faster and faster, until they were nothing but clatter and a blur of motion.

While the guide spouted figures ranging from the speed of the presses, to the number of papers coming out per minute and per hour, to the circulation of the *Truth-Examiner*, I listened with only half an ear. More numbers than I cared to remember. I was concentrating on the spinning wheel of death below me, thankful I was behind glass walls.

Below us, rows of suspended lights shone from the ceilings. A maze of catwalks hugged the sides of the gigantic room, the better not to obscure the presses at work. Still, I observed, a fall from one of those catwalks *could* land you directly in the revolving wheels. You didn't stand a chance: the press would suck you up and crush the life out of you instantly. It must have been awful, not just for Blasingame, but for the pressmen below.

"What are those rails for?" I asked the guide, pointing to one of the catwalks.

"Those are used by the machinists who repair the presses and inspect them."

"Can you get a better view of the presses from there?"

She gave a nervous laugh. "Oh, we can't go there, sir. This is the only place we view the presses from."

Two of the teenagers snickered. "Where did the guy fall from?" one of them inquired, making certain to ask nobody in particular.

"Splat!" whispered his friend, and the two snickered again.

The guide, embarrassed by a member of her own generation, swallowed nervously. "It was a very unfortunate accident, and not at all the fault of the newspaper. And now," she continued, her voice shaky, "we'll go down to the ground level and see the papers as they come off the press."

If the lights on the presses shone twenty-four hours a day, it seemed unlikely that an enemy could get behind Blasingame and push him without being seen. That's the way I had sized up the situation from the top. Once down at the bottom, I was forced to add qualifications. I didn't know the exact spot Blasingame had pitched forward from, but most of the catwalk was not all that visible from the ground. I could make out the bottom of the walk and part of the railing—the rest was obscured by long, dark shadows.

"Sir, your newspaper." Thrusting a fresh newspaper into my hand, the guide seemed to want me to pay attention to her talk. I took my eyes off the catwalk and accepted the free paper. Newspapers, churning out of the presses at a rapid rate, were being mechanically folded, stacked, and carried away on a conveyor belt. One of the pressmen began passing out the newspaper hats. He wore his own at a cocky angle: it failed to cover most of his sparsely haired head. I made a point of staring intently at the catwalk as he came by.

Turning his head, he followed my gaze. "What's up there?" he bit.

"I was just wondering where that guy fell from."

The guide frowned at me. Nowhere near as effectively as Marcia.

"Up there." He pointed to a catwalk that joined two parallel walks. It ran right under and parallel to the glass wall. "Corner of that walk."

"It must have been awful for you," I sympathized.

"Not me," he answered. "Night shift."

"Was anybody up there with him?" I asked.

"Not that I heard of. All alone."

The guide was now tugging at my sleeve, having ushered the rest of the tour elsewhere. I let myself follow.

The tour took us past conveyor belts on which bundles of papers were being tied with wire, past delivery trucks, and back to the public relations room. My mind was occupied with thoughts having nothing to do with the distribution of the *Truth*. The place Blasingame fell from was the part of the catwalk most hidden from the view of the pressmen. That would support the possibility that somebody pushed him. On the other hand, once Blasingame hit the presses, it would be very difficult for anybody to come down from that catwalk unseen . . . or would it? Might everybody rush toward the presses, oblivious to somebody coming

down the catwalk and walking away? Maybe. But
it would take a very bold murderer to pull that off.

Finally, the tour was over. Leaving the public
relations room, I bumped into Marcia.

"Frank, I thought you said you weren't working
on a case." Her tone was slightly scolding.

"I didn't say exactly that, Marcia."

"Well, you let me think it, which is the same
thing. Who are you working for? Is it Gayle or
Ted? Can't you tell me?"

"No," I answered. "And it's *not* the same thing.
I've got to keep an appointment. I'll talk to you
later," I said, rapidly walking away.

Downstairs, I asked one of the guards where the
typesetting department was.

"Composing room," he corrected.

"Okay, composing room. Where is it?"

"Who do you want to see?"

"I don't want to see anybody. I want to know
where the composing room is."

"Second floor," he growled, "but you can't get in
unless you want to see somebody."

I left without thanking him and took the stairs
up to the second floor. After wandering down several dead-end hallways, one with "Personel" misspelled on the rippled glass of a dark door, I found
a doorless opening. Peering through, I saw linotype machines. (The movie *had* helped educate me
—now I knew the name of the noisy old machines
that set the type.) Stepping through the opening, I
started walking toward the machines.

"Hey!"

I turned around. Behind me, in an alcove set off
from the entrance way, was a small room with a
half-door. Leaning across it was the man who had
shouted. At first I wondered whether they had

used grease or a wedge to squeeze him in. He looked like a bear inside a mouse cage. An army fatigue tank-top shirt was all that covered his hairy upper half. Sleepy eyes peered out at me from under the fringes of blond hair hanging down his forehead.

"Whaddoyou want?" he asked, not necessarily belligerently.

"I'd like to see the composing room," I replied politely.

"You work here?" he asked.

"No."

"Only NTU members and management can come in here," he informed me.

"NTU?"

"Newspaper Typographical Union."

I walked up to him, buddy-to-buddy fashion. "You see, I just finished a tour of the *Truth,* and I wanted to see this room in particular, but they told me I couldn't."

"Right," he agreed. "Only union members are allowed here. And management. Since you ain't either, I can't let you in."

"What harm would it do to let me look around?" I reasoned.

"Can't."

"Listen," I confided. "I'm doing a paper, you know, for my Ph.D., on modern composing rooms. Isn't there somebody I can talk to to get permission to look at this room?"

"Nope."

"Now, look," I implored, "be reasonable. I came to you first. I'll bet I could get permission from a *Truth* executive."

"Then get it. Our contract states that nobody

comes in here without our permission. The floor of the composing room is ours."

I promised to walk only on the ceiling, but the hairy giant wasn't amused. I hurled a tentative insult or two, but they bounced back, their points bent. Defeated, I left, but not without telling him that I, like General MacArthur, would return.

The *Truth* had many stairs, hallways, and catwalks. Whether a murderer prowled any of them, I was no closer to knowing than when I had walked in. I walked out into the street.

Chapter Four

TAKING THE SUBWAY to the Criminal Investigation Division for the Loop area, I wondered whether I should have called first. Police detective lieutenants aren't always in. It turned out I was lucky: Dragan Brdar was in. Dragan and I were friends from way, way back—infancy, in fact. We had become friends because our parents were friends. And our respective parents were friends because they had grown up together in the same Chicago Croatian neighborhood. Ten years ago, insular America didn't know the difference between a Croatian and a Martian. Now, thanks to a few plane hijackings by Croatian terrorists who demanded Croatia's independence from the rest of Yugoslavia, more people knew what a Croatian was. Dubious progress.

Of course, with the special election of Michael Bilandic as mayor of Chicago just a few months earlier, all of Illinois got to learn that Croatians did more than hijack planes. Nobody knew yet what kind of mayor Bilandic would be, but almost everybody agreed that if the Irish had to give up the office to the Croatians, Bilandic wasn't a bad choice.

Dragan, who still lived on the southeast side, was a lieutenant in the Criminal Investigation Division of the Chicago Police Department. He had had a chance for more rapid advancement in the special unit dealing with terrorism, simply because he spoke Croatian, but he had declined it. "Frank," he had observed, "a hell of a lot more criminals speak English."

Dragan's lifelong personal mission in the police department centered around keeping the meaning of his first name a secret. Most people thought it meant "dragon." It didn't. If you were English and your last name was Dragon, it would mean dragon. Simple enough. And if you were Italian and your last name was Drago, it would mean something like "dweller-at-the-sign-of-the-dragon." But if you were a Slav and your name was Dragan, Dragomir, Dragoslav, or something similar, your name meant "love." Not love of dragons—just love.

My last name meant something very similar— "son of Drago, or son of beloved." Like Dragan, I don't enlighten people on its meaning. I do, however, insist that they pronounce it with the accent on the first syllable—Dragovic. And the c at the end of my name is pronounced ch.

"What now?" was Dragan's greeting.

"Just a little information."

"Of course. That's understood. You only come here when you want information. Why don't you just join the police force?"

Good old Dragan, he never let up. I frowned at him and he relented. "Yeah, okay. What do you want to know?"

Leaning against the windowsill, I made myself comfortable but receptive, ready to field any important facts he might throw at me. "Blasingame," I said. "Give."

When you're a detective, you have to wear a mask. You have to fit in with those you're talking to, and you can't show emotion when you're trying to get to the facts. Dragan certainly knew how to do it. But with me, his friend, he liked to loosen the mask and exaggerate the facial muscles—sort of like stretching in order to prevent tendons from snapping. His blue eyes grew rounder and wider, and he shifted in his chair.

"Well, well, Frank. You do surprise me sometimes. How'd you get into this? Who you working for? Why do you want to know?"

I laughed. "Hey, I said 'Give' first."

Dragan cupped his hand and rested his jaw in it. "That's *my* case we're talking about, Frank."

There was a long pause, as if he had said something significant. The police tend to feel possessive about their cases.

"So, what kind of case is it? Accident? Suicide?"

"You wouldn't be here if it were, would you?"

"So it's not an accident or suicide, huh?"

"Now, I didn't say that." He backed off, resettling himself in his chair, placing his elbows on the desk and making a tent of his fingertips. I knew the pose well: it was Dragan's now-I'm-going-to-give-you-the-facts pose. "It looks like an accident, sure. Not suicide. So far, no witnesses to anybody being up there on the catwalk with him. However: motive. First, the wife. She stands to inherit everything, including a whopping $600,000 double indemnity insurance payment. We can stretch a point and say she also stands to inherit his job. Second, Ted Haapala, one step below Blasingame in rank. Bitter about being passed over for Blasingame. Maybe impatient to get to the top. Third, Suzanne Quering, paramour. You could say she was jilted and furious about it." Dragan stopped and regarded me.

"Okay," I replied, crossing my arms over my chest, "that's motive. Means? Opportunity?"

"That's the problem. I think I favor the wife. Money's the strongest motivator. But she's too puny to have pushed him. Maybe Quering." Dragan studied me. "Opportunity: Quering was in the building."

"The other two weren't?"

Studying his tent of fingertips, Dragan expelled his breath loudly. "Haapala claims he was home asleep. The wife claims she left the building some time after midnight, but before the 2:00 A.M. edition. Quering's the best bet."

"That's not much to go on, Dragan. You haven't got a shred of evidence. Looks like accident is the answer. Why isn't the case closed?"

"Who says it isn't?"

"You're making trips to the newspaper to complain about home delivery, maybe?"

"There's more. There was a woman's silk scarf in the presses with Blasingame."

"Umm. Whose?"

"We aren't sure yet. But Quering had one like it."

"Who says so?"

"Everybody in the typesetting department, that's who. She's your client, isn't she?" challenged Dragan.

"How can they tell she had one like it?" I asked, sidestepping the question. "What's it look like?"

Dragan made a face. "Red, yellow, green, and gray. Sort of like a deep-dish pizza somebody ran a steamroller over." He tapped his fingertips together. "It's all smeared with ink and blood. We're working on tracing it."

"That's still not much," I argued.

"Yeah? Well, there's still more, Frankie. Quering threatened to kill him."

I straightened up but kept my arms crossed. "Who says so?" I demanded.

"Aha!" Dragan likewise straightened, thumping his desk with an open palm. "It *is* her you're working for! I knew it! We've flushed a quail, Frankie. Admit it. When did she come to you? What'd she tell you?"

"You could be jumping to a conclusion," I parried. "Maybe I'm working for one of the other two. Maybe for somebody different altogether. Maybe for *all* of them."

Dragan made a mock face of disbelief and dismissal.

Unintimidated, I continued. "I'll tell you what my job is—to discover if it was murder, and if it was, who the murderer was." I thought I sounded silly saying it, but Suzanne Quering would probably have been proud of me.

"Yeah?"

"Yeah."

"Yeah, shit. That's our job, not yours."

"There's no reason it can't be both of our jobs.

C'mon, Dragan. You can give me more than you have. What about Blasingame?"

Glaring at me, Dragan spoke grudgingly. "From all accounts, he wasn't liked. Hard to get along with. Moody. That's what everybody beneath him said. Those above liked him. Said he put in long hours, always there when you needed him. You know the things superiors like."

"How long had he been there?"

"Five years." Twirling a pencil between his fingers, Dragan studied it, then, unable to resist, pointed it at me. "Seems he married into the job."

My raised eyebrows called for elucidation.

"Rumor has it he married Mrs. Blasingame—who was then Gayle Rybak—as a way of getting into the *Truth*."

"She worked there before he did?"

"You bet. And she raised holy hell when, a few years after the wedding bells, he was promoted over her. Seems she thought that, what with her being there longer and all *and* her being a woman, she should have been promoted."

I pondered the situation. "Did he have any enemies elsewhere?"

"Worked in First City Merchants Bank before the *Truth*. As far as we could tell, he had no enemies there—certainly not any that would wait five years to push his face into death." Dragan had a way of turning a phrase now and then.

"Any threats at the *Truth*?"

"I told you, Quering threatened to kill him. No others we heard of." After a moment of silence, Dragan continued. "We can't prove that it was murder."

"Why are you trying, then?"

My question was more than casual. It wasn't just

that I was working for a client. It was more than that. The police are not eager to prove that every death in the big city—or elsewhere—is a crime. If the death is a murder, then who has to solve it? The police, of course, and they already have their hands more than full solving (or trying to solve) countless crimes. Mind you, I'm not saying that the police deliberately look the other way whenever a seemingly accidental, unexplained death occurs—just that their first instinct isn't to yell "Murder." And this holds for private detectives, too, for the same reasons. For three years before getting my license, I worked for a detective agency. We exhibited the same reluctance to prove crime, for that meant solving the case.

Dragan stood and began sorting things on his desk. "It's just me, Frank. I've got a funny feeling about this, you know? Guy shows up on the catwalk alone in the middle of the night. For what? Nobody knows. No reason for him to be there at that time. Guy's got a lot of people who don't like him, including a wife, a jilted lover, and a passed-over subordinate. Things are funny," Dragan continued, warming up to his suspicions as he rattled sheets of paper. "The jilted lover is there. Okay, it's true she was hired to work the late shift, 9:00 P.M. to 5:00 A.M. But she could have asked to be hired then, by somebody she knew usually took Monday nights off. Not hard to do. Normally she works the one o'clock or five o'clock shift. Then a scarf's found in the presses, along with the body. Quering can't produce a similar scarf that people say she owned. Then the type she set, it comes out full of mistakes. Strange. She's a looker, probably not used to being jilted. I like her for it: motive, means, opportunity." He thumped a large batch of papers together and looked at me.

"Doesn't sound like much of a case, Dragan."

"Yeah, well, if mine doesn't, neither does yours. If I'm not onto something, why are you here, huh? Don't give me that shit. Quering's your client, isn't she?"

"Who says she was jilted? Who says she threatened to kill him?"

"You know I can't tell you that, Frank."

I knew he could tell me that. He'd told me at least that much on other cases. I also knew that Dragan was being stubborn. So was I. He wasn't going to tell me who told him that Suzanne Quering threatened to kill Blasingame, and I wasn't going to tell him—yet—who I was working for. Maybe if I told him who I was working for, he'd tell me who reported the threat. Then again, maybe he wouldn't. We stood and stared at each other. Call it a Croatian standoff.

"A genuine threat?" I asked, giving in.

"Genuine."

I waited, but Dragan didn't offer any more. "It's ridiculous," I said with more vehemence than I had intended, uncrossing my arms in an angry gesture. Dragan looked at my flailing arms and raised an eyebrow. "Maybe you could miss seeing somebody go up that catwalk at 2:00 A.M., but you couldn't miss seeing *her* go up that catwalk. Don't give me that, Dragan. It's pure horseshit." Grabbing a photocube from his desk, I toyed with it, giving my hands something to do. The cube contained photos of Gloria and the kids. Dragan was a pretty good amateur photographer.

"She is a looker," replied Dragan, as if he were

agreeing with something I had said. "It depends on how she was dressed, Frankie. Red hair can be covered up. Put on a mechanic's shirt over the shirt and pants she was wearing and go up the walk as if she belonged there. It could be done."

"You aren't going to do all that, Dragan, and forget to take off some silk scarf. And I saw the catwalk. It's a fourteen-foot drop to the ground, for chrissake."

Dragan shrugged. "Next time you see her, ask her how her gymnastics are coming along. She's quite an acrobat. It wouldn't have been hard for her to swing off the rails and drop to the ground below, then step out the back door."

I returned the photo cube to Dragan's desk, my palms sweating. I didn't like all the things Suzanne Quering had not told me. I didn't like the way Dragan was thinking. I found myself wanting to throw suspicion on his other two candidates, and we hadn't even determined that it was murder.

"The wife. You said she inherits. Could be a strong motive."

"Could be. But we can't place her on the scene at 2:00 A.M. And why the hell would he go up there with his wife anyway?" He stared at me belligerently.

"Can she prove she was home?"

"At 2:00 A.M.? Alone in bed? No. And we can't prove she wasn't. Don't worry, though, we haven't given up on any of them," he relented. "Hey, listen, Frank, I haven't got any more time. Come back when you get something I can use. And watch out for the redhead."

Funny. But I didn't feel funny. I felt angry. And worried. Frowning, I glanced at my watch: 4:20. If

Suzanne Quering wasn't working some strange shift, I might find her at home. If she wasn't home, I'd get something to eat. Then I'd go back and wait until she got home. Then she'd have to answer some questions.

Chapter Five

LEAVING DRAGAN, I walked to the elevated, taking the Ravenswood line north to the Diversey stop. If you catch yourself wondering how I remembered Suzanne Quering's address, just from getting it down once in the morning, don't be impressed. It's a minor detail. Observation, memory, deduction: these are the three most important skills a detective can have. These, plus one that's even more important—tenacity. Having observed her address as I wrote it down, I now had it stored in my memory.

Notice that I call myself a detective. You're probably aware that the trend today is to call us PI's. That's Private Investigators. And that's them, not me. Have you ever noticed that all these fancy titles in the world are ego-inflating but performance-subtracting?

You see, an investigator is not the same as a detective. You can investigate until the cows come home and not detect a damned thing. True, to investigate is to inquire into systematically—to learn

the facts. And facts are important. Without facts—
those stubborn, hard burls of reality—we would
have nothing. But the facts aren't everything. What
about the context of those facts and the conclu-
sions we can draw from them? There's something
to be *detected* from facts. That something is the big
picture.

Well, I'm getting carried away. Let's get back to
investigators and detectives. If all you want are the
facts, then you want an investigator. If you want
what the facts might reveal, you want a detective.
The choice is yours. Just don't ever call me a PI.

Suzanne Quering lived on Diversey Parkway
near the lake, probably in a high rise. Though
from the number of her apartment, 410, I couldn't
be sure.

The el on Diversey is a long way from Lake
Michigan. I could have caught a bus, but I'd have
been crushed in the coming-home-from-work
crowd; so I walked. Because it was chilly out, I
quickened my pace. By the time I got to the Half
Shell, a small bar and restaurant, I was cold and
hungry. My stomach, hungry for food, told me to
stop, enter, and eat. My mind, hungry for the
whole story, told me that Suzanne Quering had
not given me all of the facts. My mind overruled
my stomach.

The building was, indeed, a high rise. Entering, I
confronted a doorman. Somewhere in Chicago
there may be doorwomen, but I haven't confronted one yet.

"Suzanne Quering, please. Apartment 410."

The doorman's eyes widened. He looked me up
and down swiftly, and I thought he might even
have smiled thinly, as if suppressing something.
But all this happened so quickly and was followed

by his "Yes, sir," that I chalked it up to my imagination, or his facial quirks. I waited while he dialed a phone number.

"She doesn't answer."

"Okay." I thrust my hands into my pockets. "I'll try later."

Food, argued my stomach. Humoring it, I walked back to the restaurant.

The Half Shell, smaller than the hallway of many houses, wasn't filled yet. I thought of ordering a drink, then reconsidered, thinking that I wanted a perfectly clear mind when talking to Suzanne Quering. Then, considering my reconsideration and realizing that she might not be home until five in the morning, I ordered a beer. After two beers I ordered the salad and the broiled shrimp and asked for a double order of french fries. Finishing with a cup of coffee, I paid the bill and headed east again. There wasn't much light left in the sky by the time I got to her building.

The doorman remembered me. As soon as I stepped into the lobby, he said, "I haven't seen her come in, sir, but I'll ring her." I waited while he looked up the number, dialed it, and pursed his lips close to the receiver. Finally, he returned the receiver to its cradle. "Still no answer."

"I'll try later," I said, feeling that I might be repeating the line all evening long. Outside, I walked around the building and tried to figure out which was her apartment. That did no good, and no lights were on in any of the fourth floor apartments anyway. Crossing two streets, I took a position diagonally across from the lobby doors. Hunching my shoulders against the wind, I backed into a small recessed doorway and waited.

Why are we standing here freezing to death in the

wind? asked my Goofus. *Why not come back to-morrow?*

Be patient, answered my Gallant patiently. *We're here to get some answers.*

Just when I was beginning to think that the Hawk was after me, personally, and that Goofus was a lot wiser than Gallant, I saw her. She was coming from the west and walking with a nice stride. A different generation would have called it a handsome stride. What the hell—I'll call it handsome, too. Although she was on her side of the street, I moved farther back into my doorway. Under the street lights, I could just make out the colors of her clothing: a brown skirt, boots, a tweed sport coat, and a red turtleneck pullover. And, around her neck, a colorful scarf. Her hair was blowing in the October wind. She looked handsome all over.

Over her shoulder was a small purse. But no fumbling for keys in the bag for Suzanne Quering. Her right hand reached inside her skirt pocket just before she got to the outside door. Transferring something (probably keys) into her left hand, she swung open the door with her right and walked into the building. I grumbled, wishing she had done something—anything—to smack of inefficiency, fumbling, or what is called femininity. Everything about her was wrong if you were trying to clear her of suspicion. She even had the wrong color hair.

My watch read 7:20. At exactly 7:25 P.M. I strode across Diversey, then Sheridan, and walked into her building.

"She's in," volunteered the doorman. "Your name?" he asked.

"Frank Dragovic."

Nodding, he dialed the number and spoke into the phone, getting my first name right. One out of two wasn't bad, I suppose.

"It's apartment 410," he announced, walking up to the glass door and unlocking it.

An elevator was waiting. I entered, punched four. When I got out she was standing in her doorway. Goddamn it! She had done the wrong thing again: changed clothes in five minutes. Now she had on Levi's, a blue sweater, and socks—no shoes.

She looked at me without a word and stepped aside for me to enter, then closed the door after herself. We stood in a large room that faced east. Off to one side was a tiny kitchen, not enclosed. Maybe three hundred fifty square feet in all.

"An efficiency," I muttered.

"They're called studios. But it's really just a room. They call them anything but a room so they can justify the price. You can't very well ask $26,000 for a room, can you?"

"You own this?"

"No, but it's going condo soon. Everything is," she declared, waving a hand to include the properties along Lake Shore Drive, the near North, and maybe even Milwaukee. What I was aware of suddenly was that the hand included a knife.

"What are you staring at?" she demanded. There may have been a challenge in the demand, a semibelligerent undertone.

"Do you always greet visitors with a knife in your hand?" I asked. No client was going to outdo me in asking questions.

"Oh." She glanced at her hand, then laughed. "That's not a knife. It's a firmer."

"A firmer what?"

"No, no. Not a firmer anything. It's a—it's a chisel. A special kind of chisel, and it's called a firmer. Instead of being called a chisel. See?" She held it out to me, her hand flat open, the tool resting on it.

I took the damn thing and examined it, twirling the thin shank between my fingers. "You could gouge somebody's eyes out with this."

She laughed again, a playful sound I enjoyed hearing. "No, that would be a gouger. They're curved. Gougers, that is." She held her hand out for the firmer.

I retained it. "What's this used for?" I asked, having a damn good idea she didn't use it to peel potatoes.

"Carving. Wood carving." She wiggled her fingertips, indicating that I should return her property.

Slowly, I returned the chisel, firmer—whatever the hell it was—to her hand.

She leaned against the wall, putting her hands behind her, firmer and all. "Have you found something already?"

"Can we sit down?" I inquired.

She jumped away from the wall, as if reminded of her manners. "Oh. Sure. I'm sorry." She led me to a loveseat. "Excuse the mess. I just got home and was sort of doing lots of things at once." At one end of the room was a bed. Her clothes—the skirt, the red turtleneck top, the tweed jacket, the scarf—were thrown on it, her purse thrown on top of them. Her boots—one upright, the other limply folded over—lay alongside the bed. Scooping up everything—the clothes, the purse, the boots—she kicked open a footlocker and dumped the armload of goods into it. Closing the locker with a satisfied look, she inspected the bed, then turned her eyes to the small coffee table in front of the loveseat. The table was covered with wood shavings and a carving that I had been staring at. The wood cried out to be touched, its whorls and color catching the eye and holding it. Under different circumstances, I would have picked it up, but it was a carving of a woman, or I should say of a female torso, from the thighs to the neck: no arms, no head, no legs. Suzanne Quering grabbed it away and looked around for a place to put it. Finding no place suitable, she gently laid it in the footlocker. Then she knelt in front of the coffee table and swept all the wood shavings into her hand, walked into the tiny kitchen, and deposited them in a wastebasket.

She opened the oven. "I just got home from work. I'm heating up some pizza. I can put more in if you'd like some."

"No, thanks, I just had dinner."

"Coffee, then? Tea? Fruit?"

I shook my head. "No, thanks." Picking up a finished wooden carving, I examined it. It was a seal, or perhaps I should say the essence of a seal, since the shape was squared. The wooden seal was straddling a wooden rock, its flippers splayed out, its nose pointing straight up. Two realistic rolls of what must have been seal blubber rippled around its neck and shoulders. If seals have shoulders.

"I like the seal," I commented, rubbing the wood between my thumb and fingers.

"Thank you. That's ironwood. I got it in Mexico. The wood, I mean. The only thing heavier than that is leadwood. That's found in Florida. I haven't been there yet."

The wood had quite a heft to it, but the heft was secondary to the ebony gloss that highlighted the grain. "How'd you get the seal to stand still for so long?"

I heard the sound of running water, then the clang of kitchen metal. "I'm putting some water on for coffee. Lincoln Park Zoo. The seals bask in the sun for hours."

She was back in the main part of her living quarters, looking around to see whether there was anything else that had to be scooped up and thrown into the footlocker. I picked up a squirrel. "Another Lincoln Park model?" I asked.

"Um-hmmmm." She sat on a rocker and looked at me.

Resisting an impulse to ask her who modeled for the torso she had put away (but not resisting the thought that she had modeled for herself), I returned her look, wondering, now that I was here, how to begin my questions.

"Why are you here?" she asked, hacking away the supports of any bridges I had intended to build.

I had experienced such tactics before. One way across was to leap boldly from my edge of the chasm to hers. I still preferred a more oblique approach.

"Why me?" I asked.

She stared at me, trying to comprehend, then gave up. "Why you what? I don't understand the question."

"Why did you pick me to prove murder?"

"I *didn't* pick you to prove murder—I said to prove whether it was murder," she protested. "And to find out who did it," she added. "I just looked in

the yellow pages, that's how I picked you. Anyway,
that's a silly question to ask."

"Humor me. I want to know. There are lots of
listings. How did you happen to pick me?"

She sighed, as if dealing with a child to whom
something must be explained patiently, over and
over. The firmer was in her hand again, and now
she pointed it at me. "I looked in the yellow pages
under *D* for detective." She was going to be sarcastic. "The listing was subdivided into Detective
Agencies and Detectives, Private. One look at the
agencies told me I didn't want them: huge ads, ap-
pointments only, domestic matters, child custody,
voice identification. All those artificial *A* names
just to get at the beginning of the alphabet." She
examined the firmer, holding the shank perpendic-
ular to the floor and pulling the tang toward her
with an index finger. It twanged, as if dismissing
the agencies. "So that left Detectives, Private.
Yours was the first name in boldface." Pausing a
minute, she stared into space, then returned.
"Yeah, I guess that was important, that you would
pay for boldface type. A box ad would probably
have been a waste of money, after all those agency
box ads. A lightface listing would have been a sign
of defeat. So, your name was the first one in boldface: Dragovic, Frank." She pronounced my name
correctly, as she had the first time. "I liked the
sound of it. Frank's a nice name." Maybe she
blushed; I wasn't sure. "Does that answer your
question?"

"Okay." I had to remain businesslike. "So you
picked me because I have the right name. Did you
ever hear of me before? Anybody ever tell you to
come to me?"

She stared at me. "No. I told you, I looked in the yellow pages. Why, what are you, some sort of criminal?"

"Look," I said, "don't worry if I ask you all kinds of questions that seem irrelevant. Just figure that there's a method back here"—I tapped my forehead with an index finger—"and there's a reason for the questions. Just answer them truthfully."

"Well, of course! I have no reason to lie."

"Would you lie if you had a reason?"

"If somebody had a gun to my head, and I thought a lie would save me, sure. Don't tell me you wouldn't?" she challenged. I stared at her and in a few seconds it dawned on her. "Hey, don't look at me like that! You think I might have killed Ralph and so I'm going to lie to you?" She bent forward in the rocker and stared at me. "Are you serious? I thought you believed me." I didn't say anything. "Why would I come to you if I were guilty? If I were guilty, I'd cut my hair short, dye it, take my money out of the bank, and disappear. I'd go to Canada or maybe Australia." She leaned back in the rocker and waved the firmer in the air in a circular motion, as if making herself disappear. "Tell me why you're here," she asked again.

"I'll get to it," I answered.

She looked at me with a frown but didn't say anything, so I continued. "When did you break off with Blasingame?"

"Three months ago."

"Why?"

With that question, I stood firmly on her edge of the chasm. Watching, I waited for her answer.

She rubbed the tang of the firmer along the seam of her Levi's. Holding it up to the light, she examined it. Then she stood. "My pizza's ready. Would you like some coffee while I eat?"

I stood up also. "Sure," I replied, following her into the tiny kitchen. Now that I was on her side of the chasm, I wasn't about to let her get away.

Chapter Six

■

WE SAT AT a round table barely large enough for two. It was also barely large enough for the three magazines, dictionary, and paperback novel that were scattered across its blue-and-white checked tablecloth. Scooping up the reading materials, Suzanne deposited them on top of the refrigerator, where, I noticed, there were many other books and magazines. She had an unsettling way of disposing of the messes she created. I felt that, when it was time to leave, I, too, would be scooped up and unceremoniously thrown out the door.

She set the table: blue-rimmed plates, cloth napkins, heavy flatware. On her plate she dished out two wedges of thick Chicago pan-style pizza.

"Giordano's?" I ventured, looking at the pizza.

"Due's," she replied, pouring herself a glass of orange juice. To go with the pizza, I presumed, trying to keep from grimacing.

"Sugar or cream?" she asked, pouring my coffee.

I shook my head, still wondering about complementing pizza with orange juice. She placed a plate, knife, and fork before me, and about a quarter of a very large cake on the table.

"Carrot cake," she offered, sitting down and cutting into her pizza. "Have some if you want."

Should I have the cake? After two beers, shrimp, fries, and coffee? No contest: I sliced myself a wedge of the triple-layer cake, admiring the frosting (cream cheese, I hoped) and crushed pecan topping. "Jerome's?" I asked.

"Suzanne's," she replied, smiling.

"Delicious." And it was. I ate quickly, perhaps fearing that the cake would be scooped away from me before I finished.

"Good pizza?" I asked, watching her eat.

She nodded, swallowing orange juice.

Cutting myself a second piece of cake, I lifted it onto my plate and asked, "Did Blasingame's wife know about you?"

"No." Her reply was immediate. Calm. Matter-of-fact. Maybe too much so.

"Are you sure?" From where I sat, I could, if I tipped my chair a bit, stretch back and reach the coffeepot. I did so, pouring myself a second cup of coffee.

She ignored my bad table manners. Maybe she didn't even notice them. "Yes. I think so. I asked Ralph—at the beginning—if he had told his wife. He said he hadn't. I think I shocked him, asking the question."

"Why? Did you want him to get a divorce?"

She gagged. I couldn't tell whether it was a response to my question or a comment on the orange juice and pizza combination. Finally, she caught her breath. "No," she whispered hoarsely. "I didn't want him to get a *divorce*. I just wanted him to be honest."

"That's why you thought he should tell his wife?" I asked, wondering if it made any sense.

Suzanne nodded. "I thought he should tell her, but he thought he shouldn't. I felt like telling her myself at one point." Picking up the pizza crust, she bit into it, washing it down with the remaining orange juice. Then she lifted her empty coffee cup and raised an eyebrow at me.

Stretching again, I grabbed the coffeepot, poured, and placed it back on the burner, pleased with my own efficiency of motion. I even cleared her plate away and, lifting an eyebrow, indicated that if she wanted a piece of Suzanne's carrot cake, I would be willing to cut and serve. Two can play at that game. She nodded, but her thoughts seemed elsewhere.

"What stopped you?" I asked.

Pulling at the edge of a woven wood shade with a finger, she peered out the kitchen window into the darkness. "It was over," she answered, dropping the shade and picking up her fork. "I don't do things out of vengeance."

"Nemoj drugom jamu kopat jer bi mogal sam u nju upast," I quoted. When she looked at me blankly, I translated. "It's a Croatian proverb: 'Don't dig a hole under someone else, for you might fall into it yourself.'"

She stared at me in silence, then nodded. "That's one way of looking at it. Vengeance is a waste of time and effort."

"Apparently not everybody thinks so," I replied, watching her.

"What do you mean?"

"The dirty proof—the copy with your slug on it. And the scarf in the presses—*if* the scarf is yours."

"Oh." Lifting a piece of carrot cake on her fork,

she brought it halfway to her mouth and poised it
there. I thought she was going to say something,
but she didn't. She ate the bite of cake. And then
another. And another. I watched while she finished. I even poured her a second cup of coffee.
She drank it, her elbow on the table, her eyes
studying the tablecloth. "It's got to be somebody in
the composing room."

After a second or two, I figured out what she
meant: the person digging the hole. Vengeance.

"Why do you say that?"

"The composing room's the only place a person
could alter the tape to get my slug on it. And if
somebody took my scarf—well, where else would
it have been but in the composing room?"

"What about Blasingame's wife?"

"No." An emphatic shake of the head. "She
wouldn't be allowed to stand there and punch paper tape. That's union work."

"You're sure she didn't know about . . . you
and her husband." Now I was having difficulty saying the name.

Suzanne shook her head. "Ralph said she didn't
know. I . . . believe me, Ralph wouldn't have
wanted her to know."

"Why did you break off with Blasingame?"

Again, I thought I had timed the question well.
But once again she evaded it. Her eyes met mine
without blinking. They were a very clear gray,
with a darker gray outlining the irises. Without
haste, it seemed, yet without a pause, she stood
and cleared the table. With her, that consisted of
stacking all the empty plates in one hand, then
sliding them with a crash into the sink behind her.
I tried not to wince. Still standing, she pivoted and
emptied the coffeepot by pouring coffee first into

my cup, then into hers. She lifted her cup and saucer and walked out of the kitchen. Naturally I followed, wondering how long she would keep up the evasion.

She sat in the rocking chair and I sat in the loveseat facing her, placing my cup and saucer on the table.

"There are all kinds of reasons why people break up," she announced. "We just didn't get along anymore."

Goddamn it, that got me mad. "Listen, Suzanne," I said, leaning forward intently, "there's no room for games here! You're in serious trouble. If you want me to help you, start answering my questions," I shouted. "Now." Standing suddenly, I nearly spilled my coffee. "If you don't, I'll be glad to return your retainer." I wouldn't have been glad, actually, but I was glad I said it, if you understand the difference.

"Don't *shout* at me!" she shouted, placing her cup and saucer on the floor. "You're just like Ralph. He shouted all the time. I won't be shouted at any more!"

"I'm not shouting," I argued, lowering my voice to a normal, conversational tone and taking a deep breath. "Okay. Blasingame shouted at you. That's abusive."

"Don't patronize me!" She was still shouting. "I *know* it's abusive."

"Calm down. I only meant, that's obviously one of the reasons you broke off the . . . relationship." Although I needed to pace, the size of her apartment prevented it; so I simply stood there with my hands in my pockets.

She was giving the rocker a workout, rocking back and forth violently—her hands gripping its

wooden arms, her white-stockinged feet turned
heels up, toes gripping the floor. "Relationship,"
she sneered. "Relationship, affair, whatever. Mistake, that's what it was. A big, fat mistake. Look."
She stopped rocking. "Look. I told him to leave. To
go. To never—I . . ." She breathed deeply. "Yes.
Okay. I broke off with him because he shouted at
me. He was abusive."

Studying her, I thought that her feelings seemed
a long way from the not-love, not-hate she had spoken about in my office that morning.

"Was he physically abusive? Did he ever hit
you?"

"No! Yes! No, he never hit me. What do you
think shouting is if it isn't physical abuse? Psycho-
logical, I suppose. I think it's physical abuse. It's
like being hit."

She was wrong, of course. I'd been shouted at,
and I'd been hit; and believe me, I'd much rather
be shouted at. But now was not the time to argue
the fine points of abuse with my client—especially
this client. Sitting down again, I sipped the warm
coffee. "What else?" I prodded.

She glared at me for a few more seconds, probably just to make sure I wouldn't start behaving like
Blasingame again. Then she unfurrowed her eyebrows and picked up her coffee cup. "He was
moody," she offered. "I couldn't stand that. Whatever mood he was in, that's the mood that domi-
nated our being together—excited, morose, angry,
funny. I couldn't take all those moods."

Sipping her coffee, she made a face and put the
cup back on the floor. "And another thing. He
hated cabbage, beets, barley, and lentils. Anything
that was a peasant food, he hated. I once told him,
'You know, Ralph, you hate all the peasant foods,'

and he said, 'That's not true, I love asparagus.' It wasn't a joke: he thought asparagus was as plentiful as cabbage. He had no appreciation of anything that didn't cost a lot of money. Ralph was . . . obsessed with making money. He never had enough of it. He was always looking for schemes to—for schemes to make more money. He wouldn't eat here. He always wanted to eat out, only in the most expensive places. And then, because he didn't want to be seen, we'd have to drive to Milwaukee or someplace to eat. He wouldn't let me take him out—he always had to pay. He was a fool for money."

She picked a curved carving instrument off the floor and twirled it between her fingers. I watched, thinking that I could live on nothing but barley, lentils, cabbage, and beets if I had to. Why, I practically grew up on cabbage! I'd let anyone pay who had the money. But it was no good, comparing myself to him. Where could it get me? Suzanne Quering's reasons for breaking off with Blasingame seemed genuine enough. That is, the emotions and reasons she expressed seemed to come from deep within. But there might have been more.

Switching directions, I asked her when she had started the affair with Blasingame.

"About three months before it ended—say about six months ago."

"Why?" I asked.

She stared at me as if I were the sphinx.

"Why?" she repeated finally. "I don't know. Maybe because he was intelligent . . . energetic . . . good looking. . . ." Her voice trailed off. "The reasons hardly seem enough . . . now."

"Were there any other reasons you broke it off?"

I asked, switching back to my earlier question,
knowing there had to be more if she had threatened to kill him.

"Why do you want to know all these things?"

"The police will want to know. They'll ask you
the same questions, if they haven't already. If they
suspect murder, then they look for motives." I
paused, watching her. "If you expect me to help
you, you've got to give me the advantage of the
truth." I waited, expecting another reaction, an
outburst; but she simply sat there rocking, fingering the gouger, and staring at me. "Were there?" I
prodded, somehow disliking myself for it.

"I've told you. Ralph's character was the most
important reason. I've just given you examples of
it." She stood, bending first to collect her cup and
saucer, then mine. Her walk was graceful, shoulders straight, hips gliding—the kind of walk that
makes you think there's a layer of air that you, too,
could be walking on, if you could just take the
time to find it. Much as I admired her carriage,
however, I sensed that she wanted to dismiss me. I
didn't want to go.

"Are you a dancer?" I asked, standing and following her to the kitchen.

Dropping the cups into the sink with a clatter,
she turned on me. "Don't tell me you want to go
dancing?" she challenged.

Fleetingly, I wondered if it *were* true about the
temper of redheads. "No," I answered calmly. "I
was admiring the way you move, and I wondered
where you acquired the skill."

Several seconds passed before she replied.
"Gymnastics. I work out a lot."

"When did you break off with Blasingame?"

She looked startled—and disapproving—at the way I had come back to the question.

"About three months ago. Like I told you."

I nodded.

"Look. Are you almost done with your questions?"

"Why did you threaten to kill Blasingame?"

I was standing quite close to her—it was unavoidable in her tiny studio—and I swear I saw her pupils dilate, then contract. "What?" she asked, her voice a whisper.

"Why did you threaten to kill Blasingame?"

"Who says so? Where did you hear that? Who says I threatened to kill him?"

She had gone from soft to hard, from mild to vehement, in about two seconds.

"The police."

Her face drained of color, and she sank against the counter behind her. She started to say something, but stopped. I waited; but she simply stared at me, then turned her head and looked at the window shade.

"I think you should tell me about it, Suzanne."

She turned and glared at me. "What makes you think it's true? I didn't kill Ralph. If you don't believe that, there's the door." She extended an arm and pointed a finger, as if I could possibly miss the door. "I told you what I wanted," she continued. "To prove whether it was murder. That will clear me. Do you believe me?"

I felt like asking her what she wanted me to believe: That it was murder? That she was innocent? That she hadn't threatened to kill Blasingame? Just those three possibilities alone could be mutually exclusive, partially overlapping, or entirely coincidental. "I took the job because I wanted to take it,"

I replied, choosing my words carefully. "I want to prove whether it was murder and, if so, who did it. I want to 'clear you,' as you put it. Those are strong enough reasons for me to stay on the case."

She nodded her head slowly, but what she was agreeing with I wasn't sure. "I see," she said. Straightening, she brushed by me and walked to the door. I didn't want to leave, but I didn't think she would answer any more questions tonight.

Then she turned toward me. "I've told you as simply and honestly as I can. I think somebody is trying to frame me. Shouldn't you be asking questions in the composing room?"

She had turned resilient and resourceful when I had not expected it. "Yeah, I should. And I will. I was going to bring it up. How do I get past the gorilla in the cage?"

A tired smile indicated it could be done. "He's not a gorilla, he's a nice person. Jeff. I guess I could meet you there and tell him who you are and that I'd like you to be able to look around. Would that help?"

"Yes. I'll call you tomorrow." I started to move toward the door, but she blocked it.

"Is it because of the color of my hair?" she asked.

I thought I knew what she was getting at, but it made me uncomfortable. "Is what because of the color of your hair?"

"Is that why you don't believe me?"

She had thrown me a question I couldn't handle easily. Combing my fingers through my hair, I stalled. With my fingertips I brushed back my mustache. A nervous gesture. "I want to believe you. I'm not saying I don't. Listen, let's just forget it. Maybe my name should be Philip Trent. I'll call you tomorrow after I check out Blasingame's wife."

"Who's Philip Trent?"

"Nothing, forget it. And it's not your hair."

She didn't push it. "Good night, then." She opened the door.

"Good night."

In the lobby, I stopped at the desk to talk to the doorman; but the one who had been on duty earlier in the evening was now off duty, so I asked my questions to the man behind the desk, showing him my ID. Did he remember a man who used to visit Suzanne Quering?

"Umm." The doorman scratched his chin. "Used to. Yes, sir, a gentleman like that used to call on her."

"Do you remember the last time you saw him?"

"Can't say exactly. Must have been, . . . oh, a couple of months at least. I enjoyed seeing him. Kind of miss his visits."

"What do you mean?"

"He always came with a package. Real pretty, nice wrapping paper, ribbons and bows. A real gentleman, he seemed."

"Ummm." Now it was my turn to think. I stared out the lobby door. In the end I asked a few more questions, the doorman let in a few more visitors, and we parted amicably for the evening.

Stepping out into the October evening, I realized that the temperature had dropped significantly. Turning up the collar of my sport coat, I crossed the streets to Diversey, then turned south to walk the fifteen or so blocks that lay between Suzanne Quering's home and mine.

As I walked, I thought confused thoughts about Suzanne Quering. Kicking an empty pop can vi-

ciously, I listened to it tumble down the empty
street with a tinny rattle. It was a mistake to get
involved with a client. Not because the client
wouldn't pay or anything mundane like that, but
because when your emotions become involved,
you don't see clearly.

Yes, I felt like Philip Trent, the fictional painter-
journalist-detective who fell instantly and totally
in love with the widow of a murdered man. Based
on the evidence, he thought she was the murderer's accomplice. So Philip Trent left the country
rather than solve the case. Unlike Trent, I would
solve the case. Regardless. Lost in my resolutions,
I stepped off the curb and a pizza delivery truck
nearly hit me. My fault. I looked at the truck, then
looked again. The lettering on its side said "Tomb-
stone Pizza." An awful name for a pizza company.
I hoped it wasn't portentous.

Chapter Seven

AT SEVEN O'CLOCK the next morning, Wednesday, I
woke up without the alarm. As I lay in bed, combing my fingers through my hair and staring at the
ceiling, I reviewed my plans for the day: see Ted
Haapala, see Gayle Blasingame, and walk all over
the floor of the composing room. Before jumping
into all that activity, though, I first jumped into a
long, hot shower. Then I fixed myself a breakfast

of scrambled eggs and mushrooms, with sausage
on the side, followed by two cups of hot, black,
French Market coffee, which contained chicory
and thus reminded me of the coffee my grand-
mother used to keep in a big enamel pot on the
back of her wood-burning stove. As a kid, I had
tried it once, thinking that anything adults drank
all day long and forbade me to drink must be
good. It wasn't then. It was now.

Out of my kitchen window I observed the paved
parking lot below and the backs of three old three-
flats some contractor or owner was trying to re-
model. I say "trying to" because he hoped to save
himself money by skimping on the windows. True,
he replaced the old windows with new ones, but
he didn't knock through the walls anywhere for
new windows. But, I guess some people want dark
places. Not me. I loved the floor-to-ceiling windows in my apartment. So did my plants. Absentmindedly I pinched the leaves of a kalanchoe, giving its pot a quarter turn in the bargain.

Down behind the three-flats, an obese, middle-
aged woman in slippers, housedress, cobbler's
apron, babushka, and a tattered black sweater
made her daily round of the trash bins. Every
morning she opened the lid of each trash bin and
peered inside. Although I'd lived here two years
already, I'd never yet seen her take anything out.
Either she was the world's pickiest antique collec-
tor, or she was simply a voyeur, getting her kicks
out of other people's garbage.

Stacking the dishes in the dishwasher, I thought
of Suzanne Quering throwing her dishes into the
sink. We seemed opposites in so many ways. I
shook some soap powder into the dishwasher,

flicked on the switch, and turned off the kitchen light. Shrugging into my sport coat, I left.

The walk to the *Truth-Examiner* took me just over half an hour. That included a quick stop at my office to check on any mail and phone calls. Once at the *Truth*, I had no difficulty getting into the editorial offices, which all seemed to lead off of a large rectangular room full of reporters working at silent computer terminals. Ted Haapala was pointed out to me when I asked for him: he was a formidable-looking man, talking to two other men and a woman. As I waited for Haapala to finish, I looked at his office. One of two large ones, it contained a large window that looked out into the newsroom. Through that window I could see larger windows beyond, overlooking the Chicago River.

Haapala was beefy, with a definite beer belly. But the beef didn't seem flabby. He was maybe six feet tall, though his weight made him look shorter. Early forties, I'd say. Sand-colored hair, flecked with gray, but there wasn't much of it—the hair, that is. He kept it cropped quite close to his scalp, a throwback to the 1950s. From where I was standing I could see the ridges and furrows of his scalp. His head looked like a rippled bowling ball covered with sandy fuzz. His red face was already covered with perspiration. His teeth clamped tightly on a cigar.

As soon as he was alone, I walked up to him, flashed my private detective's license, and told him I'd like to ask him some questions.

"Again?" he growled.

Again? I asked myself—then realized he must have thought I was the police. Since it was his mistake, I took advantage. "We're never through. I need to go over some information."

"What do you mean? No, wait, come in here," he commanded, leading the way to his office. As I followed, I noticed that Haapala walked with a pronounced limp.

Closing the door, he took command from his desk. "Well, what is it? I've told you this is the worst time of day for you to come."

"Sorry. It can't be helped. I'll try not to take more than half an hour."

"Half an hour!" he bellowed. "More like ten minutes is what you'll get, and be damned lucky at that. I'm getting sick and tired of all this bullshit!" Removing a white handkerchief from his pants pocket, he wiped the sweat off his brow. Off his scalp, too.

Taking out a pocket notebook so that I would look more like the real thing (a police detective), I began: "To your knowledge, did the victim have any enemies who would want to see him dead?"

"Yes. No! Hell, I told you, nobody liked Ralph. He was a pompous ass. Phony, through and through. He didn't belong in the newspaper—no, nobody would kill him. We've been through this."

"Did he have any violent arguments with any of the other editors or officers here?"

"No."

"Did he suffer from vertigo?"

"What?"

"Did he suffer from vertigo?"

"How the hell—" He stopped. "How the hell am *I* supposed to know that? Did you ask Gayle? You think maybe he got dizzy and fell?"

The police didn't say what they thought. In my notebook I sketched a figure: a face, very round,

fuzzy on top. I continued. "Did you ever hear him
or anybody else say anything about heights or diz-
ziness?"

Haapala stared at me belligerently, but I thought
he looked relieved. "I don't remember." Either he
was a man of few words, or he fully intended to
rush me out in ten minutes. Drawing three holes
in the face, I made it look like an animated bowling ball. I kept fishing. "What was Blasingame doing here the night he died?"

"I don't know." Haapala's naturally deep voice
rose a notch on his answer.

I didn't believe him. "Was something wrong with
the presses that night?"

"No. I mean, how the hell do I know? Ask the
pressmen."

"Have you ever come down here at 2:00 A.M. for
any reason?"

"No."

Again I thought his voice rose.

He must have seen the doubt on my face.

"I told you—some nights I *stay* here until after
midnight. But that wasn't one of them."

"Had Blasingame ever come down here that late
at night before?"

"Sure. Probably. Ask Gayle. He was often out all
night."

"How do you know that?"

Haapala shifted in his chair, straightening himself to his full round height. I tilted my notebook
toward my chest.

"I didn't mean it like I knew it. Gayle says he
was. Listen, I don't want to get her into trouble,
see? I don't know what she told you. Did she tell
you he was often down here at night?"

Ignoring the question, I continued. Dragan

would have been proud of me—after he got over being pissed off, of course. "Where were you at 2:00 A.M. on the morning of Tuesday, October 4?"

"I told you, home in bed."

I raised my eyebrows, then drew a four-poster bed around the bowling-ball head, wrote a question mark above the pictograph, flipped back the pages of my notebook, searched with my fingertips for something that wasn't there, then pointed my pen to the supposed item in my notebook. "We have a witness who says you were seen down here that evening, Mr. Haapala." What the hell—why not?

"Who?! Who says so?!"

Now he sounded like Suzanne Quering: not denying, not confirming, just demanding. "Mr. Haapala"—the police always called people Mr. or Mrs. or Miss—"we've been through this before. You know we don't reveal the names of witnesses. Why did you say you were home in bed when you were down here? What were you doing here?"

He fidgeted with his cigar, took a long puff of it, then answered. "It's not true. I told you, I was home in bed. If you've got proof otherwise, take me down to the station. I know my rights," he growled, exhaling a long stream of smoke in my direction.

No wonder the cops play hard-cop, soft-cop. The guy was lying about something. Maybe something insignificant, maybe something important. *Bože moj.* (My god.) The stuff you have to go through to get the truth. It seems it would be easier to beat it out of people. Except that wouldn't work—they'd tell you lies to make you stop beating them. Why the hell hadn't Dragan concentrated on this guy?

Possibly because Dragan hadn't conjured up a nonexistent witness.

"I'll probably have to do that, Mr. Haapala. Let's come back to the question later. Maybe you'll realize that there's a perfectly innocent explanation as to why you were here that evening." I looked down at my notebook, placed it on my knee, and sketched in a fuzzy bowling ball rolling down an inclined catwalk. I looked (with what I hoped was a very pointed look) at him, then back down at my notebook. "How did you feel when Blasingame was promoted to vice president and sales/marketing director?"

"It was a mistake, that's how I felt. Sure, I was personally involved because *I* should have got the job. Go ahead—prove I murdered him."

"What makes you think it was murder?"

Haapala was sweating even more than before. At his back the sun shined on his barely protected head. He took a deep breath. "I *don't* think it was murder. I believe it was an accident."

I'll be damned. He sounded so convinced, so sincere, that I was taken aback. "What makes you so sure?" I wanted to know.

"Nobody thinks it was murder. Nobody here would murder to become a director. I told you; you're bothering busy people for nothing. Ralph fell. It was an accident, a horrible accident."

"I see," I muttered, more to fill an empty space in the conversation than anything else. "How did you say you got that limp?"

If Haapala had had longer hair, it would have bristled at this point. Well, his hair didn't bristle, but the furrows of his scalp seemed to stand at attention. Crushing his cigar into a large ashtray that already held the remains of two previous cigars, he folded his hands across his chest and sighed. "I told you before. I slipped and fell off the loading dock."

"Ah, yes," I agreed, using my pen to point to absolutely nothing in my notebook. "That was what day?" I doodled a humpty-dumpty-type bowling ball, with a cigar in its mouth, sitting on the edge of a dock.

"What day do you have, for chrissake? If you were a reporter, you'd be fired, you know that?"

"These aren't my notes," I commented in an injured tone. "I'm simply here to check on the facts. Purely routine. What was the day?" I repeated.

"Last week." He ran a hand across his scalp, then returned it to his chest, so that he sat there looking at me as if he were a modern-day Buddha. "It was Tuesday morning. I remember because it was a painful fall. I was going to see the nurse after I got in, but then . . . Ralph had fallen into the presses just a few hours before. Naturally Gayle didn't come in. I stayed on the job. I didn't see a doctor until late that evening."

"What time did you come in that morning?"

"The usual, seven o'clock or so. No. No, a little earlier, I think. Say about six-thirty."

"The *Truth* didn't call to tell you about Blasingame?" I inquired.

He seemed offended. "Of course they did." And then, anticipating my next question, he offered, "The nightside editor called about 5:00 A.M."

"Did you rush right down?"

Haapala hesitated. "Well, no. I woke my wife to tell her. Then I called on Gayle. She lives a few blocks away. I told her that Inga, my wife, could drop by and stay with her if she needed it. By the time I did all that and drove down, it was maybe six-thirty."

I nodded, filling my notebook with a few words as I listened. I finished jotting down the information, then put the cap on my pen, put the pen in my pocket, and assessed Haapala. "Okay. Tell me why you were down here at 2:00 A.M. Tuesday morning last week." I lay the words down—not like a gauntlet—gently, but firmly, so he knew I *knew* he was there. I don't mean "knew" with facts and witnesses. There are different kinds of knowing.

"Goddamn it, get out!" He had not exactly jumped to his feet, but he had moved fast enough to surprise me. His hand was gripping the heavy glass ashtray. Cigar butts spilled out. "Take me down or get out!" he threatened. "I've had enough of this!"

And he looked as if he had. I rose nonchalantly to my feet, unthreatened by the ashtray, and tucked away my notebook. "I'd put that down if I were you."

He stared at the ashtray in his hand as if it were some foreign substance growing there, a fungus he had just noticed.

"I can't take you down to the station for more questioning. But I'll see that my information gets to the police, who most likely *will* take you down."

I was halfway through the door when his bellow stopped me.

"YOU!" he roared. "Who the hell are you? I thought—" He left it unfinished.

"I know what you thought. But I'm not. I'm a *private* detective, working on the Blasingame case," I informed him. Watching the look on his face, I added, "A good reporter would never have jumped to the conclusion you jumped to." It left him speechless, providing me with a good exit.

Down in the lobby, I gave Dragan a call and told him what I had. He didn't like it but said okay, he'd question Haapala again about being at the *Truth* the early morning of Tuesday, October 4. Dragan acted as if he were doing me a favor; I thought I was doing *him* a favor.

Haapala had seemed nervous, far too nervous to be innocent. The question was, what was he guilty of? The police could do a hell of a lot more than I could when it came to tracing Haapala and discovering whether or not he had left his home sweet home and crept into the doors of the *Truth*—or elsewhere—that night.

He was lying about something, but it wasn't necessarily murder. I found it hard to believe that Haapala would push Blasingame over the railing just to become vice president and director—although murder has been committed for just such reasons. Supposing Haapala had been at the *Truth* that night, why? *Why* had he been there? What could have caused two of the head honchos (bitter rivals if reports were correct) to return to the paper in the dead of night?

I went to the back-files desk located off the main lobby of the *Truth-Examiner* building and bought a copy of the paper for Tuesday, October 4. Then I spent the next hour or more reading it from front to back, but nothing hit me as being remotely connected with murder motives. I threw the *Truth* into a convenient trash barrel, convinced that the answer wasn't in the discarded newspaper.

Why? Why had Blasingame been down there? Haapala had tightened at the question. Tomor-

row I'd check back with Dragan, but today I'd
check out Haapala's neighbors myself.

I glanced at my watch: 10:35. There were plenty
of pay phones in the *Truth*'s lobbies. I used one to
call Suzanne Quering. We agreed to meet in the
composing room at five o'clock the next evening.

Chapter Eight

JUST BECAUSE TED Haapala had assumed I was a
cop didn't mean I could expect the same mistake
from Gayle Blasingame. First off, Haapala might
have already told her who I was. Second, it's the
bluff-and-gruff type (like Ted Haapala) who make
quick assumptions. Gayle Blasingame might be an
entirely different proposition.

From the lobby of the *Truth-Examiner* I phoned
Gayle Blasingame and asked for half an hour of
her time, explaining that I was a private detective
hired by somebody who was unjustly suspected of
murder in her husband's unfortunate accident.
Since I also told her I was in the lobby, she said
she would see me.

Her office was across the wide open spaces from
Haapala's. I suppose they always met in the middle: neutral territory. She had had blinds of thin,
vertical slats installed over her office window. Was
it so she could see into his office, but he couldn't
see into hers? Stepping into her office, I observed

that it was painted a golden shade of beige, with color-coordinated wallpaper behind her desk. The furniture was a coordinated shade of brown with golden chrome tubing for arms and legs. In one corner was a bentwood coatrack. Hanging from it was a light coat with a green scarf draped around its neck and a nylon tote bag out of which protruded a pair of jogging shoes. Silk scarves must have been the latest in fashion—jogging shoes, too, for those who walked to and from work. As Gayle Blasingame told me to be seated, she twirled the lucite baton that closed the blinds. Dragan had called her puny. Had she known, she would have surely resented it. She was the size that dress designers call petite. Her honey-colored hair framed her face in swirls. I found myself wondering if she could have possibly pushed her husband over the railing. It seemed next to impossible.

"Whom do you represent, Mr. Dragovic?" she asked, pronouncing my name with a hard *ick* ending as, sitting on the edge of her chair, she adjusted herself in front of a pad of paper and a pencil.

"I can't tell you that at this time, Mrs. Blasingame."

"Who has been accused of murder?" she asked.

"Nobody yet. But I believe there's suspicion of murder."

She raised an eyebrow—a trick I hate, probably because I can't do it. "I'm not *surrre*," she began, dragging out the word, then stopping, tapping her pencil on the pad of paper. "No. No. I'll see what you have to say before I make any judgments."

Thanks a lot, lady. I had taken an instant dislike to her. "Thank you," I replied, clearing my throat.

"First off, could you tell me why your husband was down here at two o'clock in the morning?"

"No, I can't."

That was all. The rest was silence.

"Do you *know* why your husband was down here at that time?"

"No, I don't know." She was writing on the pad —probably my questions and her answers, but her desk was too wide for me to see across. On the other hand, maybe she was composing today's headlines or her shopping list.

"I see. Did you know—before you were told— *that* he was down here?"

"No, I did not."

Feeling as though I were questioning a robot, I had half a mind to pull out *my* notebook and imitate her. I decided against it. Let her feel superior. It might make her trip up, if she had anything to trip up on.

"I understand that you were here, at the *Truth-Examiner,* that evening. To your knowledge, your husband wasn't here?"

She answered my question first with a nod, then with words. "He may have been here, I don't know. The fact is that I didn't see him here."

"What were you doing here that late in the evening?"

Her frown was so severe that I thought she wasn't going to answer the question. But she did.

"I was in a meeting."

"What kind of meeting takes place that late, Mrs. Blasingame?"

"In the newspaper industry, almost any meeting can take place that late. When the Watergate story broke, we had meetings twenty-four hours a day."

"Right. What kind of meeting did you have here that Monday evening?" I asked.

Again she frowned at me. "I was meeting with several reporters."

"About what?"

"In regard to a story." She sighed in exasperation. "The police have asked me all. these questions. I suppose, given your profession, you must ask them also. All I can tell you is this: I'm handling a big story. In pursuing it, I have several reporters working undercover, you might say, and we have weekly meetings late in the evening. I will not tell you what the story is, and I will not give you the names of the reporters. They have nothing to do with Ralph's death."

I mulled over this information for a while, then continued. "When did you leave the building that Monday night?"

"A little before midnight."

"Did anybody leave with you?"

"I left alone. I went directly home. And I fail to see how these questions can help your client, Mr. Dragovic."

Taking a deep breath, I considered how to ask the next questions. While it was true that I sensed an antagonism between us—perhaps mutual, perhaps simply based on my inexplicable dislike of her, or hers of me—I had to acknowledge that her husband had died just last week. Whether she was genuinely bereaved or not was hard to tell. I didn't want to walk in with seven-league boots where tiny footsteps would do a better job. "Who called to tell you of your husband's accident?" I asked.

She seemed to doodle something on her tablet. "Nobody called. I was awakened by the police. They came to the door to tell me."

"What time of the morning was that, do you remember?"

"Yes. A few minutes after three o'clock."

"Were you awake?"

She glared at me. "Of course not. Why would I be awake at three in the morning?"

"Then what?"

"I'm sorry?" she said, raising an eyebrow as well as her voice.

"Then what happened? Did the police stay with you?"

Gayle Blasingame stared out the window, the one that faced outdoors, not into the newsroom. I wondered whether she resented the fact that Haapala's window had a view of the river while hers didn't. "Yes," she replied at last. "I wanted to come here, to the paper, but they told me they . . . they had asked somebody else to identify the body. They said there was nothing I could do. I thought I should go to the hospital . . . or wherever they were taking Ralph. They insisted there was nothing I could do. A policewoman stayed with me."

"Did anybody from the newspaper come to see you that morning?"

"No."

Hadn't Haapala said he called on her? "I'm sorry, let me rephrase the question. Didn't Ted Haapala come to offer his condolences that morning, on his way to work?"

Gayle Blasingame stood, walked to the indoor-facing window, and toyed with the vertical blinds. "Yes," she answered, her back to me. "He did call on me briefly. I didn't want to see him, not so soon after. . . ."

I waited; but when she didn't finish, I prompted.

"After? After your husband's death? After seeing Haapala the previous evening?"

Her back was still to me. "Both," she replied.

"I see. Ted Haapala was also here, at the *Truth-Examiner*, that evening." The words I spoke were a statement, not a question. Haapala had told me he wasn't here.

She turned toward me. A corner of her mouth turned up. It might have been a self-congratulatory smirk. "I'm sure he was."

Sure she was. "Did you see him?" I asked.

Lifting a shoulder in an elegant shrug, she raised an eyebrow at the same time. Lifting a particle of minuscule lint off the shoulder of her black jacket, she offered me the reasons for her statement. "Ted spends most evenings here. I'm sure that evening was no different."

"What's he doing? Working on the secret story?"

"Not on *my* story, Mr. Dragovic. I can handle it without Ted's help."

"His own story, then?"

Again she lifted her shoulder slightly. "Perhaps. Perhaps he's working on a book. Maybe having a few beers. Maybe listening to a baseball game. I don't know what he does down here. And, Mr. Dragovic, forgive me for saying so, but I'm not sure what you're doing here, either. Your questions seem to imply that Ted or I may have done something wrong."

It's interesting how people always react defensively to questioning by cops or detectives. Suzanne Quering had. Haapala had. And now Gayle Blasingame was taking it the same way. "Did your husband have any enemies who might want to kill him?" I asked, ignoring her remark.

"He had plenty of enemies," she responded

promptly. "But I certainly can't think of anyone who would have wanted to kill him."

"Who were some of these enemies?"

"I've named them—reluctantly—for the police, but I'm certainly not going to name them for you. They should be obvious."

I tried raising an eyebrow. It must have had some effect, for she looked at me in exasperation.

"Ted Haapala, for instance. But such professional jealousies exist everywhere: they don't result in murder."

"Sometimes they do." I wondered whether Gayle Blasingame herself had been an enemy of her husband's at work. "Did your husband suffer from vertigo?" I asked.

"Ralph's aspiration for heights never made him dizzy," she answered bitterly.

It was as good a lead-in as any. "Who do you think will get your husband's job?"

"I will, of course."

I stared at her. "Is that a fact?"

"There are facts, and there are facts, Mr. Dragovic." The *ick* ending grated my ears. "No decision has been made, no. But I'm certain the person most qualified for the job will get it." She smiled at me, then completed the syllogism in case I was too dense to get it. "That's how I know I'll get the job."

"I see. So you think your husband was better qualified for this job than you were?"

I watched her closely, but all she did was walk to her chair, sit in it, and fluff up her hair with one hand. "No. But the board thought he was."

"How do you know the board won't make the same mistake again?"

"I won't let them. I've been here longer."

"Longer than Haapala?"

"No. I meant . . . longer than Ralph. I should have been promoted instead of him. The only reason they didn't promote me was because I'm a woman. I won't let that happen again." Glancing at her watch, she looked at me, then at the door.

"Do you accept that your husband's death was an accident?" I asked.

Hesitantly, she answered. "I think so. I mean, yes. I'm convinced it was an accident. It's ludicrous to think otherwise."

"Why?"

Gayle Blasingame stared out the window for a few moments, then she began to play with her pencil and pad again. "It seems . . . it seems impossible to believe that somebody could . . . murder somebody else in that way. And how could they do it without being seen? And *why* would they do it?"

She seemed genuinely bewildered and hurt, and for a moment I felt sympathy for her.

"The police," she continued. "Do they always ask so many questions?"

"In cases of accidental death, yes. They want to be satisfied that it was accidental." As she absentmindedly twirled a pencil in her fingers, lost in whatever thoughts she was having, I pursued my questioning by asking the big one again. "Mrs. Blasingame. Do you know why your husband was here at two o'clock that Tuesday morning?"

The question pulled her back from wherever she had been. In a clipped voice, she answered. "No."

"When did you last see your husband?"

"Around five o'clock. I told him I was going home for dinner and asked if he was coming. He said he wasn't. That was the last I saw of him."

"Did this happen regularly?" I asked.

Placing the pencil she had been twirling in her fingers on top of her desk, she studied me. *"Mister* Dragovic. I don't see how these questions are going to help your client."

"I do, Mrs. Blasingame. Just tell the truth and the innocent shall be helped. Did your husband regularly not come home for the evening?"

"No."

" 'No, he did come home,' or 'No, he did not come home?' "

"What are you getting at?" she snapped. "I don't like your questions."

"I can see that, since you aren't answering them. I'll repeat the question: Was your husband usually home with you or out with you in the evenings? Were you usually *together,* Mrs. Blasingame?"

"We were married."

A classic nonanswer. "He didn't love you, did he?"

She turned an angry red. "How dare you speak to me like that!"

"I dare because I'm after the truth. Unfortunately, few people volunteer the truth. Most have to have it dragged, tricked, or kicked out of them. Some might need all three. I don't know whether you loved your husband, but his feelings for you were questionable. He was having an affair with somebody. Did you know that?"

She stood and walked toward the door. "Get out."

I beat her to it, blocking the door. "Outraged dignity won't get rid of me, Mrs. Blasingame. Did you know your husband was having an affair?"

Swiveling on her high heels (they must have added three inches to her height), she reached for the telephone receiver. I stepped to the desk and depressed the plunger. "Sit down and answer the question."

"Get out, you . . . you . . ." Covering her face with her hands, she began to cry.

I felt like a heel, a heel in seven-league boots. Taking her arm, I guided her to the chair. Even feeling like a heel, I caught myself wondering whether the tears were real. She took a tissue out of the desk drawer and blew her nose.

Maybe I should have apologized and left. But I didn't. I sat down again. "Did you know your husband was having an affair?"

She made a sound of annoyance. "Yes. He was having an affair with that redhead in the typesetting department. Ralph always enjoyed slumming."

"How long had he been having this affair?"

"How would I know? He certainly didn't report such information to me!"

"How did you know he was having an affair?" I demanded.

She drew back, and it was obvious she thought she had said too much already. "That, Mr. Dragovic, is none of your business." Straightening in her chair, she continued. "Not only is it none of your business, but these questions have nothing to do with Ralph's death. Now I want you to leave. I consider that you have invaded my privacy under false pretenses."

I walked toward the door. "Did you hate your husband?" I asked.

She compressed her lips, and I thought she was going to scream at me; but she answered. "Let's say that I had no respect for him. Ralph . . . the thing you have to understand about Ralph is that he used women. He used me to get a job at the

Truth. He used my contacts to get himself promoted. That was at my expense, Mr. Dragovic. *I*
wanted that promotion."

I left wondering how Gayle Blasingame knew
about Suzanne Quering, wondering whether Ted
Haapala had been at the *Truth-Examiner* on the
evening of Blasingame's fall, wondering what
story Gayle Blasingame had been working on.

I've said that I think best on my feet, and I do—
especially when they're moving. So I moved them,
heading north on Michigan Avenue, savoring the
crisp, sixty-two degree day. I found myself in the
Gold Coast area, where both Haapala and Gayle
Blasingame lived—Haapala on East Chestnut and
Blasingame in Water Tower Place. That's not the
place that survived the Chicago fire, just in case
you aren't familiar with our city. They built a new
marble building called Water Tower Place, one
block north of the old stone water tower. The first
seven floors and front of the new Water Tower are
a shopping mall. The back high-rise section con-
sists of condominiums and the Ritz-Carlton Hotel.
I guess if your condominium is the wrong shade of
pearl white (or chic mauve, or flat gray, or whatever shade is in vogue), and you're having it
painted, you can rent a suite at the Ritz until the
job is finished.

I hadn't come anywhere close to knowing
whether Blasingame's death was an accident or a
murder—or even a suicide. Haapala had been nervous about something, and I thought it had something to do with why Blasingame was down there
—or why Haapala himself was down there, if, in
fact, he was. What could Haapala possibly have
been doing down there that he wanted kept secret?
Maybe he was having an affair too. Christ, I hoped

not: the case was bad enough already. Maybe, though . . . What about Haapala and Gayle Blasingame?

Nah, I dismissed it. But then I turned it over and considered it again. Why not? The two rivals to Blasingame. Neither of them liked him. It would be poetic justice if they'd been having an affair. But that would mean their nervousness stemmed from not wanting it known. All things considered, that was innocent enough. I was looking for something not so innocent.

Turning west on Ohio Street, I headed for Pizzeria Uno, where, legend has it, the Chicago deep-dish pizza was invented in 1943. Once there, I settled into a chair and ordered a midget pizza. No, it's not for midgets. It's a little pizza, supposed to serve two if you stretched it with a salad. However, I had both the salad and the midget pizza, which goes to show I have the strength of two because my heart is pure.

It was possible that Gayle Blasingame didn't believe her husband's death was an accident. On the other hand, she wasn't hounding the police to prove it was murder. Dragan, at least, had given no indication that she was.

Dragan liked Suzanne Quering for murder. If it was murder, then I liked Gayle Blasingame for it because I disliked her. She was a dangerous woman. But the fact remained that if Blasingame had been pushed, she wasn't the most likely candidate to have done it.

Ralph Blasingame had been a vice president and in charge of circulation for the *Truth-Examiner* before being promoted to vice president and director of sales, marketing, and advertising. Quite an array of titles. From all accounts, he was climbing

to the top. But the climb to the top is never easy.
There are always those behind you seeking to sur-
pass you. Should I concentrate on the three princi-
pal suspects Dragan had, even though one of them
was my client? A client who had, after all, *not*
hired me to prove her innocent? Should I concentrate on Blasingame during the last three months?
What about his previous jobs? And, the two big
questions: why had he been on the catwalk, and
was it murder?

With my stomach heavy from the pizza, my feet
rested, and my head spinning with questions, I
headed toward Water Tower Place. I would do
what I could to check out Gayle Blasingame and
Ted Haapala, starting with the assumption that
one or both of them had something to hide about
the night Blasingame died. They didn't act innocent.

Neither, I reflected, did Suzanne Quering.

Chapter Nine

I SPENT MOST of the afternoon checking on Ted
Haapala and Gayle Blasingame, but I got nowhere.
If you've ever tried to get into the tightly guarded
houses of the rich, you know what I mean. They
surround themselves with people who protect
them against the likes of me. What I managed to
glean in the way of information was this: Gayle

Blasingame came home from work Monday afternoon around five-thirty. She left her apartment around seven o'clock and returned after midnight. Nobody saw her leave after that. Ted Haapala also came home around five-thirty. The doorman didn't see him leave again that evening.

By 3:30 in the afternoon I was ready to call it a day. The morning's sixty-two degrees was a memory that no longer kept me warm. Up Michigan Avenue I headed, walking briskly. Michigan merged with the Inner Drive along Lake Shore. I followed it to North Avenue, where the street ended. Turning left, I followed the southern-most edge of Lincoln Park. At La Salle I turned north again and was home. Saying hello to Ed, the day-shift doorman, I wondered how I would like it if somebody flashed a license and asked him questions about me. I decided I wouldn't like it one bit. Checking my mailbox, I pulled out bills and a Land's End catalog. Throwing the mail on the kitchen table, I washed up, grabbed a coat, and took the stairs to the parking lot. Five minutes later, I was driving down La Salle, and five minutes after that I was on the Kennedy, heading south.

Every Wednesday that I could, I visited my parents. If I had plenty of time and money, I'd call before noon to let my mother know I was taking them out to a neighborhood restaurant—Croatian, Italian, Serbian, or Polish—or perhaps Phil Smidt's, across the state line in Hammond, Indiana, serving the best pan-fried perch anywhere. If I was short on time or money, I'd just drive down and make myself at home at the dinner table.

The Kennedy became the Dan Ryan. At 65th I took the Chicago Skyway toward Indiana. Where the Skyway passes over 95th Street, I was above Chicago's main Croatian neighborhood, just a few blocks northeast of the Calumet River. This is the neighborhood of Chicago's steelyards, and if you're entering Chicago from the east, coming across the Skyway, you look down on the factories, storefronts, and homes and wonder how anybody could stand living there. Well, Poles, Serbs, and Croatians have stood it for practically a century, working in steel to help make Chicago the giant that it became.

After paying the Skyway toll, I crossed the Calumet River. At the Illinois-Indiana border I got off the expressway, took Indianapolis Boulevard south, then turned back west toward Chicago on 106th. I turned south on Avenue G and pulled into the driveway of my parents' home. Here, on Chicago's Southeast Side, I had grown up, just a few blocks from Hammond, Indiana.

Also just a few blocks from Wolf Lake, where in 1924, Nathan Leopold and Richard Loeb, after picking up Bobby Frank at 50th and Ellis as he was on his way home from school, murdered him for kicks and then disposed of his body. The killers poured hydrochloric acid on Bobby Frank's naked body, then stuffed it into a culvert at Wolf Lake. Carelessly, the killers left Bobby Frank's feet protruding from the culvert. Even more carelessly, Nathan Leopold dropped a pair of his expensive eyeglasses into the culvert, giving grist to the process of detection. The murder was solved in a matter of days. Nobody had dropped eyeglasses into the *Truth*'s presses when—*if*—they pushed Ralph Blasingame into them. But somebody had dropped a silk scarf into those presses. Was the scarf, like

Leopold's glasses, dropped inadvertently, or was it dropped deliberately?

I walked in the back door and into the kitchen. My mother was at the kitchen counter tearing lettuce for a salad. Kissing the top of her head, I lifted the lid of a pot from which came the inviting smell of good food.

"*Sarma,*" she said, unnecessarily.

That was not a Croatian greeting, but the name of a Croatian stuffed cabbage dish.

"How have you been?" my mother asked.

"Good," I replied, opening a cabinet and taking out plates.

"When are you going to get married?"

"Not this week," I answered. "Are Stefanie and Aaron coming?"

"No."

I began to set the table for three.

"You're twenty-eight years old." My mother stirred the *sarma* and thumped the wooden spoon on the pot rim unnecessarily.

"Dad was twenty-nine when he got married." It always helps to throw a little family history back at them.

"People get married younger nowadays. Besides, we had been going together for five years before we were married. You don't have five years." She went back to tearing the lettuce.

"Where are the napkins now?" I asked, looking around and not finding them where they used to be.

"On the shelf by the stove. Have you seen Marcia Paxton lately?"

My mother asked me this question every week. The answer was usually no. Today the answer was yes.

She was surprised. "Marcia sure can cook," she managed to say after a few moments. "Did she cook anything for you?"

"No. It was strictly a business call."

"Oh." She was clearly disappointed. She recovered. "Well, then, are you interested in any woman, at least?"

"I met two interesting women this week," I offered, changing slightly the intent of my mother's words.

That pleased her. "Tell me about them."

"One works as a typesetter at the *Truth*. She's also a gymnast. She whittles wood and has red hair. The other is a business executive. She's a very rich widow and has light brown hair."

I grabbed a beer, a Budweiser, from the refrigerator. My mother finished the salad and considered the information.

"A business executive. That sounds good. But a widow. That could be bad. I don't know about a gymnast. Although Mrs. Burkovich's daughter is an acrobat, or something like that. Which one do you like better?"

I swallowed some beer. "The redhead."

"I don't know," offered my mother, considering it seriously. "A redhead could mean trouble. Why don't you bring one of them to dinner?"

"Maybe. I've got a question for you."

She put the salad in the refrigerator and sat at the kitchen table. "What?"

Straddling a kitchen chair, I also sat. "There's a man, see. We'll call him Teddy. And there's a woman. We'll call her . . . Galina. Teddy and Galina and Galina's husband all work together, in the same business. Galina's husband has an accident at work late one night—morning, really. It's fatal. Galina's not there at the time. Neither is Teddy. Somebody from work calls to tell Galina, of course. And somebody calls to tell Teddy. Are you with me so far?"

"I'm only fifty-two years old, Frank."

She meant, of course, that senility had not yet set in.

"Right. Now, I'm questioning Teddy. Teddy is often at work late at night. But Teddy insists he wasn't at work that night. In the course of the conversation, Teddy says that the morning Galina's husband was killed, he—Teddy—called on her to offer his condolences, then he went to work."

"There's nothing wrong with that. Somebody has to run the business. He did the right thing."

Swallowing the last of the beer, I reached backward, placing the bottle on the counter. "Now, I also question Galina. Galina *was* at work the evening her husband died. But she left before his accident. Galina says that Teddy *was* there that night. When I push her for proof, though, she backs away. And when I ask her what time Teddy came to see her that morning, she says he didn't come to see her. When I tell her Teddy says he called on her, she mumbles that he did; but she didn't want to see him." I paused. "Now, why would she lie about something like that?"

My mother thought about it a while. "Maybe she wasn't lying. She was in shock. Maybe she heard your question wrong. She probably just wasn't thinking. On the other hand, maybe she wants to get Teddy in trouble. Is this a murder case, Frank?"

"I don't know," I replied. "Could be." I thought about things a bit more, then pushed them to the back of my mind. "Where's Dad?" I asked.

"He's putting in new cement steps for the Croatian Hall."

"He was doing that last week."

"He had to put the roof on Mr. Yenerich's garage
while it was dry."

"I'll go help him load the truck," I said.

"Tell him to come home, it's time to eat."

The Croatian Hall at 96th and Commercial now
contained the offices of the 10th Ward Democratic
Club. My father, who preferred not to get involved
in 10th Ward politics, would not have sought out
the job of putting in new steps for the Croatian
Hall. But Croatian Hall and the 10th Ward preferred giving all such work to 10th Ward voters
(and good workmen), and so my father was asked
to do the job.

Commercial Avenue and 96th being too far to
walk, I drove, taking 106th west and catching
Commercial. Crossing the bridge over the Calumet
River, I looked down on the slips where barges
and freighters from the Great Lakes docked and
workers unloaded their industrial cargo for southeast Chicago and northwest Indiana.

Legend has it that back in the early 1800s, when
the federal government sent a survey party to
choose the site for a Lake Michigan fort, the party
considered first the mouth of the Chicago River,
then the mouth of the Calumet River. Whether out
of whim or wisdom, the survey party chose the
Chicago River: Fort Dearborn was erected there in
1803. During the War of 1812, the fort was burned
by Indians. But in 1816, Fort Dearborn, like the
phoenix, rose again, and in much shorter time.
Around the new fort grew the city of Chicago; the
Calumet section remained an undeveloped area
far from the heart of town until the 1870s, when

the first steelworks opened at 109th and the Calumet River. So, but for historical accident, the Calumet River, and not the Chicago, might have been the center of town. Then Croatian, Serbian, Polish, and black Americans would probably have been living at Michigan and Oak.

My father was troweling the steps one last time. "Hello, Frank. Mom send you to get me?" he asked, inspecting his work.

"Yep. Looks good."

"Want to put your initials on it?" he chuckled.

He was referring to the time I had ruined a set of freshly poured and troweled steps at the Serbian Eastern Orthodox Church (almost across the street from where we now stood) by writing my initials, FAD, on each step. Even then, at the age of ten, I had been thorough. My father hadn't noticed until the cement had set. I got a tanning I'll never forget. It would have been bad enough, he'd lectured, had I done it to fellow Croatians—but what would the Serbians think of us?

"No, thanks," I replied. "I'll put up the signs." Walking over to the pickup truck, I pulled out the "Wet Cement" sandwich-board signs my mother had bought for my father to use. But my father never used them, believing that anybody should be able to tell wet cement from dry concrete simply by looking. The wooden forms surrounding wet cement meant nothing to most people though, and many was the time Southeast-Side citizens had stepped into wet cement, only to complain to the proprietor. One day my mother got tired of getting phone calls from irate citizens, each one of whom knew our phone number, and took preventive action. But my father still didn't use the signs.

After setting up the signs, I helped my father

load the truck: trowels, forms, buckets, bags of sand and cement, hose, ladder, scaffold. As we loaded up, I told him the same story of Teddy and Galina that I had told my mother. It was my father's opinion that Teddy had lied (about being at his place of work in the evening and about calling on Galina), but for no particular reason: perhaps simply because a lie came to him more easily than the truth. Interesting.

We drove back home: my father in his truck, me in my car. I unloaded the truck for him, storing the things in the garage, while he went into the basement to take a quick shower and put on clean clothes. We ate dinner and watched the evening news on television and talked. Around eight-thirty I said I would go over to see Dragan.

I walked through our backyard and then through Mrs. Spikovic's backyard, turned down N street, and walked up the sidewalk to Dragan's house. I knocked and then, without waiting for a reply, walked in. Dragan never locked his doors until he went to sleep. "It's me—Frank," I shouted. From upstairs I could hear the sound of the kids squealing and water splashing.

Gloria's blond head appeared around the banister. "Hi, Frank. We're giving the kids a bath. Dragan will be down in a minute. Have a beer."

Dragan came pounding down the stairs, one of his shirt sleeves rolled up above the elbow, the other flopping loosely over his wrist. Both were soaking wet. "Frankie! You've come to tell me it was murder. You've come to tell me who did it!"

I glared at him. "I've come on a visit, Dragan."

"Yeah, yeah," he mumbled, heading for the refrigerator and returning with two large bottles of beer. "Have a beer."

"You have it, Dragan. I just had one before dinner."

"Come on, Frank. It's Niksic *pivo*—brewed in Yugoslavia." He shoved the opened bottle and a beer mug at me.

Accepting them, I poured the beer into the mug. I'd had his Niksic *pivo* before, and it was great beer—very grainy in taste. "Niksic is in Montenegro, not Croatia," I commented.

"So?" he challenged. "It's from Yugoslavia. We can't be partial to provinces, Frank—I don't want you thinking like a terrorist." Dragan took a large swallow of beer. He still had plenty to go, since a Niksic *pivo* (*"pivo"* is beer) held one pint, five fluid ounces.

I didn't really want more beer, but I drank it.

"So. What gives? You working for the redhead?"

"Yeah," I replied grudgingly. "You made any progress?"

"We always make progress."

"Um-hmm. Was it murder?"

"Not that much progress."

"Tell me more about Haapala's limp," I suggested.

Dragan shrugged. "What's to tell? Says he fell off the loading dock. The morning Blasingame fell into the presses." He swallowed more *pivo*. "Too much falling that day if you ask me."

"Um-hmmm. Did you check it out?"

"Of *course* we checked it out, Frank. Three or four guys saw him fall. The doctor examined the sprain later in the day."

"Later. Enough later so it didn't have to look recent?"

"Frank, come on. We're working on it." Dragan

poured the rest of the one-pint-five-ounces into his beer mug.

"What did Haapala do the morning of the . . . accident?"

"Nothing. He went to work. What do you mean?"

"He said he stopped to see Gayle Blasingame first."

"Oh, that. Yeah, he showed up," snorted Dragan. "We had a female officer inside the apartment. Mrs. Blasingame didn't want to see him. So he left. What's wrong with that? You think it means something?"

So he had stopped by to see her. "I doubt it." I rubbed a hand over my face, trying to wipe away the tiredness—*pivo*-induced, no doubt. Nursing it so that Dragan wouldn't pour me a second, I watched Gloria come down the stairs. She waved to me silently as she stood there, cocking her head to listen for any sounds of activity upstairs.

"Are you two talking business?" she asked, apparently satisfied that the kids weren't escaping from behind the bars of the cribs.

"Frank started it," blamed Dragan, getting himself a second beer.

"I'll bet. I'm going next door to see Patty then. Keep an ear out for the kids."

We watched her go. Dragan eyed me as I sipped the beer. I licked my lips, trying to show that I appreciated the full twenty-one ounces. Dragan was getting a very slight, but very definite, gut. I eyed it. He sucked in his stomach, patting it. "A few workouts down at the track, and it'll be gone," he prophesized.

"How did you know that Suzanne Quering had been Blasingame's lover?" I asked.

"Mrs. Blasingame told us. When we asked the redhead, she didn't deny it. Admitted it." Dragan shrugged.

"How did Gayle Blasingame know?"

Dragan wiped the condensation off the beer bottle by rubbing it across his pants. "Now, Frankie, you know I can't tell you that."

I knew he could. Everytime Dragan said "you know I can't," I knew he could—he just wanted me to agree that he couldn't. Which I didn't—agree, that is. "So she told you that Suzanne Quering threatened to kill her husband."

"Who?" asked Dragan too innocently.

"Gayle Blasingame. First she told you that Quering and her husband had had an affair. Then she told you that Quering had threatened to kill him."

The only sound was that of Dragan swallowing more beer. "You know I can't tell you that," he finally replied.

"The question is, how would she know that? How would Gayle Blasingame know that Quering threatened to kill him?"

Dragan smiled. "Ah, Frank. The real question is why would I *believe* she threatened to kill him. Hmm?" Looking smug, he took a large swallow of beer, wiping the foam off his lips.

He had me there. It *was* the real question. Why did Dragan believe that Suzanne Quering had threatened to kill Blasingame? I asked it to myself, knowing he wasn't going to tell me, no matter how many times I might ask it aloud.

"I suppose Gayle Blasingame was at home at three in the morning, or whenever the police came to tell her about her husband?"

"She was."

"I suppose she answered the door quickly?"

"Not too quickly. Not too slowly."

"How was she dressed," I asked.

"You know I can't—ah, what the hell. Skirt, blouse, sweater. Nylons, slippers."

I stared at Dragan.

He continued, pleased with the impression he had made. "Says she fell asleep on the couch."

"Skirt, blouse, sweater. Nylons, slippers," I repeated. "No silk scarf?"

Dragan needed another swallow before he could answer the question. "No, no silk scarf. No scarf of any kind. The scarf belongs to Quering. All we have to do is prove it."

"Ummm." I finished my beer and declined another. We sparred over the case for another half hour, but I got nothing more out of Dragan. Finally, I said good night and, after dropping by my parents' house to say good-bye, drove home. I felt bloated with beer.

Chapter Ten

WHEN THE ALARM went off at 6:00 the next morning, I shut it off with a groan and rolled out of bed. Stretching, I turned on a light, fetched the *Truth*, which had been delivered outside my apartment door, glanced at the headlines, studied the weather, and, still carrying the *Truth*, stepped into the bathroom to weigh myself: 172. Three pounds

too many. Even ditching the *Truth* didn't affect the
reading on the scale. I blamed it on Dragan's *pivo*.
Dialing the weather (not trusting the *Truth* to be
anything more than general), I heard that the
lakefront temperature was forty-eight degrees. So
I pulled on a jockstrap, long underwear, a T-shirt,
running shorts, socks, and shoes, did some warm-
ups, and went for a five-mile run.

The fallen leaves—wet with dew, dark with dirt,
and flattened by the pounding of 'many feet—
smelled inviting in the early morning air. This
must be what hunters smelled as they waited for
the innocent beasts to come by in the early morning. Thinking about it made me glad that if I was a
hunter of anything, it was of people, not animals.
The people, at least, had done something wrong—
or had done nothing wrong, but had to convince
the right people of their innocence.

Before I knew it, I had reached Diversey
through the Lincoln Park running trails. Not slow-
ing as I passed Suzanne Quering's apartment, I ran
as far north as Barry, then turned around and
came back. Sixty minutes after I had started my
run, I was stepping out of the shower, toweling
myself dry, and checking my weight. The scale still
read 172, but it seemed to be leaning toward 171. I
felt lighter. Since I had to appear in court, I had
time only for a cup of coffee and a few pieces of
gibanica (nut roll) that I sliced from one of the
three rolls my mother had given me the previous
night. Maybe, I thought, chewing and sipping, the
extra weight was not all due to Dragan's beer.
There had been the midget pizza yesterday, as well
as the *sarma*. Perhaps I should go on a diet of cabbage, lentils, and beans.

By 2:30 P.M. I was out of court. I called Suzanne

Quering to confirm our 5:00 meeting at the composing room, but there was no answer. So I took the subway to the Criminal Investigation Division to see Dragan.

He wasn't at his desk. Joe Flynn, a buddy of Dragan's, told me that Dragan was questioning somebody.

Although it sounds strange (because it's not pleasant to watch), there's something that has always attracted me to watching the police question somebody. What I liked was standing behind the observation glass unobserved. Because that glass was in front of you, you seemed detached from what was happening. You could see how the subject was reacting much better than the cops inside the room could.

Clipping on an identification tag, I wandered down to the questioning rooms until I stopped in my tracks. It wasn't Dragan I spotted first; it was her red hair. I don't think I heard anything for the first thirty seconds. The shock of seeing her there gave me a horrible feeling in the pit of my stomach.

She was wearing a gray sweatsuit, white socks, and blue running shoes, her hair held back by a green bandana. That worried me: if they had pulled her right off the running track, it was bad. Her face was tense and white; she had her heels hooked on the chair rung and was rubbing the palms of her hands on her thighs.

The shock passed and I started to hear them—Suzanne, Dragan, and another cop.

". . . and you still claim you didn't set this story, even though we found the tape on it this morning." That was Dragan.

Suzanne frowned. "I don't *claim* it, I say it.

'Claim' makes it sound like I'm lying. I *didn't* set
that story." She paused, as if thinking. "And I still
haven't seen this tape you found."

"Blasingame was your lover, wasn't he?" asked
the other cop.

"*Yes!* How many times are you going to ask me
that?" she asked in exasperation. "You probably believe in sin, don't you?"

"If we show you the tape, how will you know it's
yours?" asked Dragan.

Turning back to face Dragan, she took a deep
breath, then answered nervously. "If it's the story
you say it is, the one on Colorado, then I didn't set
it. So it won't be mine. I'll be able to read the codes
on front of the tape."

Dragan motioned his head to the other cop, who
left the room.

"Found your scarf yet?" asked Dragan casually.

Suzanne frowned. "No."

He stared at her without comment, then
switched back to the topic of the paper tape. "And
what if the codes say the tape *is* yours?"

She shook her head. "I told you last week. Whoever set that story was a terrible operator. She
could have punched the wrong code. Operators
make more mistakes when they hit numbers than
when they hit letters."

"Why 'she'?"

"Why not?" Suzanne asked. "It could be a he, I
suppose, though most men type too slowly to
make any mistakes. But I told you, the person who
sets dirty proofs in there is Ruby. It's probably
Ruby's tape. What makes you think it's my tape,
anyway? *You* can't read paper tape." She looked at
him with sudden comprehension. "You think it's

mine because somebody told you that! Didn't they?"

Dragan didn't say anything.

Suzanne seethed for a few seconds, then filled the silence. Just like Dragan wanted her to. "Well? How do you know?"

"It's yours. Your number is sixteen, isn't it?"

"I'm sure you know it is," she answered with sarcasm.

"Well, the number on this tape is sixteen. Here," he said as the other cop came back with a piece of yellow rolled-up paper tape in his hand. "This is your tape."

Suzanne put her hand out for the tape, but Dragan moved back. Not quickly, just surely. I caught myself wondering whether he had known last night that he was going to pull her in today—whether he had known it while he was plying me with his imported *pivo*.

"Nothing doing," he said. "Steve, watch her. We don't want her tearing this."

Naturally he expected nothing of the kind. He was trying to implant fear in her. Sweat dripped down my back, where it seemed to collect in a small, damp depression, creating a cold sensation.

I thought this guy was your friend, said Goofus.

He's just doing his job, advised Gallant.

He's making me very angry, replied Goofus.

As I watched, Dragan unrolled a small segment of the tape and held it up for Suzanne. She leaned forward, hands on her thighs, and Dragan stepped back again. "Put your hands behind your back."

That was really going too far. Did he think she was stupid enough to wrestle him for possession of the tape and shred it to bits right before his eyes?

"Don't be ridiculous," she replied in a nervous voice. Instead of complying, she folded her arms across her chest. Dragan stepped forward, holding part of the yellow paper tape unrolled so that she could see it. She squinted.

"Okay," Dragan announced, "tell me what you see. You see your number, don't you? Sixteen. You set this story, didn't you? You set it the night Blasingame was killed, didn't you?"

The one-way glass I stared through was framed in moldering wooden molding. My hands were on the molding over my head; I peered at the scene from between my arms. My mouth was dry. I was hanging there, waiting for Suzanne to answer.

But she was silent.

Pressing his advantage, Dragan softened his voice. Dangling the tape from one hand, he placed his other hand on Suzanne's shoulder. My fingers tightened their grip on the molding. "Miss Quering," he said, "this is your tape, isn't it? You set it very early Tuesday morning, October 4—the Tuesday morning Ralph Blasingame fell into the presses. In fact, you set it after he fell into the presses, didn't you? That same evening, you lost your silk scarf—the scarf that Blasingame had given you. Admit it," he encouraged.

Suzanne looked up at him. He had an honest, open face, a kind one: blond hair, blue eyes. I would trust him. Suzanne, don't trust him for a minute, not for a second! Don't say anything! Especially, I thought, if he offers you his beer.

"It's my number," she answered softly. "It's number sixteen. But I didn't set that story. I didn't punch that tape."

"You did, though. This is your tape." Pulling up a stool, Dragan sat facing her. Again he placed his hand on her shoulder. "Come on, now. There's no crime in setting this tape, is there? We both know that. This is your tape."

She brushed his hand off her shoulder. "*No*, it *isn't* my tape because I didn't set it. Somebody else put that number on there. Maybe—" She stopped abruptly, studying the floor. Dragan's feet were the only thing there.

"Maybe what?" he asked skeptically.

Don't *tell* him what, my fingers tried to communicate, pressing the molding, the shredding wood splintering beneath the pressure. Don't tell him *anything!* Goddamn it, get a lawyer! There was a cop standing next to me. He gave me a glance, then looked again and studied me. I ignored him.

"Maybe . . . I thought maybe somebody changed the number by hand."

"What do you mean, by hand?"

"A couple of people there—the foremen, copycutters, and some others, those who used to work at job shops—have little clips. They're paper-punching clips, so you can punch holes in the tape by hand." She had been looking at Dragan, but as she spoke she looked back at the floor, her voice fading into a whisper. The classic signs of defeat. I wanted to slam my fist through their goddamn one-way glass.

"C'mon," challenged Dragan, standing and kicking the stool aside. "Why would anybody want to do that?"

"Because somebody is trying to frame me! I keep telling you that."

"Do *you* have one of those little clips?" Dragan asked pointedly.

Suzanne opened her mouth to speak, stopped, then finally replied. "Yes. I have one."

"I see." Dragan gazed at her silently for a minute, then leaned back against the wall. "So you're saying this hole could have been punched by hand, huh?"

"Yes. But it probably wasn't. It's too straight. Too perfect. It was probably done by machine. But it *wasn't* done by me!" she almost shouted, her voice now louder and defiant once again. Sweat was dripping down her forehead. She wiped it away. Unconsciously, I made the same gesture.

Dragan kept studying her. The other cop still stood behind her chair. His presence must have made her uncomfortable, for she turned around just to make certain he was still there and not up to no good.

"You can change a three to a six, you know," she said to Dragan.

"So?"

She hesitated, running her tongue over her lips. "Ruby's number is thirteen, mine's sixteen. Paper tape has a six-hole code. See those columns? Three holes on top, three on bottom, with those little feeder holes across the middle." Dragan studied the tape as she talked. "The code for a three is holes in the first and second rows. The code for a six is holes in the first and second rows and the fourth and sixth. All you'd have to do is punch two extra holes—the fourth and sixth rows—and the three becomes a six."

"Yeah, but this wasn't done that way," the other cop announced. "You said this was done by machine. *Your* machine."

"I don't have a machine. I'm a sub, so I work on different machines."

Suzanne, shutup! Goddamn it!

Having found his voice, the other cop was now

gathering steam. "He was your lover. He left you, you were jealous. You pushed him off the rail. Your scarf fell with him. You could cooperate with us, get a reduced sentence, maybe five years—who knows? You didn't plan it." Suzanne placed her hands over her ears and bent forward, thrusting her head between her knees. The other cop bent over her, still talking, but she hunkered down tighter, like a child.

"Hey! Wait a minute!" she shouted, jumping up from her crouch, the top of her head clipping the second cop's jaw. "Ouch!" She rubbed the top of her head.

"Sonofabitch!" The cop rubbed his jaw, then his lip. I could see the blood where he had bit it. It didn't look nearly bloody enough to me.

Dragan, still leaning against the wall, waited.

"I want to see that tape again," she demanded. Then, perhaps recognizing that better manners were called for under the circumstances, she tacked a grudging "Please?" to the end of it.

"Why?" asked Dragan.

"Let me see it and I'll tell you."

Dragan was in charge, but he stepped forward. First, however, he unrolled the tape for himself and looked at it very carefully. Suzanne shuffled her feet impatiently. I got a splinter in my thumb from the goddamn rotten molding.

After what seemed like forever, Dragan shrugged his shoulders and gave the tape to Suzanne. Unrolling a portion of it, she held it close, peering intently, as if reading hieroglyphs. Then, with a slight smile, she held the tape out to Dragan. "I don't have to see it any more." Relaxing my grip on the molding, I listened. "I knew somebody was trying to frame me," she explained, looking at

Dragan. "That tape," she said excitedly, "has never been run."

It seemed as though there were only the two of them in that room, Suzanne and Dragan. He looked only at her, she only at him.

"Translate."

If I had been less tense, I might have smiled at Dragan. He hadn't expected this. He was supposed to run the show. But I didn't know what Suzanne meant, and I didn't feel safe for her.

"Okay. These paper tapes," she explained, pointing at the one he held, "are 'read' by the linotype machines. See, we set the stories on regular typewriter keyboards that punch out paper tape. The tape and copy are sent out to the floor—that's where the linotypes are—where each piece of tape is hooked up to a machine called a reader. The reader activates the old linotypes, which cast lines of metal type." She studied Dragan to make sure he was following her exposition. Maybe, I thought, she should give guided tours of the composing room to cops in her spare time.

"*That tape,*" repeated Suzanne, stabbing a forefinger at the unwound tape dangling from Dragan's hand, "has never been read. It's never gone through a reader machine. See those feeder holes? They're perfect, just like when they were punched by the keyboard. If a reader read those, the feeder holes would be larger. They'd be elongated, bigger —big enough so that you could look at them and tell that the tape had been run."

"Oh, yeah?" demanded the other cop, still touching a finger to his cut lip. "Then where did the dirty proof come from, huh?"

Suzanne turned to shake her head at such denseness. "It obviously came from *some* tape—but not from this one."

"I don't believe it," he announced.

"I don't care if you believe it. It's the truth." Defiantly, she turned to Dragan. "Somebody's trying to frame me."

Dragan kept up the questions for another half hour, but you could see his heart wasn't in it. Perplexed, he kept glancing down at the tape and frowning. My heart felt lighter. Dragan was a good cop, an honest man. Right now he was thinking what I was thinking: if that paper tape was not run, then it was planted. By whom? Why? Where did the dirty proof come from? Who set it? And how did Suzanne's slug get on it? And none of those questions answered the big one: Blasingame. And the scarf.

Finally, Dragan gave in to Suzanne's insistence that she had to call the newspaper to see if she had a hire. He waited until she stood up, then took her arm and led her toward the door.

I stepped around to meet them, standing where they would come out, my hands in my pockets, blocking their way.

Suzanne saw me first. "Frank!" She grabbed my arm with both her hands. "What are you doing here?"

It was like an electric charge. Reaching out, I put my other arm around her shoulders, pulling her around to my side. We stood facing them, with me glowering at Dragan.

"Was this necessary?"

He seemed taken aback, but the words were out and I was hot. "Yeah. Yeah, Frank, it was necessary. What we do on our job is always necessary." He brushed by us without another word. I wanted to call out after him that, on top of making me spend a miserable afternoon in front of his two-way mirror, he had made me gain three pounds—but even I realized that it sounded foolish.

The other cop spoke to Suzanne. "You can go now, but we may have to call you in for questioning again."

He was the one I really itched to punch, but my fingers pressed into Suzanne's shoulder instead. If she noticed the pressure, she didn't mention it.

"How did you know I was here?" she asked, turning around to stare at me. "Am I late? I don't even know what time it is. They found me running in Lincoln Park." She looked down at her jogger's watch and pressed a few buttons. "Worst time of my life. Ha! That's a pun. What have you found?"

I looked at her. Her capacity for recovery was phenomenal. There were many things I wanted to say. All I said was, "It should be ten-to-four."

"Oh. Right. Oh! I've got to call to see if I have a hire. Where's the phone?"

She returned in a few minutes, exclaiming excitedly that she had a hire. "Maybe my luck is changing," she reflected. "I've got to take a cab home and change clothes," she added, already running out the door and down the steps. "Come with me, then we can go back to the *Truth* together."

I followed in her wake.

Chapter Eleven

■

SUZANNE RUSHED INTO her apartment, kicking off her running shoes as she entered. "We can have steak sandwiches if you make them," she suggested as she grabbed an armful of clothes from the closet and disappeared into the bathroom. As I listened to the shower water running, I tried to imagine Clark Kent stopping for a quick shower between costume changes. My imagination wasn't up to it.

In the kitchen I looked around and spotted an electric grill on the counter. In the refrigerator I found some prime thin steaks and plenty of tomatoes, along with a bag of Italian rolls. I heated the bread, grilled the steaks, sliced the tomatoes, and set the table. As I worked, I wondered how I could persuade Suzanne to hire a lawyer: I had tried again when we left the police station, but she had adamantly refused.

She stepped out of the bathroom wearing a dark blue skirt and a blue and tan shirt. As I watched, she pulled on leather boots and slipped on a camel blazer. She sat at the table. A gold chain dangled around her neck. Gold chains turn me on. I tried to concentrate on the food. Her perfume interfered.

"This is delicious," she said, interrupting my silent daydreaming. "If I don't eat now, I can't eat until lunch. That's at ten-thirty on the five o'clock shift. Thanks for making it." She ate silently for at least half a sandwich, then added, "Thank you for being there. I felt better when I saw you."

"I'll feel better when I get somewhere," I muttered. "Got any suggestions on who I should talk to tonight?"

She shrugged, then reconsidered. "Well, if somebody's trying to frame me, it wouldn't be one of my friends. So there's no sense concentrating on them."

"Who are your friends?" I asked.

"Well, there's Jeff Barton. You've already met him; he runs the office. There's Chandra Robinson. We went to school together and go back a long way. There's Carl Wahl, Adrian Venable, Frederick Douglass Williams. There's Ellen—" Seeing my hand in the air, she stopped. "What's wrong?"

"That's not the way it's done," I answered. Recognizing her blank stare as one of incomprehension, I explained. "I don't avoid questioning people's friends—chances are it's the friends who . . . know something."

"Phooey. My friends didn't even know Ralph."

"Everybody knew who he was," I corrected.

"That's different. They didn't know him enough to want to kill him."

We ate the rest of the quick meal in silence as I pondered whether knowing Ralph Blasingame automatically meant wanting to kill him. When we finished, Suzanne scooped up the dishes and dropped them with a crash into the sink. In two minutes we were on our way, in her car.

She drove like she changed clothes.

"My god, you're lucky to be alive!" I shuddered.

"Don't be silly. This is nothing."

Screeching to a halt by the loading docks of the *Truth,* she asked me to tell the gorilla that she would be a few minutes late. She also reminded me that his name was Jeff Barton, as if I couldn't remember. I obliged. It was safer outside the car than in.

When I gave the message to Jeff Barton (the man in the cage), he told me that I couldn't enter the composing room until Suzanne got there. Maybe he thought I'd slip or trip on the floor without somebody to hold my hand. He seemed too busy to bother with questions at the moment, so I went back down to the loading dock to wait for Suzanne.

The toes of my shoes lined up with the edge of the dock, and I swayed back and forth in thought, studying the street below. It would have been a four-foot fall for Haapala—enough to twist an ankle seriously. But why would anybody be walking that close to the edge of the loading dock, which was at least eight-feet wide, to begin with? From a long way off, I saw Suzanne coming and walked down to meet her.

"If somebody's framing you, why didn't they run that tape so it would look authentic?"

She shook her head as she walked briskly along. "You heard that? Well, something dawned on me after the police questioned me." She grabbed me by the arm as we walked along. "A proof appears in the proofreading room, a dirty proof with my slug on it. I told you about it: it's the proof they found after Ralph . . . died. *I* didn't set it, so somebody else must have. Maybe it was an accident. Maybe somebody hit the wrong code number." She shook my arm, practically rattling my teeth. "But maybe it wasn't an accident. Maybe somebody did it deliberately."

"Um-hmm." I knew her point. She'd said it often enough: somebody was trying to frame her—but it wasn't one of her friends.

"Yes. That's what I think."

As we walked I moved her out of the way of other hurrying pedestrians, more for their sake, I think, than hers. "If somebody's framing you, why didn't they run that tape—the tape they showed you at the police station—so that it would look authentic? You know what I mean, so that the feeder holes would be elongated."

She shook her head, the red hair bouncing back and forth. "That's too risky. You see, anybody could have *set* it. There are more than fifty keyboards in the composing room. Anybody could sit there at any hour of the day or night and pound out that little piece of story in less than ten minutes. But if they took it out to run it, they'd be noticed. If they just sent the tape out with the others and let it be run, the story would be set in metal and a makeup man would try to put it into the paper, or check where it went. Then somebody might remember that the story was cast a week ago: what's the tape doing here again?" She paused, then concluded. "The way I see it, the tape that the dirty proof came from is not the same as the tape Lieutenant Brdar showed me today."

"What do they do with all those tapes?" I asked, pulling open a heavy metal door after a guard motioned us through. "Can we find the original?"

She led the way up some back stairs. Through the wall I could hear the pounding of the presses.

"They throw them away, usually within twenty-four hours. Job shops—those are shops that set magazines, books, pamphlets, brochures, that sort of thing—keep tapes, sometimes for years. That way, they can run a brochure over. But newspapers would have millions of tapes around, and nobody would know which was which. So the *Truth* keeps them for a few hours. Some maybe they keep for a few days at the most, then they throw them away."

"So the first tape, the one that was used to produce the Colorado travel story, is gone? There's no way we can check the original?"

"No," she replied. "The story ran in Sunday's *Truth*, so the tape is long gone."

We were now on what was no doubt the floor of the composing room without ever having gone down the outside corridors or past Jeff Barton, the bear in the mouse cage. All around were linotypes, just like in the publicity film. In real life, though, their noise was deafening, with no soothing voice-overs of narration.

As I followed Suzanne, who was rushing through the plant, following aisles cordoned with lime-green tape on the floor, I thought about what she had said. If somebody were framing her, it would be risky for them to get the original paper tape—the one from which the dirty proof came—because they would have to go to the floor or the proofreading room and ask for the tape. Too risky. Somebody might remember. But if they wanted the tape to be found without asking for it, they could just have photocopied the original dirty proof and set the new tape to match it. Plant the new tape, and somebody finds it.

"I want to talk to Ruby Good," I reminded Suzanne. "Is she here tonight?"

"I hope so." We were approaching the bear in the mouse cage after all, only from a different direction.

"Hi, Jeff! Does Ruby have a hire tonight?"

Jeff checked a large board hanging from the wall. On the board were perhaps forty names, and after each name was a metal slot with a colored tab of paper. Some of the tabs were red, some blue, some white, some green, some orange. "No," he told Suzanne. "I've been trying to get her for the last three days, but she doesn't answer. She doesn't call in either. Management wants me to take her off the board as a no-show."

"That's Ruby for you," concluded Suzanne. "Didn't she turn her tab?"

"No."

Suzanne's fingertips tapped the counter of Jeff's half-door impatiently. "I've got to talk to her. She could solve this whole thing, you know, if she set the Colorado travel story." She turned to me. "Ruby's, uh, careless. And she doesn't show up regularly."

I noticed that Jeff looked at the ceiling as she spoke, then looked at me. I couldn't read whatever look was in his eyes.

"Oh, Jeff. This is Frank Dragovic. Frank, this is Jeff Barton." She explained to him what she wanted me to do.

Jeff nodded. "Sure. Why didn't you tell me you were here to help Suzanne?" he asked me. "I'd have let you in then."

I didn't have a chance to answer because I'd have lost Suzanne if I did. She was already rushing down more green-lined aisles. I followed, waving a hand of appreciation to Jeff.

Off to one side of the linotype machines was a large, glass-enclosed rectangular room in which there were dozens of large tables with what looked like large typewriters on them. People were pounding away at the keys of most of the fifty machines; yellow tape spilled out of the machines like feed belts spill out of Gatling guns. Off to one end of the area was a high, old-fashioned-looking counter. Standing behind it were two men. One was handing somebody on our side of the counter some paper.

Suzanne introduced me, then grabbed a piece of copy and was told to take keyboard ten. She went, and I was on my own. There I stood, with a hell of a lot of questions to ask, and no idea where the answers would lead. Just to get a better feel for the situation, I studied the typesetters—perhaps forty of them. Most, but not all, were white males. There were six women counting Suzanne. Only one black man and one black woman. No Hispanics that I could tell. Three Japanese-Americans—at least I assumed they were Japanese-Americans setting type in English and not Japanese setting type in ideographs.

After surveying the scene, I started with the young guy standing behind the high desk. In his early twenties, he wore his long blond hair tied back in a ponytail. It was accompanied by a scraggly beard and wispy mustache. He had a lean and athletic build. His name was Carl Wahl; he said he was the copycutter. When I asked him to explain to me what he did, he explained that he cut the copy—the stories that came down from the reporters—into smaller pieces, then handed them out to be typeset. After asking him technical questions, I led into the night Blasingame died. Carl had been working his regular shift, 1:00 P.M. to 9:00 P.M., that day. I asked him if he could recall to whom he gave particular pieces of copy to be set. He answered that he could sometimes, but not usually.

"When sometimes?"

"Sometimes I hold out certain copy, like the race

results or baseball statistics, for certain operators."

"Why?"

"Oh, because some nights we're busy, and those take long to set, so I give them to the good operators."

"Who are they?" I interrupted.

"Oh, Frederick Douglass, Suzanne, and Adrian. Anyway, other nights we're not so busy, so I hold race results and baseball statistics back and give them to the lazy operators. There're some people here, you know, who don't take copy in the order it's on the hook. They take easy copy behind the hard copy." Carl Wahl laughed. "Fair is fair. When we aren't busy, I give them the hard stuff. And they don't like it."

A cutter with a sense of justice. "Do you remember whether you gave the Colorado travel story to anybody on Monday, October 3?"

"Nope," he said definitely, but nervously. He was a nervous guy, his fingers always busy—if not putting copy out on the hook, then beating a tattoo on the wooden counter top, or tucking a stray hair behind his ear. "I don't think I gave the story to anybody. I think it came in late, after I left. We usually set news up to eleven or twelve o'clock. Travel, things like that, they usually get set when there's no news, after midnight. Maybe Jack gave it to somebody. Most likely, though, Lee did."

"What about this Ruby Good, who everybody says sets dirty copy?"

"Dirty proofs. The copy is the stuff that comes down from the office. We set it, and then we pull a proof of what was set. We ink the type, which is in lead, put a piece of paper over it, and run a roller over that. What comes out is called a proof, just like what you'd get in the newspaper. Then we read the proof. That's proofreading, see? I don't know if Ruby took the story, if that's what you mean. I leave at 9:00." He paused and traced his fingers around a wire in-out basket. "Of course, the tape had Suzanne's code on it. I know. I was here when Lee found it."

My glance reappraised him. "You saw who found it?"

Carl nodded.

"Did this Lee give it to the cops?" I asked.

"No way, man," he replied, getting defensive. "He just happened to find it."

"So how'd it get to the cops?"

Licking his lips nervously, he explained. "Lee and I were standing here, see? This was yesterday. Lee had come in early. The tapes were on a hook here," he said, pointing to a pronged hook set into pegboard. Six or seven small rolls of yellow perforated tape were looped over it. "Jack Morton—he's the five o'clock foreman—asked him what it was. Lee just shrugged, you know? It takes a while to read those holes, you know. Anyway, Jack took it from Lee and started to read it. Then he got busy and slipped it over his wrist. Later, he came back and said it was the tape the cops had been asking about, and we had to give it to them."

"Are you sure he gave the same tape to the cops?"

"Hey, man, what do you mean?"

"I mean, did you get to read any of the tape?"

"Oh. Well, I read the code. It was number sixteen, Suzanne's code."

"What made Lee spot the tape?"

"It didn't have any writing on it. Operators are supposed to write their initials and the date and the story title on the outside of the tape, then hand it in with the copy. Sometimes we save stories here if they're too far ahead of schedule. One of the foremen or copycutters writes on the outside of the tape what the story is and when to send it on ahead to the floor. That's mainly for features. You know—Dear Abby, Art Buchwald, that sort of stuff. Sometimes they're set weeks ahead of time, and it's easier to keep the tapes here than to run them and have the metal type out on the floor."

"So it was different from the other tapes?"

"Yeah, I told you, it didn't have any writing on the outside, so Lee wanted to see what it was. That was just before I was going to leave, around eight-thirty last night."

"Okay," I summarized. "Lee found the tape last night. Lee gave it to Jack Morton. Jack Morton gave it to the cops."

Carl nodded.

"Right," I said. "Now—who gave the dirty proof to the cops last week?"

He swallowed, shuffled some papers, swallowed again. "I don't . . . I'm not sure."

"Um-hmm. Guess," I suggested.

"No," he answered firmly. "I don't know."

He wouldn't spit out the information, so I went on to something else. "Did you see the scarf they found in the presses with Blasingame?" I asked.

"No. I heard about it, though."

"Who do you think it belonged to?"

He shrugged. "Had to be a woman."

"Which women here wear silk scarves to work?"

"Suzanne. Ruby. Chandra. Ellen. Beth. All of them, I guess. Suzanne wears scarves a lot—sometimes around her neck, sometimes around her hair."

"What do you think of Suzanne Quering?" I asked.

Again he shuffled some copy, putting it into the wire basket, patting it down. "I know what they're saying, that she pushed Blasingame into the presses. I don't believe it."

"Why not?" I asked.

"I just don't."

"What do the other typesetters think of her?"

"She's okay, man. She always shows up when she's hired, and she sets good type."

"Does anybody here hate her?"

"No, man." He laughed nervously. "Not that I know of, anyway."

"Who are her friends?"

He hesitated, then pointed a piece of rolled-up paper toward the black female typesetter. "Chandra Robinson."

"Any others?"

Carl Wahl glanced nervously back at Suzanne, who was busy at work. "You'll have to ask Suzanne," he answered.

"How about the men? What do they think of her?"

"How do you mean?"

He wasn't one to answer questions without being certain what I meant. "Do they try to put the make on her?"

He blushed, a bright red. "Yeah. Well, you know. Suzanne's really, uh, . . . you know. There's a lot of kidding around."

"Do they all get rejected? Or do some get accepted?"

"If she was making it with anybody in the union, the whole floor would know about it."

"Okay. Who's gotten rejected and is really mad about it?"

"Nobody, man. Hey, you know how it's done. Kidding, but serious. That way, if they tell you No, you haven't lost face." He offered me this advice seriously, as if it were original. You know.

"Let me rephrase the question. Who's been rejected?"

"I'm not going to tell you that," he said sternly, blushing a bright red again.

"Did you ever see Suzanne out with any man? You know, during lunch break and that." My god, I was starting to talk like him. "Any man at all, whether you knew him or not?"

"How would I see something like that? If I did, I wouldn't remember."

"If you did," I corrected him, "you *would* remember. Wouldn't you?"

"Okay, okay. I would remember, but I didn't ever see it."

There was nothing more I could get out of Carl Wahl, so I turned to Chandra Robinson next.

Chapter Twelve

■

MOST PEOPLE WHO are working at a desk or table look up when you approach them. Not Chandra Robinson. Sitting with perfect posture at her typing table, she clattered away at the keys. Upon my approach, she continued to clatter away—perhaps more loudly than before. I stood patiently, watching while she moved a sheet of paper higher up on a kind of clipboard above her keyboard. Sooner or later, I figured, she would finish the story and I could interrupt.

"Ms. Robinson?" I asked the moment she stopped.

She looked me up and down slowly, then tore the edge of the paper tape, separating the punched-out tape from the unpunched portion. Winding the yellow paper tape around one hand, she acknowledged by way of a question. "What if I am?"

"Then I'd like to ask you a few questions."

Thinking it over, she placed a paperclip around the circle of wound-up tape to keep it from uncurling. With another paperclip, she attached it to the sheet of paper that was on her clipboard. "You a cop?" she asked.

"Private detective," I answered.

"Thought so. You must be that private detective Suzanne said she was going to hire."

"That's right. Frank Dragovic."

"Just a second," she said.

I watched her walk to the high-topped desk where Carl Wahl stood. Tossing the paper tape and sheet of paper into a wire basket, she took another story from those hanging on the hook.

Upon returning she placed the new story neatly on the clipboard, sat on her chair, and crossed her legs, straightening her skirt over them. "What can I tell you?" she asked. "I wasn't here that night."

"Why not?" I asked, keeping it friendly.

"I'm a regular. Sundays and Mondays are my days off."

"Did you know Ralph Blasingame?" I asked.

"Worlds apart. But I knew what he was like—I told Suzanne he was nothing but trouble."

"You knew about—" I asked, leaving the question unspoken.

"Suzanne and him?" She lowered her voice. "Sure, I knew. Suzanne told me. I doubt that she told anybody else, though."

"When?"

"Oh, a week or two after it started. I told her then he was nothing but trouble. You could tell it by how he'd walk into this room, thinking he was better than the rest of us." Chandra Robinson looked me up and down again, perhaps concluding that I, too, was nothing but trouble. "Suzanne is too naive about men for her own good."

"You've been friends with her for a long time?"

"Um-hmmm. All through high school, then college. We were both gymnasts in school, so we hung around together."

"You still work out with her?" I asked.

"No," she laughed, "Suzanne keeps asking me, but I've got a husband and two kids. Maybe I should take the time, though," she added ruefully, glancing down at her waist and pulling at an imaginary roll of fat with two fingers.

Suddenly she turned serious, all laughter gone. "Just because Suzanne can swing on the bars doesn't mean she pushed Ralph Blasingame into the presses. Put that out of your head. Don't even *think* that about Suzanne."

Easy advice to give, I thought. After several more questions, I left Chandra Robinson and headed for the general path of Jack Morton, the five o'clock shift foreman. When he slowed down enough for me to talk to him, I convinced him to show me around the composing room. Make 'em feel important, and they'll eat right out of your hand. I had him show me twice what happened when the typesetters got a story.

First, the copy came down from the reporters—usually an editor carried it down to the composing room and handed it to a foreman or copycutter. At the copy desk, the copycutter or foreman divided the copy into sections and put the sections on a hook. The typesetters walked up to the desk and took the copy off the hook, or were handed it by the copycutter or even the foreman. They took it back to their machines and, in their jargon, set it into type. Then they placed the rolled-up and paper-clipped tape, along with the copy, in a wire basket near the copy desk. So far, so good: I had observed Chandra Robinson doing this. In charge of the basket and the copy, the foreman sent the pieces that were turned in by the typesetters along an overhead conveyor belt, which dumped them on a desk in the proofreading room. Not so the paper tapes: those the foreman personally took out to the linotype machines.

At the linotypes, another foreman handed out the rolled-up paper tapes. Workers standing in front of machines fitted the tapes on small rectangular "readers"—computers that read the light emitted through the holes in the tape. Driven automatically by the computers, the linotype machines dropped out long slugs of metal type, line by line. A few of the linotypes had operators sitting at them, old men with cotton sticking out of their ears.

"They set the lines of correction," Morton shouted at me when I asked him what they were doing. Shouting was the only way to be heard above the rattle and clank and din of the machines.

We walked over to where several young men wearing printers' aprons stood inking rows of slugs that were now a "story." They placed pieces of paper over the ink; when they pulled them away, the pieces of paper were inked proofs. The proofs were then collected and taken to the proof-reading room, where they were matched against the original copy and proofread.

Following Morton into the proofreading room, I asked to see the dirty proof that Suzanne had set. Morton frowned but gave me a photocopy of the proof. "The cops have the original," he said.

"Who mentioned it to them?" I asked.

"Lee Hubbard. He was the foreman on her shift."

I studied the dirty proof, a short article on the vacation opportunities in Colorado. The proof was full of proofreader's marks, each referring to a particular error. And the proof had plenty of errors: letters missing from words, transposed letters, missing sentences, misspelled words. I handed the proof back to Morton, thinking that whoever set the stuff was either daydreaming of Colorado or under a great deal of stress. Or quite a frame-up artist.

We continued our walk through the plant.

"This is a historical tour," said Morton, waving a hand to encompass all the ground we had covered.

"Yeah? In what way?" I asked it only halfheartedly, my mind spinning with the possibilities of how many different ways, and in how many different places, a typesetter's story could be tampered with.

"All gone. It'll all be gone in another six months. The whole paper will switch over to floppy disks. Get rid of the linotypes." He waved a hand at the machines. "Get rid of the operators. Get rid of the makeup men." He pointed to the men rapidly assembling the slugs of type into what even I recognized as the reverse image of a newspaper page. "And then," he said with scorn, "they'll paste up paper galleys and take photographs of them and make printing plates. But even that won't last long. FPM. That's the future. FPM."

I rolled it over in my mind. Future Printers' Movement? Fading Printers' Memories? Fraternity of Printers Moribund? Morton stared at me, his head tipped to one side, waiting. I had to ask. "Which is?"

"Full Page Makeup. Some reporter will type a story in the editorial offices and punch it into a computer. The computer will format it on a page, put in the pictures, and spit out a plate. Eliminates typesetters altogether. We'll lose our jobs section by section, but we'll lose them altogether."

Maybe Morton pushed Blasingame into the presses because Blasingame was trying to hasten along floppy disks—or Full Page Makeup, whichever was worse. I asked Morton how and why he had turned the yellow paper tape over to the cops yesterday. He was stubborn about his reasons. Yes, he had read the tape that Lee and Carl had found.

Yes, he had turned it in to the police. Why? Because they had asked him to call them if he ever found it, that's why. No, he didn't dislike Suzanne Quering, he was simply doing his duty. No, he didn't consider checking with any of his superiors before turning the tape in, he was doing his duty.

Jack Morton had rounded the corner of forty years and would soon meet fifty face-to-face. The right age, maybe, for taking a rejection pretty hard? Maybe. Might Morton have pulled a frame-up out of revenge? It was possible but not probable. He had not been nervous about showing me around, nor had he been nervous about turning the tape over to the cops. He was, in all things, dutiful.

There was one question I asked Morton that he couldn't answer. If the tape that he gave to the cops was the tape that had been run out on the floor the night after the murder, how did it get back to the copy desk more than a week later? Let me explain it this way. Somebody, let's say Suzanne, dropped the tape off with the copy at the desk on the early morning of Tuesday, October 4. There, the nine o'clock shift foreman, Lee Hubbard, glanced at it, took the tape out to the linotypes, and sent the copy to the proofreaders. Now, once the tape was run, it was left dangling from a large hook at the linotype, streaming loose like so much exhausted tassel at a parade. That was standard procedure. It was *not* wound back up and returned to the typesetting department. So, how did it get back there on Wednesday, October 12? (I knew that it didn't: the tape given to the cops had never been run. But I didn't know if Jack Morton knew that.)

Morton didn't know how the tape got back to the

composing room. He suggested, however, that it was probably returned because it may have fallen off the hook out on the floor, from where, because it had no identification, it was rolled up and returned. I suppose it was a likely explanation—except that the tape he turned over to the cops had never been run.

Leaving Jack Morton out on the floor, I made my way back to the composing room to speak to other typesetters. It was slow going. Nobody knew anything; nobody had seen anything; nobody had heard anything. By eight o'clock I had been on the job three hours and realized that in another hour a new shift would start work.

As I stood between tables, writing in my notebook, one guy, whom I had eyed and marked as a definite talk-to, called me aside before I got to him. "I hear you're asking questions about Suzanne," he said.

When I acknowledged it, he introduced himself. "Name's Adrian Venable," he said in a British accent. "Don't leave me out." He was a short man, maybe five-five, with arms and legs like the mighty oak tree under which the sinewy village smithy stands. He had a large chest and a shock of reddish orange hair. He also had a limp, which was why I had marked him as someone to talk to.

We walked to his machine, which was in a back corner, behind a thick pillar. His eyes twinkled. "The foremen assign the machines. You have to be a good worker to get assigned back here. But I can talk to you and still give them as many keystrokes as they want every night. For Suzanne, I'd do anything. We redheads have to stick together." He winked.

Slouching against an empty table next to his, I

glanced through my notebook, my head spinning with information about copycutting, typesetting, foremen, shifts, and linotypes. "Okay, Venable. I appreciate your help. Let's start with Suzanne's typesetting."

"Let's," he agreed, the twinkle still in his eyes.

"What kind of typesetter is she?"

"Good. Very good. Too good to be working in a newspaper. Same as me." He pointed a well-manicured, thick forefinger at me. "Too good to have set that dirty proof they're all interested in."

"You know about that?"

He nodded. "I know everything that goes on here, just about."

"Maybe she had a bad night," I offered.

Venable shook his head. "We all have bad nights now and then, but bad nights do not make us into our opposites."

"Bad nights make us careless—make us make mistakes," I offered.

He continued to shake his head. "When a juggler has a bad night, does he drop all six plates? When an acrobat has a bad night, does he fall with every flip turn? He does not. A bad night for a pro is imperfection. A bad night is not catastrophe."

Scratching my chin, I felt a strong stubble of beard trying to take over. " 'Catastrophe' seems a strong word for some typewriting mistakes."

"Typesetting," he corrected automatically, hitting a key on his keyboard, sending the yellow tape spewing out of the machine. Taking his finger off the key, Adrian Venable pulled the yellow tape toward him, pulled a stubby pencil out of his shirt pocket, and wrote something on the tape. Dropping the tape, he looked up at me. "Watch. You talk to me, ask me questions. I'll answer. And I'll set type at the same time. I'll make far more mistakes than usual. But my stuff will still be quite clean." He began to type.

I watched, saying nothing. Despite the noise, I could fall asleep in this room without half-trying.

"You know," continued Venable, typing away, "sometimes the linotypes malfunction. I should say the readers, not the linotypes. Sometimes the tape is askew on the reader; and so the reader reads wrong, and the linotype spits out what the reader has read. It's rather like having your keys on the wrong fingers of the keyboard and typing away."

"You think that's what happened?" I asked.

"No. What comes out then is pure garbage. The travel story the cops are so suspicious about—that was set by a bad operator."

Reserving judgment on that, I thought I'd follow the path Venable was leading me down nonetheless. "Like Ruby Good?" I asked.

He stopped typing, or typesetting—or whatever —spun around on his padded typist's chair, and looked at me. "Who suggested that?" he demanded.

"I don't remember," I lied. I waited, but he said nothing. "I take it you are about to defend the typesetting abilities of the legendary Ruby Good?"

He blew air through his lips, making a sound like a horse neighing in derision. "That's a job even Sir Galahad would refuse."

"Listen," I complained in exasperation, "why doesn't somebody just ask Ruby Good if she set the goddamn story?"

He chuckled and typed a few more lines, moving a metal bar that held his copy up. "Ruby doesn't show up every night. She's a sub."

"Like Suzanne."

"Not like Suzanne. Ruby has . . . Ruby doesn't have to set type to make a living."

"But she was here the night Blasingame went into the presses."

I thought he shuddered, but I wasn't sure. "Absolutely. She was here. I'm sure she won't deny it."

The thought of having a job you didn't have to show up for a week at a time intrigued me. I'd have to meet Ruby Good. "What does Ruby think of Suzanne?" I asked.

Staring at his keyboard, or his copy, or entertaining visions of Sir Galahad, Adrian Venable pursed his lips and grasped them with a thumb and two fingers, slowly pulling on them. Finally he turned to me. "Ruby doesn't like Suzanne."

Hallelujah! Somebody was admitting that somebody else didn't like somebody else, if you follow me. "Why not?"

"You've seen Suzanne."

I think I got his drift. "Competition?"

"Ruby makes men's heads turn. They turn less when Suzanne is also around."

In my notebook, I doodled an hourglass figure next to the name Ruby Good. "And how does Suzanne feel about Ruby Good?" I asked.

"Ahh."

I waited.

"I don't think," he replied slowly, "that Suzanne is jealous of Ruby. Suzanne isn't that type of person," he said with emphasis. Perhaps too much emphasis, making me conclude that Suzanne was indeed jealous. Venable ran more tape out of his machine, then tore off the tape altogether. "Back in a minute," he assured me.

Limping to another desk, he attached one end of the tape to what looked like a giant fisherman's reel. He turned the handle of the reel, and in a few seconds the tape was wound up. Interesting, I thought. Chandra Robinson had wound hers around her hand, disdaining the use of the reel. But just as she had, so Adrian Venable also paper-clipped the tape, set it on top of the copy, and walked up to the tall copy desk. There he dropped both into the wire basket. Grabbing another piece of copy off the hook, he sauntered back to his desk.

"How'd you get the limp?" I asked him.

"Accident. Ten years ago—longer, even."

I let him get settled, run out the tape, write on it, and tap out a few lines of story. "Suzanne Quering doesn't like Ruby, does she?" I commented.

"Suzanne does not," he agreed, nodding his head to the rhythm of the keystrokes.

"Why?" I asked. "Not because Ruby apparently can't set clean type."

Adrian nodded vigorously. "Oh, yes. Yes, that's a large part of the reason why. Suzanne doesn't like . . . shoddiness."

I straightened from where I had been leaning against the table, flicked any flecks of lint off my sport coat, readjusted my tie, and ran a hand through my hair. No shoddy detective I. My grooming finished, I asked Venable the obvious question. "What's the other part?"

"Beg pardon?" he asked, stopping his typing and looking at me.

"The other part of the reason why Suzanne doesn't like Ruby Good."

He hesitated. Peering at the copy on his keyboard, he stalled for time. "I believe that *shoddiness* encompasses it all."

"What exactly do you mean by that?"

"You'll have to ask Suzanne."

I doodled in my notebook. What I could use was some sleep. Or some food. Or both. "What do you know about Suzanne's love life?" I asked.

That stopped his typesetting. With a quick thrust of his leg, he spun around on the chair again and faced me. "I am able to put two and two together and get four, which is more than what most people here can do."

"Meaning?"

"Meaning it's pretty obvious her love life must have included Ralph Blasingame. It's no crime to set dirty copy. That's not what you're here for."

"If she had had an affair with Blasingame, she would have kept it quiet. So how would you know about it?"

Apparently, it was the wrong question.

Standing to his full short height, Venable ripped the tape off the machine, crumpled it in his fist, and threw it into a wastebasket. "I told you before that whatever goes on around here is obvious to someone who uses his eyes and ears." His voice was low but quite angry. "I'm trying to help you help Suzanne. If you don't believe that, go ask your questions elsewhere."

"Look, I'm sorry," I offered. "It's my job to ask questions."

He mulled it over but made no offer to accept my apology.

"Do you know why she broke off with Blasingame?" I asked.

"Ask her. She probably had excellent reasons."

Right. And I'd get them out of her in about a hundred years. "Look, let's get off the subject of Suzanne for a while. Tell me something about the subs. And the regulars. Is there a lot of competition among the subs? How does it work?"

Venable expounded on the system of hiring at the *Truth*, allowing that there was competition among some of the subs, particularly those who wanted to work a full five-day week. These subs, he assured me, cozied up to the regulars to be named as their replacement for the day or evening.

I wanted to ask whether there was such competition between Ruby Good and Suzanne Quering; but it didn't seem likely, and I felt it might set him off again, so I simply listened. In listening, I learned more than I thought I needed to hear. I learned, for example, that the days of the tramp printers (printers who tramped around the country taking jobs wherever they pleased) were gone. Now printers were forced to take "situations," or, in other words, be full-timers.

"It's getting so bad," lamented Venable, "that soon we won't have any subs to hire. Then the newspapers will have us by the balls. No subs to hire, you can't take time off. You take time off, they fire you. That's what they want. They don't want workers, they want machines. Automation. Get rid of the whole working class, that's what they want." He sat back in his chair. "Why, ten, fifteen years ago, I used to travel across the states with my union card. I'd work summers in Portland, Boston, New York, Albany, Philadelphia, Chicago— wherever I damn well pleased. Winters, I'd head down to Florida. I wasn't the only one. Jack Morton, too. And Lee. The three of us worked with the circus. Jack and Lee, they worked with the trapeze crew. Me, I worked with the circus strongman."

He flexed a muscle. "Bent bars with my bare hands. Can't do that anymore."

I yawned, not out of boredom, but tiredness. I'd been up since six, had run five miles, sat through court, sat through a grilling session, shuddered through Suzanne's driving, and had now been questioning typesetters for—I glanced at my watch —nearly four hours.

"Buck up," encouraged Venable, as if reading my thoughts. "Here comes the nine o'clock shift. Time for you to ask more questions." Adjusting his copy on the clipboard copyholder, he ran out a length of tape and attacked the keys, making them chatter rhythmically.

I wondered whether I would get at least a free newspaper out of the evening's work.

Chapter Thirteen

IF THE CREW coming into the typesetting area— pardon me, composing room—was the nine o'clock shift, then it was a small one. I counted six people: four men, two women. Leaning against the back wall, taking some of the weight off my feet, I thought about how tired I was. It would have been nice to call it a day and a night, go home, and get some sleep. Instead, I let the new crew get settled, thinking I would question Frederick Douglass Williams while they did. But Williams was even more

elusive than his namesake: every time I looked
around to question him, he wasn't there.

One man, part of the group of six that had just
come in, walked up to the copy desk and started
shuffling papers behind it. He could have been
Carl Wahl's twin, at least in build. But not in hair.
His was darker, a medium brown, and cut short.
No wispy ponytail for him. He had a long face, a
long, narrow nose, thin lips, and prominent eyebrows. He must have stood six-two. Everything
about him was long and lean, like a whip. I assumed he was Lee Hubbard, the nine o'clock foreman. Still leaning against the wall, I flipped open
my notebook and drew an Ichabod Crane figure
on a clean page.

Unlike Carl Wahl, Lee Hubbard didn't speak to
the typesetters as he handed them the copy, nor
did he smile. Hubbard wore crepe-soled shoes
that, along with his silent nature, must have allowed him to sneak up on typesetters who weren't
putting out their full quota of keystrokes for the
day. A small metal clip dangled from a long
keychain on his belt. Although it looked like a
strange nail clipper, it was the punch that operators used to change the holes in the paper tape
they worked with. I had noticed, in the last four
hours, several others using the clip: Carl Wahl,
Chandra Robinson, Jack Morton, Suzanne Quering, and Adrian Venable.

When I introduced myself to Hubbard and explained what I was doing, he didn't even grunt—
just kept on working. It was not in order to ask
him if I could ask a few questions. With people
like him, you just plunge in without seeking permission. "Do you remember giving the Colorado

travel story to anybody on the night of Monday,
October 3?"

"No." He stared out over the high desktop, not
even looking at me. Suzanne came up to the desk,
and he handed her a piece of copy. I found myself
wondering what it was—race results? basketball
statistics? Dear Abby? Yugoslavia travel?

"Do you know if the story was handed out on
your shift?"

"No."

"Did you see anybody setting it?" I persisted.

"No."

In my notebook, I added a padlock to the thin
man's mouth. "When did you give the dirty proof
to the cops?"

Lee Hubbard was silent for a while. "That morning. Tuesday." I could sense his peripheral vision
on me.

"Why?" I asked.

He jutted his jaw out, snatched a piece of copy
from the hook, and thrust it into the hands of
Frederick Douglass Williams, who had suddenly
materialized out of nowhere. Williams examined
the copy Hubbard gave him. Directing a slight
sneer at Hubbard, he walked away with the copy.
Glaring at Williams's back, Hubbard replied, "The
cops asked me to report anything . . . unusual."

"And so you thought they were interested in how
a story was typeset."

He didn't rise to the bait.

Scratching my chin with the tip of my pen, I
continued. "Are you sure the Colorado travel story
was set after Blasingame fell?"

He didn't answer.

"Hey. I'm asking you a question."

"It came back from proofreading just after four o'clock."

"Uh-huh. Does that mean it had to be set after, say, 2:15 A.M. ?"

Hubbard went from laconic to silent again, so I prodded him by tapping him on the shoulder with my pen.

"No," he admitted.

"You know, Hubbard, you should take up gambling. The laws of chance seem to suspend themselves for you. You find a dirty proof that has Suzanne's slug on it. Then, a week later, you just happen to find the missing tape that goes with that slug—a tape that should have been thrown away days before."

Naturally he had no comment to make. Though I prodded him a while longer with pointed questions, all I got was no or silence. Hubbard answered questions as if words were water and we were lost in the desert, with him in charge of the water. Did he remember Suzanne taking a break around 2:15 the morning of Tuesday, October 4? No. Did he remember whether, when he heard about Blasingame, Suzanne had been present in the composing room? No.

It was when I asked him whether Suzanne had any relationships with any of the men that he surprised me. No, he didn't break forth in a tirade. He stumbled. Silently. He tried to say something, a word—once, twice . . . three times. Finally, it came out. "No."

I'd had my fill of Hubbard. He, Morton, and Venable must have made an unusual trio tramping across the country, dropping into newspapers now and then to keep up their typing skills. Just for the hell of it, I asked Hubbard how much trapeze work he had done in the circus, hoping that the question would get a rise out of him. It didn't. With something approaching a stiff smile, he told me that he had done as much as he could.

"Um-hmm. Who was the flyer—you or Morton?"

He hesitated. "Me. Jack caught."

"What time do you normally get off work?" I asked.

"Five A.M."

"When does Morton get off work?"

Looking me over, Hubbard smiled his thin smile: "1:00 A.M."

"When did your friend Venable get the limp?"

"Ask him. It was an accident."

"Who's in charge during the overlap, from 9:00 until 1:00? You or Morton?"

"The five o'clock foreman's in charge until his leaving time. Just like the one o'clock foreman's in charge until he leaves at 9:00."

What a speech.

"So you were in charge here after 1:00 Tuesday morning—after Morton went home."

"Right."

But Hubbard had hesitated just long enough to make me realize he wasn't answering truthfully. I thought about the question I had just asked, then did some fishing. "So Morton didn't leave at 1:00 the morning of Tuesday, October 4, did he?"

Staring out over the top of the tall wooden copy desk, Hubbard watched the approach of Adrian Venable. Venable winked at me, grinned at Hubbard, and snagged a piece of copy off the hook.

"Any special reason Morton didn't leave?"

Hubbard remained silent.

"Look, I'm going to find out one way or another.

Any special reason Morton didn't leave? Overtime, maybe?"

"No."

"Why did he stay, then?"

"He punched out. He wasn't here on company time. Down in the bindery, where the papers are bundled, there's usually a card game going on. If you tell Jack I told you, though, I'll deny it. Everybody knows it goes on, even the company."

After finishing with Hubbard, I turned back to the typesetters, looking for Frederick Douglass Williams. I couldn't find him. So I did the next best thing: talked to the remaining typesetters.

I don't know how my questions left the typesetters, but they exhausted me. Leaning against a pillar, I wrote in my notebook in what I knew was an unobtrusive manner. I knew it because by this time I had become like yesterday's news: nobody paid any attention to me.

Nobody from the nine o'clock shift could say for certain that Suzanne had or had not been in the composing room area when they had heard about Blasingame. Since some operators on the nine o'clock shift claimed to have known about Blasingame's fall as early as 2:15, others not until 3:00 or 3:30, I got nowhere.

As I said, I was leaning against the pillar, dog tired. My thumb was starting to fester from the splinter. Absentmindedly, I gnawed away at the thumb, trying to relieve the itch. I looked up and Suzanne was standing by me, staring at me with a slight frown on her face. I jerked upright and pulled the thumb out of my mouth. "Don't sneak up on me like that," I admonished, feeling foolish.

"I'm nervous," she confided. "I've been making all kinds of mistakes."

I wondered whether she realized the significance of what she was saying, but I let it go.

"Maybe we can speed this up by finding Ruby," she suggested. "If she set the story and will tell the police, I'll feel a lot better. But she never answers when I call."

She looked at me with those gray eyes. How could I resist?

Sighing with weariness (or was it resignation?), I straightened my shoulders and put away my notebook. "I'll go see her right after I talk to the pressmen."

"I didn't mean you should go tonight. You look so tired."

"Where does she live?"

"On Leavitt, I think, somewhere south of North Avenue. Jeff should have her address."

That wasn't more than two miles out of my way. I could hit it on the way home.

"Where can I get some decent coffee?" I asked Suzanne. "That stuff from the machines is undrinkable."

"Come on," she offered. "I'll get you a good cup."

She led me through a chasm of linotype machines that were clattering away. There were no women back here, only men—older men, most with big battings of cotton sticking out of their ears. Apparently the *Truth* hadn't heard of foam rubber earplugs.

We came out the same door we had entered at five o'clock. Suzanne opened it, and we descended a flight of stairs, twisting through a narrow maze and coming out in the room where the papers were bundled. Thousands of papers lay there on pallets, ready to be bundled and shipped. I wondered whether I could fall asleep on a wooden pallet.

We turned a corner and stopped. There was Frederick Douglass Williams, upside down, walking across a long, wooden table on his hands.

He saw us, lost his balance, and toppled off the table, landing askew on a hand on the concrete floor.

Suzanne stepped forward and, bracing her legs, held out an arm to Williams. "Frederick! I've never seen you fall before. What happened?"

Pulling himself up with her help, Williams stood. "He made me lose my balance," he blamed, pointing at me. "Who is he?"

Suzanne performed introductions.

"Oh," said Williams. "I thought he was some kind of new foreman."

"That's some feat," I commented. "Do it often?"

"Not really."

"Walter Payton can walk the length of a football field on his hands," said Suzanne. "He's Frederick's hero."

"Sports hero," specified Williams, studying me and rubbing his wrist.

"Payton doesn't have as far to fall," I offered. "How's the wrist?"

"Good enough to set type."

"Hey, Frederick, I'll buy you a cup of coffee," offered Suzanne.

"No, thanks. I'd better go upstairs and make myself visible."

Williams departed, and Suzanne led the way to another long wooden table. "Hi, Mack," she greeted, smiling at the tall man polishing a stainless steel percolator. She pulled some change out of her pocket and dumped it on the counter—separating a quarter, a dime, and a nickel from the rest —pushing it across to him. "Two big ones." Scooping up the rest of the coins, she shoved them back into her pocket. Then she took them out again and looked at me. "How about a doughnut or some pastry? They're good."

"How about one of each?" I replied, hoping she appreciated the fact that I was letting her pay. I hoped she noticed it, at least.

"Pick 'em out," she offered, nodding her head at the pastry and counting out more change to Mack, who had poured two tall Styrofoam containers full of hot, black coffee. I stacked a longjohn on top of a cherry Danish. Suzanne took the two coffees aside to still another plank table, this one covered with unused newsprint. On the table rested sugar in a two-pound box, wooden stirring sticks, and some real cream in a half-pint container. She put a small amount of sugar and a larger amount of cream in hers. I took mine straight.

We sat on the steps and drank. I also ate. The coffee was what I needed. The longjohn and Danish weren't bad, either. Sitting so close to her seemed best of all.

"Thanks," I said when we had finished. "That helped."

Suzanne went back up the stairs. I walked across the bindery and into the pressroom. People looked pretty busy—probably getting ready for the midnight edition. Nobody was there to introduce me, but people seemed to accept me without question once I showed them my license.

As I questioned the pressmen, it didn't take me too long to learn why Dragan had a funny feeling about the case. Two pressmen *thought* they had caught a glimpse of somebody up on the railing.

They weren't sure—they didn't spend their time studying the catwalk, they informed me. Still, after the cops began asking questions, they thought they had seen something. Maybe it was a shadow. Maybe it was nothing. Maybe it was a person. I coaxed, confided, and led, all to no avail.

It was understandable. Somebody screams and falls. You look up, but only quickly, because your eyes are riveted to the horror in front of you. That's what would normally happen. In this case, though, it was different. The presses were so loud that, even if Blasingame had screamed, nobody heard him. They *saw* him—after he had hit the presses. But they didn't hear him. So that gave the murderer (if it was murder) a few precious seconds to get away. If it was murder, the murderer had taken a hell of a gamble, assuming he (or she) could escape unobserved.

The pressmen were a dead end. You can't build a case on shadows on catwalks.

Climbing back up the stairwell with the support of the railing, I followed the lime-green tape on the floor until I found the union's office. Jeff was no longer in the cubbyhole, but another steward gave me Ruby Good's address when I explained who I was. He first called Suzanne on the phone to check me out. I approved of that. You may have to let a guy walk all over your floor, but that doesn't mean you have to stop patrolling the house.

Outside, the *Truth*'s time-temperature display indicated that the true temperature was forty-one degrees. I took several deep breaths to help myself wake up, then I hailed a cab and gave the driver Ruby Good's address.

Chapter Fourteen

■

RUBY'S LAST NAME may have been Good, but she lived in a bad part of town. Zigzagging to Division, the cab driver headed west toward the Wicker Park neighborhood. People like Ted Haapala and Gayle Blasingame, living in their lakeshore high rises, were strangers to Wicker Park. Not that there was anything wrong with Wicker Park that lots of restoration and extermination wouldn't cure. The neighborhood traced its roots back to the Chicago Fire or, rather, to the mad building spree that followed the 1871 conflagration. Wicker Park was where the German beer kings, meat packers, and shoe merchants had built comfortable homes for themselves. The homes on the Croatian Southeast Side were nothing like this.

Then, as things are wont to do, Wicker Park deteriorated. The wealthy moved out, the lower middle class stayed, and in moved the working class. After that, the poorest of the poor moved in. Today the papers (including the *Truth)* advised that Wicker Park was a "revitalizing" neighborhood. The old homes that still survived did boast some of the best Victorian architecture of the period: stained glass, wrought-iron, columns, arches, and gingerbread trim.

The "revitalization" hadn't reached Ruby Good's end of Leavitt Avenue, where large old houses now sported plywood boards for windows. The neighborhood here was Latino, ex-hippie, and street bums. Many of the street signs were down, and most of the houses had no numbers. The driver grumbled when I had him stop at a dark house

that should have been Ruby Good's and told him
to wait.

I didn't like it. A dog started to bark somewhere
as I went up the cracked sidewalk. I knocked, but
nobody answered. In the mailbox were five pieces
of mail, all addressed to Ruby Good. I liked it even
less. Since the sidewalk continued along the side
of the house, I went with it. I knocked again at the
side door, with no result. Several houses away, the
dog kept barking. Again I followed the sidewalk,
this time to the back door. Peering through the
windows, I saw nothing but curtains. I rattled the
knob. No answer. So I took out a handkerchief,
wiped my prints off the knob, and took out a credit
card. Slipping it between the door frame and the
faceplate, I pressed against the latch bolt. In a few
seconds, I was inside. There was a deadbolt on the
lock, but nobody had turned it. Standing stock
still, I listened so closely that I could feel my muscles protest against the rigidity. Enough light
filtered through the diaphanous curtains to enable
me to see where I was going. I walked slowly
through the downstairs rooms: kitchen (which I
had entered), dining room, living room, and some
sort of sitting room—probably a front parlor.
Ruby Good was making some haphazard attempts
at remodeling. Some of the wallpaper had been
scraped off, and some of the fireplace marble had
been restored. But a film of bleakness and dust
covered the practically barren rooms: the inside of
the house was in keeping with the outside.

My silent tour brought me to the front foyer and
a stairway that led up. That was when I became
aware of the smell: a putrid, overpowering, over-
ripe odor that seemed to flow down the stairs in a
wave. You don't have to have smelled more than

one long-dead body to recognize the smell again. Covering my face with my handkerchief, I took the stairs two at a time, unworried about any noise. Nobody alive was going to hide upstairs with that smell.

The body lay in a bedroom to the right of the stairs. I glanced in only long enough to verify what I knew to be true, then went back down the stairs and out the back door.

"Nobody home," I told the driver, handing him a five for the fare and tip. "But I'm going to wait on the back porch. He should be home any minute. Just in case, though, will you come back for me in half an hour?"

"I don't know, man. Don't know what fare I'll have."

Opening my wallet, I took out a five, holding it up for him to see. "If you're back here in thirty minutes, you'll get this in addition to the fare and tip to take me back to Michigan Avenue."

He checked his watch. "I'll be here at 12:30."

After the cab drove off, I walked slowly to the back porch, trying to keep my movements unsuspicious-looking in case anybody was watching out their windows. After I let myself back into the house, I went over the downstairs rooms once more; but all I found was a drooping schefflera, bone dry. I watered it, carrying the water in a cooking pot, making certain I left no fingerprints. At the foot of the stairs I covered my nose and mouth with my handkerchief again. At the top of the stairs, I found a wall switch and turned on the light.

Four doors led off the upstairs hallway: two to the left, one at the end, and one to the right. The first door on the left was slightly ajar. I flattened

myself against the wall and slowly pushed the
door open with a knuckle, peering in. As I said, I
doubted anybody alive was upstairs; but I wasn't
carrying a gun, and I'd rather be careful than shot.
Clicking on the light, I saw a room that, like those
downstairs, was basically empty. An old stuffed
chair and a broken table sat in one corner. Here,
too, somebody had started to remove the wallpaper and strip the stain from the windows. If this
was an example of Ruby Good's work, then Venable's use of the word "shoddiness" had not been
overly harsh. My father would have used stronger
language.

Clicking off the light, I entered the second room
on the left. What I saw made me release my breath
in a whistle. The walls had the same torn-off ap-
pearance as the others, and the old carpet on the
floor was threadbare and filthy; but the room itself
was filled with racks of clothing. I mean racks, too
—the tubular chrome contraptions that dry-
cleaners and clothing stores use to wheel clothes
back and forth.

Letting my fingers do the walking through the
clothing, I examined it quickly: see-through nightgowns in short, medium, and long; lacey robes;
long silky pants that looked as if they came from a
belly dancer's costume. The clothing was sorted
according to color: blacks on one rack; whites on
another; blues, greens, and golds sharing a third.
The reds won, taking up three whole racks. There
was nothing subtle about Ruby Good's interest or
taste.

The door at the end of the corridor was the bathroom, and although I didn't whistle this time, I
was again surprised. The room was large and
newly remodeled. Looking around, I took in the

mirrored floor-to-ceiling walls, the oversized,
sunken tub, the two shower heads, the lavish sink,
the stacks of plush red towels and washcloths, the
two white terrycloth robes hanging on wooden
knobs, the tiled floors with thick throw rugs, the
portable heater, the hand massage unit lying on a
counter top. I wondered what my father would
think of the remodeling job. I doubt he ever had
call for one like this down on the Southeast Side.
Six, seven grand, easily, went into this bathroom,
and it was a cinch Ruby Good didn't do it herself.

Lifting one of the clean washcloths from a built-
in shelf, I stuffed my handkerchief back in my
pocket and put the washcloth against my mouth
and nose. The only room left was the bedroom,
and it wasn't going to be pleasant.

Flicking on the light switch with a knuckle, I
stepped into the bedroom. I blinked. The lights
were very bright. Ruby Good (I assumed it was
she, based on Adrian Venable's description) lay beyond revitalization, sprawled across an unmade
kingsize bed, dressed in one of the red nightgowns.
Her body was bloated, the face swollen. Stepping
close to her, I noticed the discoloration in the forehead and the bloodstains on her chest. She had
been shot twice, with what appeared to be small
caliber bullets. I didn't see a gun or empty shells
lying around, nor had she had time to leave any
clues that I noticed. I didn't envy the men who
would have to bag the corpse and remove it.

Moving away from the body, I stood and looked
around the room. As in the bathroom, no expense
had been spared to make the bedroom fit somebody's ideas of comfort. The ceiling was mirrored.
The wall immediately to the left of the door was
also one long expanse of mirror. The other walls

were wallpapered, professionally, in a ruby-red paper. Two dressers in the room were cluttered with cosmetics, and over in the corner was a clothing rack built to hold a man's suit, shoes, wallet, coins, and keys. I walked over to the clothing rack. There was nothing on it now, but I had no doubt it had been put to frequent use. A large television with a video cassette recorder atop it faced the bed. The recorder was empty. Using the washcloth to prevent prints, I pulled open the dresser drawers: bras, pants, slips, knit sweaters—and brightly colored silk scarves.

Something bothered me—something besides the dead body, that is. With a pencil, I swung the door closed, looking for a closet entrance. There wasn't one. I looked at the inside wall of the bedroom—the long, mirrored one. I stepped out the door, back into the hallway. I looked at the wall, wishing I had X-ray vision to see through it. Back I went to the bathroom, flicking on the light and standing there in the hallway, looking at the bathroom, the bedroom, and the hallway.

I didn't have to be a builder's son to recognize that something was missing, but it helped. Two rooms on the left of the staircase, one room at the end, and one room on the right. As large as the bedroom and bathroom were, they didn't take up all that space. Nor would the house originally have been built like that. It would probably have had four bedrooms and a bath. So how did I get to the hidden room? Never mind what was in it—I already knew.

First I checked out the bathroom for any hidden doors.

Then the hallway.

Finally, I went back into the bedroom and

checked the long mirrored wall. And then I jumped back, turned off the light, and practically broad-jumped into the hallway. I could feel the sweat trickling down my armpits. It had just dawned on me that, if the hidden room housed what I thought it did, then the mirror I had been standing in front of was most assuredly a two-way mirror, and all my fingering of the glass was as vain as the flapping of a moth's wings against a window—and as self-exposing. *If* the mirror was two-way, and *if* there was somebody behind the glass, and *if* that somebody had a gun—well, I thought, calming myself as I walked (crept is more like it) slowly down the stairs, then I would be dead.

Thus cheerfully reassuring myself, I gave the downstairs another quick once-over. It was quick because I knew where I would put the entrance to the hidden room if I had been the builder. In the kitchen, I opened the door that went into the basement. Feeling for a light switch, I found it and threw it. A dim bulb lit the descending stairway. It also lit a door opposite the one I had just opened. Taking a deep breath, I turned the knob slowly, washcloth in hand. Peering inside, I found not a broom closet but another staircase. The builder and I concurred. This staircase was, as I had known it would be, ascending. Clicking on still another light switch, I started slowly up the stairs, keeping my back to the wall. At times like these I wished I had brought my gun.

As my head cleared the second-floor level, I saw that the hidden room was empty. All it contained was a metal folding chair and a metal bookcase, and what I had thought it would: a video camera mounted on a tripod. The camera and chair faced the two-way mirror. On the other side, of course, lay Ruby Good's bedroom—and Ruby Good's body.

The recording unit was empty, the room stuffy. Removing the washcloth from my face, where I had been pressing it almost as if it were a part of me, I got down on my hands and knees and checked the bottom of the chairs. Nothing was taped there. That left only the metal shelving, which was almost empty, containing only three videotape cassettes. I read the titles without touching them. They were all so-called adult films—sex films, in case you thought they might have been something like *War and Peace.* An orange label pasted to the top cassette told me it had been rented from a store on Clark Street.

Glancing at my watch, I realized that the cab driver should be back any minute. I stared at the dust on the shelving. Even Watson would have been able to conclude that more cassettes—lots of them—had lined the shelves. Now they were gone —and not, I'd bet, back to the shop on Clark Street.

Moving quickly, I descended the stairs, turned off the light, closed the doors, wiped off any fingerprints, and stopped to check the schefflera. It had already perked up.

In another minute I was out the back door, leaving it as I had found it. I strolled nonchalantly down the sidewalk and out to the front. My cab was just pulling up.

"Water Tower," I said, not wanting to return to the *Truth* without a chance to walk and think.

At Michigan and Chestnut I got out, paying the fare, tip, and the promised five. Thinking, I walked south toward the *Truth,* thrusting my hands into my pockets.

Shit. The washcloth was still in my pocket.

At the intersection of Michigan and Chicago, I dropped the washcloth into a trash barrel. At a nearby Walgreen's, I found a phone booth, dialed 911, and reported there was a dead body at Ruby Good's address on Leavitt. Before the cop could ask questions, I hung up and left.

I had less than fifteen minutes to make it to the back door of the *Truth-Examiner* to catch Suzanne Quering as she came out of work.

The case had changed. Did we now have two murders, or one murder and one accident? Either way, were they related? Had Suzanne Quering known that Ruby Good was dead when she asked me to see her? I wondered.

If somebody wants to make it look as if they're being framed, they can plant the evidence themselves, with enough doubt left so it does, in fact, look as if they're being framed. Why? Who knows. Maybe they like to feel persecuted; maybe they want attention; maybe they're trying to protect somebody else. Maybe they want to be tried and found innocent in order to protect themselves: double jeopardy.

Well, whatever the answers to my many questions, one answer seemed obvious: Ruby Good was dead because of the tapes. But the question that followed the answer was which tapes: the paper tapes or the videotapes . . . or both?

Chapter Fifteen

■

By 1:00 A.M. I had reached the *Truth*'s back door and parked my weary body against the *Truth*'s solid support.

Suzanne came bouncing out at 1:05, a prompt leaver.

"Hello," I said. "I'll walk you to your car."

"Oh." She registered surprise. "Where have you been? I thought you were done."

Too tired to tell her that a detective's work is never done, I simply asked, "Tell me about being a gymnast."

Adjusting her bag more comfortably on her shoulder, she stuck a hand into her skirt pocket and settled into a long stride. The wind blew back her hair gently. If she thought there was anything strange about the question, she didn't let it show. "Well, I like to work out. I've been doing gymnastics since I was eight or nine years old. I like to run, too, though. Why?"

"Just tying up loose ends. You'll have to bear with me again. Have you ever . . . worked out . . . with anybody from the composing room?"

"Sure. Chandra. We went through school together."

"Did she know Blasingame?"

"Only what I told her about him."

I wondered about that. "Anybody else?"

"Anybody else what?"

"Did you work out with anybody else from the composing room?" I repeated tiredly.

"No. Why?"

"Did you know that Jack Morton and Lee Hubbard used to perform on the trapeze in a circus?"

"Oh. Sure, I remember that now that you mention it." She stopped walking abruptly, and I had to turn around to face her. "You don't suspect— What are you leading up to?" she demanded.

"Trust me," I assured her. "I'll put it all together in time. But first I've got to run around to see what's unconnected."

She stared at me, then started walking again. "Well, okay. I guess. No, I've never worked out with Jack. Or Lee."

We were walking along underground Michigan Avenue. Above us, I could hear a car go over the bridge. Below us, I could smell the river. "How did you meet Blasingame?"

"He called me up." She grimaced. "He said he'd seen me in the typesetting department and wanted to meet me."

I waited; but nothing more seemed forthcoming, so I prodded. "And?"

She picked up the pace as if she were trying to walk away from the question, but I had no difficulty matching her stride.

"Why—*why* is it important? About Ralph and me."

"It's something you'd rather forget?"

"It's something I'd rather not talk about. I won't forget."

"I think you've got to talk about it, the sooner the better. He called," I prompted, "and you said yes."

"No," she replied.

"What did you say?"

"I said no. I don't have to give a *reason* when I say no." She glared at me, but I pretended to miss the point. "I just said no. I don't have to justify it."

"So how did . . . so what happened?"

"A couple of days later he called again. I didn't know him and had no desire to meet him. So I said no again. But a couple days after that, he showed up at the apartment. Well, he seemed decent." She slowed and shook her head. "So I let him in and we talked. You know," she said, stopping and thereby forcing me to stop, "the other night . . . I don't want to give you the impression that . . ." Again she shook her head. "Ralph had a good sense of humor, and he was intelligent. At first he was interesting. He'd been around a lot, done a lot of things. It was like seeing the news from the other side."

I waited silently.

She continued. "I'm talking about how I first saw him, the kind of person he seemed to be."

"Okay," I replied. "I see." I thought I saw, but I wasn't sure. "Is it important to you—to tell me that?"

Suzanne looked away from me, down at the sidewalk. But then she looked back. "Yes. It's important what you think of me." She hesitated. "It's important to me," she repeated.

We stood there for maybe half a minute, looking at each other. Finally I took her arm and said, "Come on. Where's your car?"

"Down this way," she answered, pulling her arm away, not ungently, and turning on North Water. "I don't mean," she continued, "whether you think I'm guilty. I can't believe that you think I might be." She shook her head in disbelief. "If you thought I was guilty, you'd just drop the case, wouldn't you?" she asked.

I ignored the question. We walked farther—a lot farther.

"I never did get to question Frederick Douglass

Williams," I informed her. "I'll have to talk to him tomorrow."

"Can't," Suzanne answered.

"The next day then, or the day after."

"Can't," she repeated. "He'll be on vacation. That's why he was having so much fun tonight."

Great. "How long will he be gone?"

"Two weeks."

"Where?"

"I don't know—wait, yes I do. He's from Baltimore. He's going back there for a while to visit his family. Then to, uh . . . Halifax. He has more relatives up there."

Well, I'd have to question Williams when he returned. "Do you know Ted Haapala?" I asked, shifting mental gears.

"No. Who's he?"

"An editor. Jesus Christ, Suzanne, *where* did you park?" We were walking east along North Water, toward Lake Michigan. Parked cars lined both sides of the street; but the street was deserted, the pavement no longer existent, replaced by packed dirt. Old railroad tracks ran through the streets at intervals. Two large tanker trucks passed us as we walked.

"It's down a ways yet."

"A *ways* yet!? What are you doing parking down here all alone?"

"I'm not alone." She waved a hand at two men in work clothes sitting outside a sugar factory. They waved back. "See. There're people here. There're truck drivers. Anyway, I was late today. I don't usually park this far down."

It's strange, the things that run through your mind. Earlier I had found myself wishing that she had put the dishes carefully into the sink (or, better yet, dishwasher) instead of tossing them in as if they were hubcaps in a junkyard. Now I was wishing that she had paid to park in the lot next to the *Truth* rather than park for free in some ridiculously dangerous place. But I knew I would gladly accept all her foibles if only she would be innocent.

"Why didn't you just park out on Navy Pier?" I asked.

She glared at me. "Ralph was sarcastic when he didn't approve of something. Why should I pay three dollars a night to park, anyway?"

"Okay, okay. It's your life," I warned. I had lost track of where I was going with my questions. We walked in silence. The factories and railroad tracks had disappeared, replaced by weed-covered lots. Ahead of us loomed the giant stone arches of the S-curve of Lake Shore Drive. I hoped to god she hadn't parked *that* far down, but I bit my tongue. "More questions. Who on the floor wants to put the make on you—bad? And don't," I interrupted before she could speak, "tell me you have no idea. This is important, Suzanne."

"But I *don't* know! How am I supposed to be able to tell who's serious, and who isn't—who'll back off if I come on? Huh?"

I kicked a stone with my feet: first with the right foot, then with the left, then with the right, then the left. The three of us were the only moving things down here. "Okay. I'll ask you who you think *has*, uh, propositioned you. Carl Wahl?"

She laughed, amused. "Well, yeah, okay."

"Jack Morton?"

"Yes. But he tries to put the make on all women."

"Lee Hubbard?"

She cleared her throat, then shivered her shoulders together in repulsion. "Ugh. Yes."

"Now we're getting somewhere. Did you tell him *no* in exactly that manner?" I imitated her shivering. Actually, I just wanted to hear her laugh.

She did, but it passed. "No, of course not. I wouldn't want to insult him. But . . . he probably knows I dislike him. You can't really keep things like that from people, you know. Don't you think?"

"You're right," I answered absentmindedly, finding myself wondering whether Lee Hubbard, out of revenge, planted the tape of the dirty proof. After a while, I found myself paying more attention to the empty fields and looking back over my shoulder to see if we were being followed. "How often did he try?"

"Oh, at least once a week, up until several months ago. Now he doesn't even speak to me."

"Why's that?"

"I don't know. Maybe he just got tired of trying. Maybe he is speaking to me, only I don't recognize it." She laughed at her own joke. "Lee's not the world's greatest talker, you know."

"Adrian Venable?"

"No. Not that I could tell, anyway. I'm not sure Adrian's interested in women. Why are you asking?"

"Sex is a strong motivator."

"You mean lack of sex. Or do you mean rejection?"

"At the moment, I'm not sure which I mean. But there's either sex or money behind this. Or both," I added casually, watching her out of the corner of my eye. She stared straight ahead, and we walked in silence again. I could see her car, down under the viaduct of the S-curve. No other vehicles were around it. Taking her elbow, I hurried her on.

"What makes you think that Ruby Good might have set the dirty proof?" I asked, wondering whether my hand on her elbow, or rather her elbow in my hand, would transmit information to me like a Ouija board.

Suzanne frowned. "I'm not saying Ruby set it. Anybody *might* have set it, I guess. But Ruby sets the worst copy in the composing room. She's the obvious first choice."

"You think she might have accidentally typed your number rather than hers?"

"Sure," she answered. A bit eagerly.

"Or do you think she might have done it deliberately?" Ahead of us, her car was a shape in the darkness. Silently fuming over the stupidity of parking down here at night alone, I didn't realize at first that she hadn't answered me. I looked at her, then jiggled her elbow.

"I'm *thinking,*" she replied in annoyance, removing the elbow from my grip.

"Think out loud," I suggested, likewise in annoyance.

"It's hard to say. She *might* have done it deliberately—after she heard about Ralph, I guess. But then, that would mean she knew about me and Ralph. I don't see how she could know: I didn't tell her, and Chandra certainly wouldn't. She might have done it deliberately having nothing to do with Ralph. Isn't that your job, anyway, to find things like that out? I thought you were going to see Ruby tonight."

Ignoring her implicit question, I asked one of my own. "What do you think of Ruby Good?"

She stopped to stare at me, but I placed my hand

across her back and shoved forward gently, hinting strongly that we should continue.

"Are you in a hurry?" she asked.

"I'm in fear for my life," I replied. "What do you think of Ruby Good?"

Expelling her breath in annoyance, or exasperation, she answered. "Not much."

"Why not?"

She made a second sound of exasperation, as if dealing with a simpleton. "Because she wears ruby-colored clothes to work. Because she sets sloppy type. Because . . . This is ridiculous."

"Um-hmmm. Was the feeling mutual?"

Opening her handbag, she reached inside, pulled something out, closed the handbag, and held on to what she had pulled out: keys. "I suppose so. I don't wear ruby-colored clothes, though." She chuckled to herself.

I blew out my breath—to keep from strangling her. The car was right there in front of us. Of course, there was no telling how many would-be thieves, rapists, or murderers were crouched down behind it, ready to spring. I stopped her at the car.

"Suzanne, listen. I know you won't like what I'm going to say. You're crazy for parking down here all alone in the middle of the night. It's not safe. You know what Thoreau once said? It's an act of desperation to do foolish things. This is foolish. You know how many rapes there are in the city? Grant Park, North Avenue Beach, Cabrini-Green, Dan Ryan, even down on lower Wacker."

"Well, so what am I supposed to do? Pay to park just because people commit crimes?"

"Yes. It's safer."

"No. It's not right. I should be free to go where I want to. Men are free to go where they want to."

"No they aren't."

"Well, I'm not foolish."

"Okay. Sorry. I used the wrong word. What would you do if somebody attacked you back here? Yell for help? Nobody back there would hear you," I said, motioning with my thumb to the factories and tractor trailers we had left behind. "Would you use karate on them?"

"I don't know karate," she replied. "And don't be sarcastic. I have a gun."

That stopped my sarcasm for sure.

"What do you mean?" I asked incredulously.

"Just what I said. I have a gun."

"I don't believe you," I said, not because I didn't believe her, but because I didn't want to.

It was pretty smooth, the way she pulled the snub-nosed revolver out of her purse. She didn't point it. It just lay there flat, on the palm of her hand. A thirty-two.

I swallowed. "Suzanne, that's illegal."

"No it's not. I have a permit. It says I'm not permitted to commit a crime with a gun."

Bože moj. (My god.) "That's a permit to own. Do you have a permit to carry?"

"No."

"Then what you're doing is *dangerous*. Jesus, if you ever had to use that thing, if you *could* use it, and if you *did* use it, you could go to jail."

"Not for defending myself," she said defensively.

Running a hand through my hair, I recognized that the situation threatened to get out of control. Every time I headed in one direction, she threw a log in front of the path and rolled me over. Taking a deep breath, I asked, "Do you bring that gun every day you come to work?"

"No. Just on the night shifts."

"It must get pretty heavy dragging it around."

"Of course not. I put it in my locker until I'm ready to leave."

I hit my forehead with my fist. "You put it in your locker. That's nice, *draga moja*, that's nice." Forgive me. *Draga moja* means "my dear." I sometimes slip into Croatian when I'm sarcastic. My mother would be proud of it.

"Goddamn it, I lock it up! Nobody's taken it yet!"

Oh, Suzanne, I hope to god you're right, I thought. I had to calm myself. "C'mon," I cajoled, "let's get in the car."

"By all means," she replied, unlocking the door. "It's not safe out here."

"I thought you didn't like sarcasm," I muttered, going around to the passenger side.

As she put the key in the ignition, I placed my hand over hers. "No. Not yet. There's something I want to tell you."

She pulled away, and the look on her face told me she thought I was going to proposition her. Here. Under the S-curve. In the middle of the night.

She turned her head and stared out the driver's-side window. I filled the silence. "I went to see Ruby tonight."

"You *did?*" She turned toward me, and I could swear her face lit up with hope—or relief. "What did—" She stared at me a moment and then said disappointedly, "Oh. I see. She said she didn't set it." Starting the car before you could say *Yugoslavia*, she was in first, then second, the gravel spinning away from the tires like pedestrians scattering from a falling beam at a construction site.

Buckling my seat belt, I took a breath. "She didn't say that," I offered, hoping it would slow her down.

"Oh. I thought—never mind. What did she say?"

"She didn't say anything."

Suzanne snorted in disbelief and turned east on Illinois. Leave it to her to take the deserted way home after midnight. I put my hand over my eyes, as if from weariness, so that I wouldn't have to watch the street rush up to meet us as she swerved and twisted to avoid the potholes. At one point I was convinced we were going neither to the left nor the right of the massive pillar that loomed in front of us, but right into it.

"That's not like Ruby," Suzanne commented quite calmly, swerving into the empty left-hand lane and zipping by the pillar as if it were made of marshmallow.

Just as I thought we had made it safely through the worst of the obstacles, she slammed on the brakes with such force that I pitched forward against the belt.

"*Jesus!* What are you—"

"Wait a minute! Wait just one minute!" she demanded. "What exactly did you do at Ruby's? Did she . . . What . . ." She hit the steering wheel with her fist. "Did she invite you into her bedroom?"

I was amazed. Stunned. Flattered.

"I didn't know you cared."

"I care about my two hundred dollars a day!" she shouted, pounding the steering wheel and sounding the horn. "I'm not paying you two hundred dollars a day for that!"

Reaching over, I removed her hand from the horn.

"If you want—if you want *Ruby,* you can stand in line with everybody else. On your own time!"

My mother was right. Stay away from redheads. "Okay," I shrugged, unable to resist. "I'll refund you a hundred for tonight."

She stared at me speechless for a very long moment—her mouth rounded into an *O*, her eyes blazing, her hair a mane of dark red curls. And then she thrust the car into gear. The force threw me back against the seat. She had rounded Streeter Circle and zipped through the stop sign onto Lake Shore Drive before I could recover my breath.

"Where do you live?" she demanded through clenched teeth.

"It doesn't matter. We're going to your place."

"No you aren't!" She turned to glare at me.

Pointing to the road, I hoped she would take the hint and keep her eyes on it. "Yes, we are. There's something I have to tell you."

"Tell me now."

"Not while we're in a moving vehicle."

The tires screeching, the car careened down the La Salle Street exit. She pulled into an empty parking lot by the lake. "There. We're not moving. Tell me."

"Suzanne, I *saw* Ruby tonight, but I didn't talk to her. She couldn't talk. She was dead."

She looked at me with a lack of comprehension. "Say that again?" she asked, confused.

"Ruby was dead."

"But . . . nobody said anything. Dead? How?"

"I found her dead. I found the body. I called the police," I added as an afterthought.

She looked sad, her face pinched. She was biting the nails of her left hand.

"Suzanne," I said, gripping both her shoulders, "she was murdered. Shot." I wanted to add, *and I hope to god it wasn't with your gun,* but I didn't have the heart.

Chapter Sixteen

■

SHE DROVE SILENTLY (even slowly) the remaining short distance to her apartment and parked the car on a side street. We walked together through the lobby, Suzanne too preoccupied to do more than nod to the doorman.

"Coffee?" she asked automatically after we had entered her apartment and I had made myself at home on the loveseat.

"Please," I replied, knowing that if she answered tonight's questions anything like she had answered the previous ones, I would need lots of the black stuff. Lots just to stay awake, lots more to keep myself from shaking the truth out of her. Pulling a pillow from behind my back, I pushed it up against the armrest. The sounds of Suzanne making coffee seemed gentle. Perhaps she was taking my tired body into consideration, or perhaps her clatter simply sounded soft compared to the pounding of the printing presses. I lay back against the pillow and pulled my notebook out.

Flipping through the pages, I thought that none of my notes or doodles made any sense: a sure sign of fatigue. The coffee would help that. I could smell it brewing.

The coffee smell floated away, the molecules dissipating into the nippy October air, their smell replaced by that of the lake shore. The waves sloshed around me. Suzanne and I were in a rowboat on Lake Michigan, trying to reach the shore, trying to get to her car, which was out there somewhere, on the land side of the S-curve. But the waves grew higher and choppier, and the buoys clanked around us. Then the rowboat turned into a birchbark canoe. Gayle Blasingame came along with a tape punch and began punching holes in the canoe.

"That's my number!" shouted Suzanne, pointing to the code that Gayle was punching. "Leave my number alone!" As we started to take on water, a pirate galleon drew up alongside us, captained by Adrian Venable on a peg leg. Jack Morton was swinging loop-the-loops from the masthead of the ship while Lee Hubbard swung from the rail on the ship's deck, hanging by his knees. I shouted to him to help us. "No," he mouthed. Suzanne started shooting at him with a gun. Ted Haapala appeared and began throwing ashtrays at Suzanne. I swatted them away.

In the distance I heard police sirens. "Dragan!" I shouted. "Save Suzanne!" In a police motorboat, Dragan came speeding to the scene. "I like her for it," he announced, scooping Suzanne out of the water-filled canoe. The police siren faded in the distance, and I was alone in the quickly sinking canoe. In my notebook I drew a bucket, tore out the page, and began bailing water. A mermaid wearing a flimsy red nightgown swam into the boat. "Hello, Frankie," she cooed, as she set up a movie projector. We were underwater now, but that didn't stop the projector. The mermaid pulled a paper punch out of her flimsy costume and attacked me with it. First she nipped my arm, then my shoulder. The sharp little bites were annoying; when I tried to get away, the paper punch turned into a pegboard hook that she prodded me with. I tried to swat it out of her hands, but my hand swept right through her; she merely laughed and continued to prod. She got me in the back, and then the buttocks. No matter how I twisted or turned, she kept prodding.

Then I woke up.

Daylight was visible in the east through the sides of Suzanne's wooden shades. I was twisted into a fetal position on the loveseat. Something was still stabbing me in the back. With a groan, I reached behind myself and pulled it out. Holding the offending piece of wood close to my eyes in the subdued daylight, I peered at it. It looked like a squirrel. It felt like a porcupine. Still groggy, I stretched out an arm and found the coffee table. Depositing the sculpted squirrel on the table, I looked around. Somebody had covered me with a blanket. Turning my head, I glanced in the direction of the bed. Suzanne was in it, presumably asleep.

Silently, I disentangled myself from the blanket. Slowly, I rose and stretched. My muscles felt as if they had been run through a printing press, folded, bundled, and wrapped, and were now ready for shipment downstate. I glanced at my watch. 7:10 A.M.

Suzanne was sleeping on her back, her hair spread out behind her on the pillow, one arm

folded across the covers. The other arm was flung
out behind her head. The glint of metal pulled me
closer. In her outflung arm was a knife. I couldn't
tell at this distance whether it was a carver or a
firmer. I think I shook my head in disbelief. I
could see her neck and the straps of a white cotton
nightgown. She looked like a cherub, or seraph—
whichever carries a knife.

On the edge of the bed, just on top of the sheet,
was a wooden sculpture. Carefully, I leaned forward and plucked it from the covers. It was the
wooden female torso. Some of the squarer knife
strokes had been smoothed away. I replaced the
torso. I needed a shower.

Taking off my sport coat, I stepped softly to the
closet, looking for a hanger. Instead, I encoun-
tered stacks of glossy boxes. Their labels told me
they came from the finest stores along the Magnifi-
cent Mile. With a finger, I lifted the lid of the top-
most box. A black camisole. A present from Blasingame? I lifted the lid of another box. A red
nightgown. I looked through several more boxes.
Garter belts, nylons, bras. Turning, I stared at Suzanne. She still appeared to be asleep. A white
bathrobe hanging on the inside of the closet door
caught my eye. Fingering it, I recognized it as
identical to the two hanging in Ruby Good's bathroom. The clothes in the glossy boxes had never
been worn. The bathrobe could be a coincidence:
white terry cloth robes were common.

Who was I kidding? Furious, I jangled several
hangers loose from the tangle in the closet and
strode into the bathroom. Instead of hanging my
clothes neatly and steaming them into some sem-
blance of presentability, I kicked off my shoes and
threw everything in a heap on the floor.

For twenty-five, maybe thirty minutes I stood under the stinging spray. When I stepped out, I picked up my clothes and hung them neatly on the hangers. When I opened the bathroom door a crack to let the steam escape, the distinct clang of metal met my ears.

Wrapping a towel around myself, I pulled open the door and peeked around the corner. Suzanne was standing at the kitchen sink, wearing a gray sweatsuit over a purple turtleneck top, white socks on her feet. She was humming something to herself. I smelled the unmistakable aroma of freshly brewed coffee.

Trying to push the glossy boxes out of my mind, I ducked back behind the bathroom door. Now that I was fully awake and clean, I realized I was very hungry. I dreamed of *palačinke*, Croatian thin batter pancakes, more like crepes than like anything else. They were my favorite breakfast meal when I was a kid. My mother would make them every Sunday, and my sister and I would fill them with jam, then roll them up. With a fork, I used to slice each of my *palačinke* into seven pieces. I think I remember naming each of the seven pieces for one of the seven dwarfs.

Suzanne Quering would not be making *palačinke*—maybe pancakes, but more likely bacon and eggs, or an omelet. Quickly, I finished shaving with her powder blue, single-blade razor. It didn't do a superior job; but, what the hell, it was adequate, I thought, rubbing my face and looking in the mirror.

Dressed, I stepped out of the still muggy bathroom.

"Good morning," she greeted me. "Feeling better?"

I straightened my shoulders and ran a finger around the inside of my collar. What was really on my mind was that she shouldn't let men sleep on her couch overnight. Although my back testified that it wasn't safe for them, I was concerned that it wasn't safe for her. But starting in on that would set us off on the wrong foot altogether. And I certainly couldn't start on any of the bigger questions, which now included the boxes in the closet.

"Much better," I replied.

Her bed was unmade, the covers thrown back, the white nightgown on top of them. The knife was nowhere in sight. Stepping closer to the bed, I peered down: wooden shavings on the pillow.

"How about some breakfast?" she called, twisting to look at me.

I straightened and walked into the kitchen, a matter of about seven steps. "Absolutely. I'm starving." Draping my sport coat over the back of a chair, I looked around the tiny kitchen, noticing that there were no pots or pans on the stove. There was no toast in the toaster. But the smell of coffee and food was in the air. Maybe we were having cold cereal. Well, I had been looking forward to something hot, but cold cereal would do.

"Can I help?" I asked, still wondering what she intended to serve up as breakfast—a plate of wood shavings, sprinkled with wheat germ, brown sugar, and raisins?

"All done. Just sit and eat."

I pulled up the chair I had sat in—when was it? two nights ago?—and sat down. Today was Friday morning. That had been Tuesday evening. Reaching into my sport coat, I pulled out my wallet. From the wallet, I pulled out one of my sister's cards: Stefanie Katz, Attorney at Law. Propping the card next to Suzanne's plate, I cleared my throat. "Suzanne. You need a lawyer."

"No, I don't. I told you, I need a detective." She poured coffee into our cups, picked up the card, looked at it, and put it back on the table. Then she turned to the oven, opened the door, and pulled out breakfast.

On the table, she placed a very large, very tomato-garlic-sausage Chicago pan-style pizza slice in front of me.

I pushed at the pizza with my fork. "This is the same pizza we had Tuesday night."

"I had it," she corrected. "You had carrot cake. It's good. Eat it."

I swallowed some coffee. Pizza for breakfast. Somehow, it was too . . . untraditional.

On the other hand, I was hungry—very hungry —and I had to ask a lot of unpleasant questions. It was best, I decided, picking up my knife, to eat her pizza.

I aimed the knife in a few silent cuts, then made six swift incisions: Sleepy, Happy, Dopey, Smiley, Doc, Sneezy, Grumpy.

The seven pieces of pizza stared at me: Dwarfs— giant dwarfs.

I speared one with my fork. "Do you know what an oxymoron is?" I asked conversationally.

She stopped chewing her pizza and stared at me. *"Oxeemoron?"* she asked, trying the word on her tongue.

Chewing, I nodded.

"Let me guess," she said, devouring more pizza and following it with more coffee. "An ox of some kind? An ox that's dumber than most? Don't tell me it's an ox that's smarter than a dumb Swede, or something like that. I don't like ethnic jokes."

If Suzanne had been a football player instead of a typesetter, she would have consistently caught the ball and run the wrong way with it. Her name would have gone into *Guinness*, and her fame would have been assured.

"Well?" she demanded.

"An oxymoron is a figure of speech. Generally, it's two terms that, put together, seem to contradict themselves: cheerful pessimist, for example."

Her brow furrowed as she chewed.

"Exciting boredom," I continued to elucidate. "Military intelligence. Giant dwarfs. Jumbo shrimp."

"Oh."

"Guilty innocence."

She stopped chewing and thought. I watched her. She picked up the crust of her pizza, brought it to her mouth, then put it back on the plate. "Okay. Come on," she demanded. "Out with it."

"Certainly. Just as we know we can't really have a jumbo shrimp or a giant dwarf, we know we can't have guilty innocence. If someone is innocent," I continued, pausing to chew more pizza and let her think about the conversation and the consequences, "then they aren't guilty. And if they aren't guilty, they shouldn't act guilty."

"Stop with the 'someone' and 'they.' You mean me. You think I'm guilty." She sat back in her chair and folded her arms across her chest.

"I didn't say that, Suzanne."

"You implied it. 'Guilty innocence.' What the hell does that mean?"

Crossing my knife and fork across the plate, I also leaned back against my chair. Dopey and Grumpy remained uneaten. "The gun. Your dislike of Ruby. Your threats to kill Blasingame. Your refusal—your *obstinacy*—in leveling with me. All the camisoles and nightgowns and god-knows-what-else in the closet!" I shouted.

"I *told* you I owned a gun! You didn't have to drag it out of me." Uncrossing her arms, she pointed a finger at me. We were so close at the little table that she practically jabbed me in the eye. "If you think I killed Ruby, you're crazy. And you had no right to look at those boxes in my closet! Whose side are you on? Who do you think you are, anyway?" Picking up her pizza crust, she bit into it savagely.

"They were gifts from Blasingame, weren't they?"

"So what?!" she shouted. "Those things aren't me. They have nothing to do with me. I meant to give them away; I just never got around to it. I'll tell you what," she said, pointing at me again, "you're so interested in them—*you* take them!"

"Tell me why you threatened to kill Blasingame."

Choking on the pizza, she coughed, coughed again, swallowed some coffee, stood up, poured more coffee into her cup, poured more coffee into my cup, put the coffee pot back in its holder, and reached for the rope that pulled the kitchen shades.

I clamped my hand over her wrist. "Come on. Out with it. I've got to know."

Pulling her wrist away, she sat down. "It had nothing to do with . . . with Ralph falling into the presses."

We were making progress, even if that's what they all say. At least now she was admitting she *had* threatened Blasingame. I wondered how. And why. "That's for me to decide. You're paying me two hundred dollars a day to gather the facts, sift them, and come up with the clinkers."

She picked up her coffee cup, wrapping both hands around it and glaring at me as if defying me to pry it from her.

I waited.

And waited.

Finally, she spoke. "You think I'm acting strange. That's why you said 'guilty innocence.' "

It was simplistic, but correct. "Yes."

She nodded, as if in reply. "Innocent guilt," she said.

I couldn't be sure, but I thought she was smiling as she ducked her head down. Her teeth were very even. I noticed once again the slight gap between her front teeth.

It was clever. I admired it. It may even have been true. But it wasn't enough.

"Okay. That's a beginning. It's innocent. Your threatening to kill Blasingame was innocent. Why?"

Her head came up. Glaring at me, she let out her breath. *"Because,"* she said through clenched teeth, "it had nothing—because, first, it happened three months ago. I was angry. If I had intended to kill him, I would have done it then and there. I had the —I didn't kill him. I didn't even *mean* it, probably."

"Tell me about it."

She stared at me in silence.

"Suzanne."

"No. I won't."

If I didn't stand up, I would throttle her. I stood up.

With my arms behind my head, I clasped my fingers around the back of my neck—might as well throttle my own neck. "I'm beginning to wonder," I said to nobody in particular, "whether this is worth two hundred dollars a day."

She glanced up, looking as if she would protest. She cleared her throat. "Well . . . you could always lower the fee."

I pulled her out of the chair so swiftly that it fell over, its chrome legs resounding against the tiled floor.

"Hey! Let me *go!"*

"Not until you come up with some answers, Suzie Q." I held her by her forearms, her back to the kitchen counter.

"Don't call me that! Let go!" She tried to kick me.

"What'll you do if I don't? Threaten to kill me?" I increased the strength of my grip.

She looked at me in alarm, then laughed nervously. "Don't be ridiculous. Not for something like this."

"What then?" I shook her.

That made her angry, and she kicked again, then tried to bite my arm. I pushed her back against the counter. What had he done? Hit her?

"Stop it! Goddamn it, Frank! Stop it! It wasn't anything like this!"

"What was it, then? What did he do?"

She gave one more squirm against the confines, then stood still. In dignity. "Why won't you believe me?"

"You're not paying me to believe, Suzie Q. You're paying me to detect."

"Don't call me Suzie Q!"

"Is that what he did?—called you Suzie Q?"

"No! You're the only one corny enough to do that!"

"Corn is good. Cheap and nutritious. Right up

there with barley, lentils, and cabbage. What did he do?" I relaxed the pressure of my grip.

She shook her head and looked down at the floor.

I relaxed my grip more. Her perfume of the previous evening lingered, drifting to my nostrils.

The knocking on the door caused me to tighten my grip and Suzanne to toss her head up, clipping me on the chin and bringing my teeth down into my lip. The saline trickle of blood registered on my taste buds and in my brain. I looked at Suzanne and released her.

She cleared her throat and called out, "Who is it?"

"Police."

Giving me a look that said *Saved*, she headed toward the door.

One hand was on the deadbolt, and the other on the knob when I reached her. Delayed reaction on my part. Clamping one hand over her mouth, the other across her chest, I pulled her away from the door.

"Mmfffff."

"Shh!" I whispered in her ear. "Suzanne, listen. When I let go, tell them 'Just a minute.' Nod your head if you understand."

She nodded and I let go.

She cleared her throat. "Just a minute, please."

Motioning impatiently with my index finger, I beckoned her to the center of her room. "Where's the gun?" I whispered.

She stared at me, and I thought I'd have to repeat the question. Then she recovered. Instead of wasting words, she grabbed her handbag from a place only she could have found it beneath the covers of her bed. Opening one of several snapped compartments, she pulled out the gun. I slipped it into the waistband of my pants, in the small of my back. I nodded to her, then at the door.

Suzanne opened the door. I heard Dragan's voice before I saw him.

"Miss Quering. We'd like to ask you some questions. May we come in?"

Pulling back the door, she stepped aside.

Dragan stepped in and then stopped. He stared at me. Shrugging into my sport coat, I straightened the shoulders and collar. I poured myself another cup of coffee, added a teaspoon of sugar, stirred, and brought the cup to my lips, blowing on the steaming liquid.

Dragan recovered. He and the other cop—the one who had been present in the questioning room —stood in front of the now-closed door.

Clearing his throat, Dragan walked into the kitchen area, taking in with his eyes all the things that cops and detectives take in. Two people had obviously eaten here. Recently. I watched dispassionately as he stared at Stefanie's card, then frowned in puzzlement over the pizza.

"Late night?" he asked.

For reply, I took a gulp of coffee—and added a burn to the cut on my lips. "Sonofabitch" I said under my breath.

Dragan stared at me. "Strong coffee?"

I wiped my lip with a finger, then examined the finger: coffee and blood. I looked up, and the other cop was staring at me, rubbing his cut lip. I looked at Dragan, who frowned as he tried to figure out the question on his mind: had I spent the night, or had I just arrived?

Stepping into the rest of the room, Dragan turned and addressed Suzanne, who had remained standing near the door. The other cop also stood there. Duty.

"Miss Quering. Where were you last night?" asked Dragan.

"At work."

"When did you get off work?"

"One o'clock."

Dragan pulled at the knot of his tie, loosening it. He stared at the unmade bed. "Where did you go after work?"

"Home. Here."

"Ummm. You came straight home?"

Suzanne left the door and walked toward the rocker. "Just as fast as I could drive."

"Fast," repeated Dragan, grabbing on to something. He stared at the unmade bed, with Suzanne's white nightgown thrown across it. "Why fast?"

Suzanne shrugged and sat in the rocking chair. "That's just how I drive."

"Umm-hmm."

Easy for him to say: he'd never had to experience it.

"Miss Quering. Do you own a gun?"

"What makes you ask that?" I demanded, putting down the cup of coffee and moving in front of the large window, where I could watch both Suzanne and Dragan.

Dragan glowered. "It's just a question."

"A strange one," I suggested.

"Not so strange," he retorted.

"C'mon, Dragan," I volleyed. "You don't walk into somebody's apartment and ask them out of the clear blue sky if they own a gun."

Suzanne moved her head back and forth, watching us.

Dragan decided to pace the apartment. Six steps later, he had finished. "We had a call," he grumbled.

"Um-hmm. From who?"

"Anonymous."

I glared at him, but he looked innocent, so it was probably the truth. "Man or woman?" I asked.

Dragan shrugged. "These days, who can tell?"

"Guess," I suggested.

"Man."

I looked at Suzanne, trying to communicate that she should be careful. "Cooperate with Lieutenant Brdar," I advised.

"Yes," she answered, looking him straight in the eye. "I do."

"May we see it?" asked Dragan, now watching me intently.

She got up and for one incredible moment I thought she was going to walk up to me, spin me around, lift the back of my coat, and produce the gun, announcing, "There's your weapon, Lieutenant Brdar. Book him." Instead, she stopped at the bed, threw some covers aside, and pulled out her purse once again. Then, for effect, she put in a hand, moved it around, followed it up with a close look into the purse's various compartments, and explained, "It's not here."

Dragan looked up at the ceiling and folded his hands behind his back. "It's not there. Well, then. Where is it, Miss Quering?"

"I don't know."

"Do you think that if you look around here," Dragan asked, indicating the room with a toss of his head, "you might find it?"

Suzanne returned to the rocker. "I don't think so. If it's not here, it's not here."

"Well, then. Do you mind if we take a look around ourselves? Just to see what we can see, so to speak?"

She stiffened in the chair. "Of course I mind. I don't want you going through my things. You have no business doing that. I'm not guilty of anything."

"You won't let us search for the weapon?" asked the other cop.

"No. I won't."

Dragan cleared his throat, pulled aside the lapel of his coat, and, reaching in with one hand, pulled out a white piece of paper. I straightened from where I had been leaning against the windowsill, and he looked at me. I'd had friendlier looks from Dragan over the years. Why, I'd say that about 99.9 percent of the looks I'd had from Dragan had been friendlier than this one.

"We have a search warrant, Miss Quering," he said to her, still looking at me. "We intend to search your apartment. It is my duty to inform you that you have the right to remain silent. Anything you say or do can and may be used as evidence against you in court. You have the right to consult with a lawyer and to have a lawyer present. If you can't afford a lawyer, one will be appointed by the court to represent you."

"Suzanne," I said, and she too looked at me. By then everybody was looking at me. "Call your lawyer. I'll be going to take care of that business we discussed. I'll get in touch with you later this afternoon."

"Good-bye," she said. She said it, I thought, with a touch of relief that the police had come to save her from my questions. Suzanne was the kind of person who could walk the unguarded rim of the Grand Canyon trail and worry, not that she might

plunge head first into the abyss, but that the solid
rock on her protected side might cause an abra-
sion or two.

"Don't mess anything up," I heard her say to
them as I was closing the door.

She sounded perfectly serious.

Chapter Seventeen

I LEFT SUZANNE'S apartment feeling the presence
of the law at my back—law, in the form of my
good friend, Dragan Brdar. Dragan did not for one
moment suspect that I had walked out of the
apartment with evidence. Up until the moment I
had stopped Suzanne from answering the door, I
myself did not suspect I would ever do such a
thing. The gun felt like an icicle against my back,
and like Lot, I tried not to look back as I walked
home.

I walked straight into the bedroom, pulled open
a bureau drawer, placed the gun in it, and shuffled
some underwear to cover it. Then I changed
clothes and caught a bus to the *Truth-Examiner.*
As the bus lurched and lumbered its way down La
Salle, turning left on Chicago and south on Michigan, my thoughts lurched and lumbered over the
happenings of the last several days. Was my strong
instinct that Suzanne's gun had been used to kill
Ruby Good right? If so, who had pulled the trig-

ger? To say nothing of why. And what (if anything) did it all have to do with Ralph Blasingame? Maybe I should be spending my time checking up on Ruby Good and the videotapes she rented—and made. But Ruby Good had worked at the *Truth,* and no matter how I looked at it, all threads seemed to lead back there.

The bus took twenty minutes to come to a wheezing halt in front of the *Truth-Examiner.* Glancing at my watch as I took the steps leading from upper Michigan to underground Michigan, I confirmed that it wasn't even 11:00 A.M. Maybe the same loading dock workers I saw now had also been working at the time Haapala took his tumble off the dock.

The dockworkers had, as I hoped, started their shifts at 6:00 A.M. Flashing my detective's license, I acted as if I had every right to be there. The workers shrugged. As I questioned them individually, I doodled in my notebook: a loading dock, a man with a bowling ball for a head teetering precariously on the edge of the dock.

Three of the men I talked to said they had seen him fall. What they really meant, it turned out, was that they had heard him shout and had seen him lying on the sidewalk below the loading dock. They had stood there watching as he got up, obviously not seriously injured. He had taken a step, then had stumbled forward and caught himself on the dock.

"Then what?" I asked the last of the three.

"Then nothing. Then he kind of limped back to the stairs and leaned against them, kind of rubbing his ankle. He kind of made sure we were looking, if you know what I mean. Probably wanted to have witnesses."

"Why?"

"C'mon," he guffawed. "My mother didn't raise any dummies. For the insurance claim. That's what this is all about, ain't it?"

Rubbing the cap of my pen against my chin, I scratched the stubble that had already appeared. If you ever need a close shave, don't use a powder blue razor. "Would you say it was possible Haapala had the sprain before he fell? That he walked up the stairs with it and faked the fall?"

"Sure," he agreed philosophically. "He might have. Then again, he might not have. Nobody can say, because nobody was watching him, see? Nobody saw him just throw himself off the dock."

"Sounds like you've talked about it a lot."

Thrusting the thumbs of both hands through his belt, he hunched his shoulders forward. "Something about it seemed different. Maybe he waited too long to make sure everybody was looking. Maybe it was the way he was lying there." He scratched the fingers that hung outside his belt against his green twill work pants. "Who knows. Just an impression."

And that was all I got: impressions. Thanking the last of the dockworkers, I climbed the stairs to upper Michigan.

It seemed to me that the *Truth* was like Michigan Avenue, divided into an upper and lower part. Or, to be more accurate, I suppose the *Truth* was divided into the day world and the night world. The day world was that of the executives, up there in their shiny glass offices, with or without fancy thin-slatted blinds. The night world was down below, where the paper was set and printed so people could read it early next morning on the subway or with their breakfast coffee.

Upstairs, in the world of glass offices, Haapala was out on the floor again, in a circle-shaped conference with Gayle Blasingame and some editor I didn't know. I walked by them into Haapala's office, as if I belonged there. He noticed, but he continued his business. No matter what else, the news must get out.

I stood and waited, and in about seven or eight minutes he came striding by. "What do you want?" he growled, standing in the doorway.

"The truth."

"It's down in the lobby, fifteen cents. Now get out." He jerked his thumb behind him to the wide open spaces, like they do in the westerns.

"No. I want the truth about you and Blasingame. There's been another murder."

The look on his face changed from one of intolerant anger to one of disbelief, or rather unwillingness to believe. "What? Who? What do you mean *another* murder? They're saying somebody *murdered* Ralph?"

For a moment, I was taken aback by his absolute conviction that Blasingame had not been murdered. I filed it in the back of my brain, remembering that I had filed it there before. In the meantime, second murders first. "Ruby Good. Did you know her?"

"Who? No. What's she got to do with Ralph's . . . falling?" Haapala stared at me, then moved into his office, brushing by me like an unfriendly whale.

He remained standing, so I did likewise. "Ruby Good. She worked in the typesetting department. She was found dead. Shot."

He rubbed his scalp. "Oh. Yes," he said wearily.

"I remember. We discussed where to put it in the morning edition."

Because I continued to stare at him, he realized that I did not accept that as an answer to my question.

"For chrissake! I didn't know her! You're overstepping your rights, whatever your name is. Now get out."

"She was a blond woman, maybe five-four. Hourglass figure. Wore lots of makeup. The hair was dyed. She wore red clothes a lot."

When he blanched and his jaw slackened for a moment, I knew I was onto something.

Haapala swallowed. "No," he said in a phlegm-filled voice. He cleared his throat. "No. I might have seen her around, but I didn't know her. For chrissake, more than a thousand people work in this building!" He stepped toward me, as if imploring me to believe him.

"Sure," I answered. "You didn't know Ruby Good, and you didn't sprain your ankle when you were on the catwalk with Blasingame."

His right hook landed square on my jaw and knocked me halfway across the office. I stumbled against his desk and landed on my ass.

"Get out!" he gasped. "Get out, or I'll have you thrown out!"

"Frank! Are you all right!"

Haapala and I both turned toward the sound of the voice. It was Marcia, standing in the doorway with a tray in her hands. It's hard to say which of the three of us was more surprised by what we saw.

I got up, rubbing my jaw. "Sure. I just fell to make him feel good."

"What are you doing here, Marcia?" growled Haapala.

Marcia looked first at me, then at Haapala. Back again to me, then to Haapala, then to the contents of the tray, which, I now observed from my upright position, were various doughnuts, buns, and other pastries.

"You know what I'm doing here, Ted," she answered very, very precisely. I recognized the tone as Marcia's you-are-in-the-wrong voice. "I'm bringing you your morning pastries, just like I always do." With that, she stepped toward him, shoved the tray into his hands, spun on her heels with a flounce of her dress, and marched out of the office without even a backward look to see whether my life and limb were in mortal danger.

Haapala glared at me. "You heard me. Get out, or I'll have you thrown out!"

It was hard to take him seriously, since he stood there in his white shirt with rolled-up sleeves holding a tray of pastries. On the other hand, it was hard not to take him seriously. He looked like an ex-convict to whom somebody had mistakenly given dining room duty.

Dusting off my pants and coat, I straightened my lapels. "Remember MacArthur," I offered. Before he could reply, I helped myself to the largest roll on the tray and left.

"Pssst!"

Turning toward the sound, I saw Marcia flattened against the wall. She motioned with her finger that I should follow her.

When we reached a corridor, she stopped and turned. "What's going on around here, Frank? Why did Ted hit you?"

I rubbed my jaw, which hurt like hell. "He didn't like what I had to say."

"Ted has a rather quick temper sometimes, but he's basically a nice man," admonished Marcia. "He couldn't possibly have murdered Ralph."

"Umm. Why would he get so upset when I suggested he was down here that night? Was he gambling? Is that it?"

Marcia looked at me as if the punch had rattled my brain. "What in the world are you talking about? Is Ted doing a story on gambling? That will never—"

I waited, but she didn't continue.

"Never what?" I prodded.

"What do you mean, gambling? Is Ted heading up a story on gambling?"

"Not that I know of. I was referring to the fact that gambling goes on here in the late evening hours—or early morning hours if you prefer. You know—card games for money."

"I *know* what gambling is, Frank! Maybe Ted was gambling. I don't know. I don't even know if he was down here. Did you take that roll off the tray? You should have chosen the coffee cake: sour cream and raisins, sprinkled with almonds. Want me to get you a square of it?"

I shook my head. "Don't try to change the subject, Marcia. What made you think Haapala was heading up a story on gambling? Is that the one you're working on for Gayle Blasingame?"

She shook her head. "No, of course not. Two editors wouldn't be working on the same exposé."

"Then what are you working on for her?"

Marcia walked out of the corridor, back into the newsroom. I followed as she made her way to the test kitchens.

"I can't tell you that, Frank," she whispered as we walked. "Besides, it has nothing to do with Ralph's death, believe me."

We stopped at the door to the test kitchens. "Wait here," she said.

In a minute she was back with another tray. To the roll I still held in my hand, she added a napkin and a very large square of coffee cake. "You've got to understand that Ted's been under a lot of pressure lately. It's not just the extra work until they hire somebody to replace Ralph, it's that Ted and Gayle are competing for the same job, maybe competing with some outsider they don't even know. And believe me, Gayle is out to get that job. I've got to go, Frank. Take care of your jaw." She turned and walked away.

Departing, I balanced the glazed roll, the napkin, and the square of coffee cake so they wouldn't flake crumbs over me as I walked down the stairs. Not bad so far, I mused. Not even noon, and so far I had been stabbed by a squirrel, had eaten pizza for breakfast, and had been caught flat-footed by a bowling ball. To say nothing of stealing possible evidence from under the nose of my best friend, who just happened to be a cop looking for it. Well, I reflected, eyeing the pastries, at least I would have something breakfast-like to eat before noon. One out of five wasn't so bad.

Downstairs in the lobby I risked drinking coffee from the concession stand. With a large Styrofoam container of the stuff in my hand, I sat on one of the marble slabs that functioned as a plant container. The roll was delicious. The coffee cake was outstanding. The coffee was drinkable. Sipping it, I knew that what I wanted to do was go back upstairs and beat the shit out of Haapala. I realized, however, that that was not the best way to make the pages of the *Truth*.

So, maybe I should try to prove that Haapala pushed Blasingame off the rails. Even with a sore jaw, however, I saw two things wrong with that. First, a detective should never function with preconceived notions of who did what. Second, even with a sore jaw I realized that Haapala was one of the least likely persons to have planted the dirty proof or punched a hole in the paper tape. To do so, he would have had to be on the composing room floor; and if he had stood there trying to punch the right one of six holes into a little yellow strip of tape, you can bet that *somebody* would have remembered it. I was beginning to wonder about the dirty proof, though: could it be entirely an accident, totally unrelated to Blasingame's death? I was also beginning to wonder about Marcia Paxton: exactly what kind of story was she working on in order to leave the kitchen and enter the newsroom?

I felt very foolish, being taken like that by Haapala. Based on his hefting the ashtray the last time, I should have been ready for his temper. But I hadn't been prepared, I thought ruefully, rubbing my aching jaw with my splinter-infested thumb and touching my cut lip gingerly with my tongue. The trouble was, I was being nickel-and-dimed to death. Splinters. Cuts. Punches. The accumulation of such details would probably kill me before the case was solved.

I felt worried. Very worried. About who had killed Ruby Good, about Suzanne's gun and my taking it, about how she would handle herself with more questioning. Strangely, I wasn't worried that she would tell the police I had taken her gun. If she had wanted to do that, she would have done it already.

She has it made, said my Goofus to my Gallant. *If she killed Ruby Good, she doesn't have a thing to worry about—they'll never find the weapon now that you took it. And if she killed Ruby Good, what are you going to say when you turn the gun in? You've goofed, Frankie, you've goofed.*

Don't listen to him, replied my Gallant quite gallantly. *You've been in the business a long time. You recognize guilt when you see it. Suzanne Quering might threaten to kill a creep like Blasingame, but you know how redheads are. That doesn't mean she would do it.*

Who are you calling creep, you creep? argued Goofus. *We don't know that Blasingame was a creep. He was probably a nice fellow—just like Frankie here. She probably shot him because he wouldn't eat pizza for breakfast.*

"Enough!" I said out loud, standing and crushing the Styrofoam cup in my hand. "We'll just find out what kind of fellow Blasingame was," I added. A woman walking by gave me one of those stares that said she considered me dangerous.

I marched back up the stairs of the *Truth*. Screw Haapala. I was going to ask questions about Blasingame of every vice president, director, editor, and office sweeper in the *Truth*.

By three o'clock that afternoon, I felt as if I had done just that. And all I had to show for it, besides my swollen and discolored jaw, was a concensus that Blasingame was a big spender, a free roller, and that he had wanted his recent promotion for the money it would bring, not because he was dedicated to getting out the news.

Back downstairs in the lobby again, I called Suzanne. There was no answer. Rather than walk back to the composing room, I called there to ask whether she had a hire. She did not.

That got me to worrying again. There were countless reasons why she might not be answering her phone. But one of those countless reasons stood out like a roll of *gibanica* on a plate of cookies. Without wasting any more time, I grabbed a cab and took it to Dragan's district police headquarters.

They told me Dragan wasn't there. The other thing they told me made Ted Haapala's punch seem like a love tap: Suzanne had been arrested on suspicion of murder—Ruby Good's murder.

Chapter Eighteen

"ON WHAT EVIDENCE?" I demanded after my breath came back.

"We think her gun was the murder weapon," Joe Flynn answered belligerently. "It's down in ballistics right now."

Gun, I thought. *What gun?* What the hell had I overlooked? Did Suzanne own two guns and tell me about only one of them? Since they wouldn't let me talk to her, I had no way of knowing. But I was determined to find out, one way or another, how the hell the police could have Suzanne's gun.

After running down the stairs of the police station to the pay phone, I pushed coins into the slot and dialed Dragan's home number. After four rings Gloria answered, only to tell me he wasn't home.

"But he left a message for you," she announced cheerily.

"Yeah? What?"

"He said he'd see you tonight. For sure. Um, let's see—yeah, that was all. He said he'd see you tonight, and he said to tell you 'For sure.' "

"Where?"

In the silence I could practically hear Gloria thinking as she tried to recall the message. In the background I heard the kids playing.

"Um, he didn't say where, Frank. But it can't be here, 'cause he said he wouldn't be home until late tonight."

"Okay. Thanks, Gloria." I hung up the phone and thrust my hands into my pockets. Jiggling the coins, I could feel the clamminess of my hands. There was one other phone call I should make, so I dialed again.

"Katz and Katz, attorneys at law," answered my sister.

"Stefanie. What happened? Why was she arrested? What gun are they talking about?"

There was a long silence on the other end of the phone. So long, in fact, that I had ample time to conclude that Suzanne had *not* called a lawyer.

"What are you talking about?" asked Stefanie.

I began again. "A client of mine needs a lawyer," I explained. On the other end of the line, I heard Stefanie groan.

"It's Aaron's turn to take one of your cases, not mine," she interjected. "I took the last one, that

Serb who broke into the Croatian Hall after the hijackings and took a list of all the members."

"He didn't break into the Croatian Hall," I protested. "He was merely *suspected* of having done so. I told you it was Chicago aldermanic candidate supporters who did it."

"Right," answered Stefanie with utter lack of conviction. "Anyway, it's Aaron's turn. I'll put him on."

Before I could protest, I was put on hold. It made me feel good, knowing I could count on the unqualified support of my family.

"Yeah, Frank?" Aaron, Stefanie's husband, was on. "Stef says it's my turn."

"She's a generous woman," I replied. "I know she's dying to handle a score or more of my cases, yet with complete self-sacrifice she gives you the next one that comes along."

"So tell me about it."

I told him everything. Well, everything except the fact that I took Suzanne's gun.

"Okay," he assured me. "I'll call district headquarters and tell them I'm coming."

"Thanks, Aaron."

I was glad that Aaron would handle Suzanne's case. But I felt terrible that it had come to this. She had wanted a detective so that she wouldn't need a lawyer. And what had the detective done? Nothing. Thanks to the detective, she needed a lawyer pretty damn badly. I wiped the palms of my hands on my sport coat. Then I went home.

"Hey, Frank!"

"Clint. How you doing?" I greeted the evening shift doorman, thinking he was greeting me.

He wasn't. He was trying to tell me something.

Something unpleasant, I judged by the look on his face. "What's wrong?"

"I think you oughta know. The fuzz was here. They asked for you; and when you didn't answer, they went into the office. I saw them show their badges, man, and next thing I know, they were getting the keys to your place. You in some sort of trouble?"

That was supposed to be my line, I thought as I hurried through the lobby and took the stairs three at a time.

Son of a bitch, I thought, unlocking the door—they hadn't even bothered to relock the security bolt.

When I stepped inside, I realized why.

Dragan was still there. Sitting in my favorite chair. *Not* drinking my *pivo*. *Not* reading my newspaper, or my magazines. Not doing anything. Just sitting there.

Carefully, I closed the door behind me. Slowly, I walked back to my bedroom. Softly, I pulled out the second drawer from the top of my dresser.

With a crash, I slammed the drawer back into the dresser, sending coins and papers chattering across the dresser top.

Back in the living room, Dragan still sat.

"Did you have a search warrant?" I demanded, standing in front of him, rolling back and forth on the balls of my feet.

Dragan lifted a hand to his nose, pinched it closed, and breathed slowly and evenly through his mouth. He'd been doing that since we were five years old: he had seen it in a movie. Then, when he had repeated it, everybody thought it was so cute for a kid to imitate such an adult gesture that, whenever Dragan needed attention, he pinched his nose and breathed through his mouth. Later, he began to do it when he was genuinely mad. Right now, I didn't give a fuck whether he was mad or needed attention. He had used his official position to come into my house and take my property, and I was plenty pissed off.

"Well?" I demanded. "Did you have a fucking search warrant to go through my house and home, Dragan?"

"YES!" he roared, removing his hand from his nose and gripping both arms of the chair. "Yes, we had a fucking search warrant! What the fuck's the matter with you, Frank, removing evidence from the scene of a crime? I can't believe it! It's the red-head. I told you to stay away from her."

"Scene of the *crime?*" I shouted. "What crime?! We were sitting there eating pizza, for god's sake, when you barged in with your search warrant. What is it with you and search warrants, you don't leave headquarters without them or something?"

Dragan stood up, probably to shout at me better. "Okay, so it wasn't the scene of a crime, but it was the premises we were searching. And you took it— a weapon you knew we were looking for! How could you do that, Frank?"

I spun away and paced the floor. "So I wanted to borrow her gun, so that's not a crime. Something's the matter with mine."

"*Nothing's* the matter with yours! It's in your nightstand, oiled and cleaned and fully loaded. You took the fucking gun because you didn't want us to find it," shouted Dragan, pacing right after me, waving his arms as he spoke. "And another thing—who called in Ruby Good's murder, huh? Huh, Frankie, huh? It was you, wasn't it? I *know* it was you!"

"You don't know," I needled.

"Oh, yeah! Oh, yeah. I know. I *know*. You know how I know? Because of the fucking *plant*, that's how I know. Who else but you would water a goddamn rubber tree at the scene of the crime, huh?"

Pinching my nose closed, I breathed slowly through my mouth. "It wasn't a rubber tree, Dragan. It was a schefflera."

"Schefflera, rubber, schmubber—they all look alike to me. Forget the fuckin' plant. You went there, removed the evidence, tidied up, then called in the schlumpy police to try to figure out what happened, huh?"

I turned and stopped him by walking right into him, our chests bumping. "You're saying I destroyed evidence, Dragan? Or altered it? Huh? Let me get this straight—is that what you're saying?"

Dragan tapped me on the chest with a thick forefinger. "You *know* you're not supposed to leave the scene of a crime, Frank. You *know* you're not supposed to remove evidence the police are searching for. What the *fuck* has gotten into you, huh? You ask me, you're acting crazy. You're acting like she's guilty, you know?"

"She *isn't!*" I shouted, slapping away his hand.

Dragan took a deep breath. "It *looks* like she is, Frank. Look at the facts. C'mon. Do what you're trained to do. I don't want to see you get in trouble over . . . something like this."

Rubbing the back of my neck, I stared out the sliding glass door of the balcony. "Where's the gun?"

"Where it *belongs!*" he shouted. "Down at the station! In ballistics!" He punctuated every sentence with emphasis, to remind me where the gun belonged.

"Look, Dragan," I argued, trying to be reason-able, "she said somebody was trying to frame her. Couldn't that be true, huh?"

"That's not the *issue,* Frank," he shouted, ignor-ing my attempt to be reasonable. "The *issue* here is that you took *evidence,* Frank. You took it right from under my nose and tried to make me look stupid!"

"I didn't try to make you look stupid, Dragan."

"Yeah?! Well, I don't know what else you'd call it."

"I wasn't thinking of you."

"Yeah. That's just the point." He wheeled around and walked out, slamming the door so hard I thought the lintel might crack or the center stile splinter.

I went over to my favorite chair and sat in it for a while. About three or four hours, I'd say. My mind told me I should have dinner, maybe heat up some *sarma* or slap together a tuna fish sandwich or go out and sink my teeth into a steak that wouldn't bite back. My stomach told me it couldn't handle dinner.

Maybe I got some sleep that night, I don't know. It didn't feel like it when I finally gave up, rolled over, and looked at the clock radio: 5:30.

I showered and shaved and brushed my teeth, but that was it. No exercise, no breakfast. How could I eat after what I'd done to Dragan? There was only one thing to do. I drove my car down to the Criminal Investigation Division. They said he was in.

He was at his desk, probably looking as bad as I felt. He looked up but didn't say anything as I sat down. Glaring at me for a moment, he got up and left the room. In a minute or two, he was back.

"What did you find at Ruby Good's?" I asked, as if by way of greeting.

Dragan looked away and studied something where the far walls met the ceiling. "The coroner places the time of death eight, nine days ago. More or less."

"Before or after Blasingame?"

"After. But we'll know better tomorrow. You know how coroners are."

"Find anything interesting there?" I asked in a neutral tone.

Dragan touched his fingers tip to tip. "There were two red hairs found under the body," he told the cornice.

I looked at him. From his tone, his look, the way he was sitting, I knew that Dragan wasn't comfortable with the evidence. Still, he wasn't uncomfortable enough not to have made the arrest. "Lots of people have red hair," I informed him.

"They match the suspect's hair." He looked away from the cornice and down at his blotter.

"Hairs can be *planted,*" I insisted. "My god, anybody could walk up to her chair at the *Truth* and select a few hairs and plant them."

I waited. Dragan was silent.

"Find anything else?" I asked.

"Where?"

"At Ruby Good's."

Dragan looked at me and frowned. "We found it. We aren't stupid, Frank. How many times do I have to tell you that?"

I nodded in contrition. "The room?"

Dragan tapped his fingers silently against each other. "Some room. I thought of your father when I saw the bathroom. Think he's ever done one like that?"

A cop came in with four McDonald's bags.

"Thanks, Jerry." Placing the bags on his desk, Dragan opened them and began hauling out the food, divvying it out with the same methodical care and neatness as he had when we were kids playing marbles or in college playing poker. "Two for you," he explained, sliding across two Egg McMuffins, "and two for me. Two for you," he said, sliding across two chocolate-covered doughnuts, "and two for me. Two for you," he finished, sliding across two coffees, "and two for me." Scooping up the bags, he threw them into the wastebasket. Then he brushed the crumbs off his desk.

I didn't feel like eating.

"Frank," he said, reading my mind, "you'll need this. Eat."

He sounded like my mother. But I appreciated it.

"Uh. Dragan," I mumbled, my mouth full of Egg McMuffin. I swallowed and tried again. "About the gun."

He stopped chewing and looked at me, saying nothing.

"I'm sorry," I said clearly, without any food in my mouth.

Dragan looked at the cornice. Maybe he was going to give up the police force and become a carpenter. He chewed. He swallowed. "Okay." He took an overly large bite of his breakfast sandwich. "Just don't do it again," he mumbled.

I felt better, even though I wasn't sure that, given the exact same circumstances, I wouldn't do it again. "You know . . . even if Suzanne's gun was—even if it's the one, it doesn't prove a thing."

Dragan stopped chewing, crumpled his McMuffin wrapper, and threw it with force into the waste-basket. "Yeah? What do you think—she loaned the gun to somebody? Somebody who just happened to take it over and kill Ruby Good?"

"It's not impossible."

"Right. It's not impossible that space aliens landed in UFOs and killed her because they didn't like the kind of movies she had." Dragan suddenly sat up straight. He looked at me, then quickly looked away.

After a few minutes of silence, it dawned on me that he had either thought of something that helped Suzanne, thought of something that made it look worse for her, or thought of something about me that he didn't like. Dragan was like that, always giving me advice on ways to change.

"Out with it," I announced. I was beginning to like that expression. I resolved to use it at least once a day.

"About that room, Frank."

"Yeah?"

He looked at the corner molding. I stood up, walked over to the molding, tapped on it with my knuckle, and looked at Dragan. "Solid. Good for another thirty years."

He paid no attention. "The room was empty when we got there," he told the wall. "Just a camera. No tape in the recorder." Dragan pursed his lips and blew air silently through them.

After about three seconds, it hit me. In rage I kicked the wainscoting that ran around the room. "*Sonofabitch*, Dragan!" I kicked it again for good measure, then paced the room, ready to throw something.

"Okay, okay. Calm down." He stood up and followed me around the room, pacing behind me. "It was just a thought. Hey, I asked, didn't I?"

"Bullshit, you asked! You *implied!* You thought I'd take something like that?!" I shouted, turning around and nearly bumping into him.

I turned again, and he fell in line behind me. "You took the gun, for chrissake, Frank! What's the difference?"

"There's a *big* difference! Suzanne's apartment wasn't the scene of a crime. There wasn't a dead body lying around! Can't you see the difference?!"

"Okay, okay, already. Hey, c'mon. You can't blame me for just thinking it, just for a minute, not after the gun."

I was furious; Dragan was contrite. Even in my fury, I managed to observe that difference between us. And it set me to thinking. I walked over to the office window and stood there, my back to Dragan, staring out at the police desks on the other side. I could sense Dragan behind me.

"Hey, Frank. C'mon. Let's forget it, okay? I spoke out of turn, okay?"

"Maybe."

"What do you mean, 'maybe?' What do you want? An apology in blood? You're not innocent, you know!"

Turning around, I faced Dragan. "I want two things. First, I want to know why you're so sure Suzanne threatened to kill Ralph Blasingame. Second, I want to know what you found about Ruby Good that I might not have found."

Clearly aghast, he stared at me. Finally he spoke. "You set me up for that."

"Give," I replied.

Dragan went back to his chair, dropped his two hundred pounds into it without mercy, propped

his feet up on the desk—likewise without mercy—
and bit savagely into a doughnut.

To encourage him, I too returned to my chair.
Taking a pen and notebook out of my pocket, I sat
facing him. To show comradeship, I too took a bite
of my doughnut. I even took a swallow of coffee.

Something like a growl escaped Dragan's
mouth. He choked it off with another bite of
doughnut. "Gayle Blasingame," he mumbled
through the doughnut.

"She told you?"

"She hired a private detective to spy on her husband."

I didn't like the use of the word *spy*, but now was
not the time to quarrel over semantics. "And?"

"And, she—the detective, Bellam—was in the
hallway outside Quering's apartment one day
when she heard a loud argument inside. Before
you know it, the door opened and Quering stood in
it, with Blasingame. She said, 'If you don't leave,
I'll kill you. Get out. I never want to see you again.'
Also," added Dragan, "she had a gun in her hand."

Jesus.

I thought about it for a while. By the time I remembered my coffee, it had grown cold. "Well.
What about the other?"

"I don't have to tell you this, you know."

"I know."

"All right, then. We searched Ruby Good's locker
at the *Truth*."

"And?"

Dragan twisted his wedding ring reluctantly.
"Damn it, Frank. This is good. This is too good to
give you without any work."

"*Daj mi,*" I said in Croatian. "Give me."

"She had a date book."

"This is like pulling teeth, Dragan."

He ignored me. "It was full of names. Men's names."

I sat up. "Whose?"

"How many you want?" asked Dragan.

He was going to make the information hard to get. I thought about it. "Give me the names of the three *Truth* employees with the highest salaries." Not bad, I thought to myself smugly as he frowned in annoyance. Damn good, in fact.

It didn't take him long to run the permutations through his police brain and come up with the answers: "Blasingame, Morton, Hubbard."

I stood up, flipped my notebook closed, shoved the rest of the second doughnut into my mouth, swallowed it, and drank the rest of the tepid coffee. "Thanks, friend."

"You're wasting your time," he warned. "You know where the evidence points, Frank."

I did. But I believed it pointed there because we were holding the compass the wrong way. What we had to do was rotate it in our hand until the needle pointed true north.

Chapter Nineteen

■

To GET WHERE I was going next, I didn't need a compass. Stefanie and Aaron lived on Superior, just a few blocks east of La Salle. This early on a Saturday morning, parking wasn't difficult to find. When I rang the bell, Peter, my four-year-old nephew, must have tried to open the door from the other side. It required little detection to surmise that. Ann and Adam, the twins, weren't even crawling yet. Goliath, the dog, would have barked. Stefanie or Aaron wouldn't have botched the job. Hence, it was Peter jiggling the handle and probably smearing jelly over the template.

A firmer hand turned the doorknob from within. "Katz and Katz, interior renovators," Stefanie greeted, blocking Peter's attempted egress with her leg. Goliath caught her unawares and slipped through, but I grabbed his collar and hauled him back into the house.

"Good morning. My interior does not need renovating. Or maybe it does, since it contains two McMuffins, two doughnuts, and two coffees."

"You've been to see Dragan."

"How could you possibly know that, Sherlock?"

"Your diet tells me, Watson."

"Hello, Peter," I said, lifting my leg out, the knee straight. Since Peter was holding onto it, he got a ride.

"Will you take me out, Frank?" he asked.

"Not today, Pete. I have to work."

"Aaron says your client's a 'looker,' to use his erudite phrase." Stefanie looked at me speculatively.

"What's he looking for?" asked Peter.

" 'She,' not 'he,' " I corrected.

Peter lost interest. He had about ten years to go, I figured, before he'd gain it. "The hammer's upstairs," he said. "Will you let me hammer?"

"Sure," I offered, knowing full well I wouldn't be around to watch him.

Stefanie and Aaron's offices were on the ground floor of the old townhouse. Now, two years after they had bought the place, the ground floor had been restored and, where necessary, remodeled. The upper floors had not yet reached that state of being.

"Morning, Frank." My father was already hard at work in the bathroom just off the second floor landing, knocking the old plaster off the walls. In the dining room my mother was nailing plasterboard to the studs. "You're here early," she said, then noticed my clothes. "Are you on a case?"

"Yeah," I answered. "Sorry I can't help today."

"Hammer!" insisted Peter. "Hammer!"

Stefanie handed him a rubber mallet. He looked at it suspiciously, realizing that it was not made of steel, but also realizing that it was quite heavy and therefore probably not a toy. Content, he took the hammer off to a lonely stud and began pounding.

"Aaron's in the basement," Stefanie informed me, pulling nails out of her carpenter's apron and joining my mother.

Only Goliath followed me down to the basement floor.

Aaron was standing in front of the incinerator, plunging an old broomstick into a pile of smoking debris.

Coughing, I took the broomstick out of his hand and used it to push some of the wood, plaster, and other clutter aside. "Oxygen," I coughed. "A fire needs oxygen to burn."

"How do you know I want it to burn? Maybe I want it to smother." He coughed and wiped his eyes.

I handed the broomstick back. "Why don't you empty this in a garbage dump instead of burning it? This is probably against city ordinances."

"Ah-ah," argued Aaron with a shake of his head. "It isn't. I checked." Brushing smoke away from his face, he poked at the smoldering materials one more time, then dropped the incinerator door with a bang.

"You left the broomstick inside."

"There will be something else to use next week." He motioned to me, and we moved out of range of the smoke. "I saw her," he said. "Pretty complicated. You have any theories about what's going on?"

"Things are still kind of smoky in my mind."

Aaron started up the stairs, followed by Goliath, the Labrador Retriever. I was third in the coughing procession.

"She's got quite a sense of humor," Aaron informed me over his shoulder as we climbed and coughed. "Wanted to know what the penalty was for jailbreaking."

I wished she had some common sense to go along with the humor.

We reached the ground floor. Aaron sat at his desk: official business. "So what do you want? To see her?"

"Right. In private. Can you arrange it?"

"I can arrange anything," he boasted, reaching for an office phone.

About fifteen minutes later, I found myself back

in the car, driving down to the Cook County jail, more properly called the Cook County Department of Corrections. Lost in thought, I walked up to the building, nearly bumping into somebody coming out.

"Excuse me," I muttered.

I tried to get around the person, but the shape stayed in front of me. Looking up, I saw Chandra Robinson.

She stared at me accusingly. Finally, with a sigh, she spoke. "I hope you're here to get Suzanne out of jail."

"I'm trying. It's not that easy," I explained lamely. "Did Suzanne ever visit Ruby Good?"

"Visit *Ruby?* At Ruby's house, you mean? Suzanne? Are you crazy?!" Chandra Robinson placed her hands on her hips and stared at me belligerently.

"Look," I asked, "what did you think of Ruby Good?"

Blowing air derisively through her lips, Chandra Robinson shook her head. "If these are the kinds of questions you've been asking, no wonder Suzanne's in jail. Ain't nobody *liked* Ruby, Mr. Detective—not even the men. Keep that in mind: men don't like the women they use."

"They don't necessarily kill them either," I argued. "Where were you the night Ruby Good was shot?"

"What night was that, Mr. Detective?"

I wish I knew. After sparring a bit more with Suzanne's friend, I entered the building, presenting my request and my identification. They spent some time verifying it. While I waited, I thought about Blasingame being one of the names in Ruby Good's book. I wondered whether that was why

Suzanne disliked Ruby Good. I wondered whether that was why she had threatened to kill Blasingame. Jealousy. It certainly looked like it. The more I wondered, the more uncomfortable I became. After about fifteen minutes, the matron in charge ushered me into a small room, empty except for a table and two chairs. I stood and waited, watching the door opposite the one I had used.

It opened, and Suzanne stepped in. Behind her, a guard closed the door.

She stood there, looking entirely out of place in an orange prison uniform. For a minute, neither of us said anything. She looked so forlorn that I felt I had botched the job even more than I had.

"I didn't think it would be you," she said.

Not knowing how to take that, I ignored it. "I'm sorry you're here," I said. It sounded dumb.

She looked at me, saying nothing.

"Did . . . did they tell you why they arrested you?"

"They think I killed Ruby."

"Did they tell you . . . what evidence they had?"

She thrust her hands into the pockets of her shabby orange polyester skirt. "They said they had my gun. They said the bullet was the same caliber as the ones in my gun. They said they found strands of my hair there! But I was never there—I was never at Ruby's."

Again I waited, and again she was silent. *What am I waiting for?* I asked Gallant. *You're waiting for her to blame you,* answered Goofus.

"Suzanne."

She looked at me, but I couldn't identify with what emotion.

"They got a search warrant for my apartment: that's how they found your gun."

"Are you in trouble?" she asked.

I swallowed, then shook my head to indicate the negative.

"I don't blame you," she said.

It made me feel better. I thought that maybe she could have walked up to me and put her arms around me. That would have made me feel better still. But she didn't.

"Thanks for sending Aaron. I appreciate it."

Aaron. Already they were on a first name basis. "He's married," I announced, surprising myself.

Suzanne laughed: a genuine laugh, sparkling and crisp.

I leaned back against the table, practically sitting on it. "Suzanne, Aaron's a good lawyer—very good. It's good to have a good lawyer. But lawyers defend people. They don't solve crimes."

She stood there, still looking at me. But the look had changed. This one was the same one she had had when I pinned her against the sink and tried to make her tell me about threatening Blasingame. When she glanced over her shoulder at the door, I knew she knew what was coming. This could have been the very first time I was glad to see one of my clients in jail.

"This morning I saw Dragan—Lieutenant Brdar. He gave me some information that you should have given me." I waited, but she waited too, and so I continued. "He told me that a private detective hired by Gayle Blasingame was in the hallway outside your apartment the day you threatened Blasingame with a gun."

This time I waited longer, but she still said nothing. When I slammed my open palm on the table, she jumped. "That is not the kind of information a detective wants to get from the *police*, Suzanne!

That is the kind of information he should get from his client!"

She glanced behind her shoulder again, then stared at the floor. "I should have told you," she said so softly that I couldn't be sure I heard her.

"What?"

She lifted her head and looked at me. "I should have told you. I'm sorry. But how was I to know what to tell a detective? You're not like a dentist. I don't hire one every six months. I didn't know."

"I'm the one who knew, Suzanne. I'm the one who told you what to tell me. Remember?"

She scuffed a shoe across the floor and didn't answer.

I ran a hand through my hair. She could, I swear, drive me to baldness. Taking a deep breath, I continued. "Okay. You thought nobody knew. But everybody knew: the private detective, Gayle Blasingame, Ralph Blasingame certainly knew, you knew, the police know. Now I know." I paused. "But they don't know everything, do they?"

Her face was pale and her lips were set.

"They don't know why you threatened him. Only you know that, Suzanne. But I have to know it too."

She made a sound like a whimper, or a groan. If I had been twins, I would have beaten up both of me. *I'd help you*, said Gallant. *You're doing great*, cheered Goofus.

"Why?" I forced the word out of my dry mouth.

From where I was, I heard her breathe. Then she walked the few steps that separated us and stood facing me. Since I was practically sitting on the table, our heights were almost equal, our eyes on the same level.

"Do you like me?" she asked.

I couldn't believe her question. "Suz—"

"Do you like me or don't you like me?" she asked, interrupting my objection. "Be honest."

"Yes. I like you. But if you don't answer my question, Suzanne—"

Again she shook her head, interrupting me. Her curls bounced back and forth even after her head was still, her eyes staring into mine. "What if we made love?" she asked.

"No." The word came out flat and cold and sounded, even to me, cruel. I stood up to get away from her, away from the anger I felt at that moment; but she pushed me back down.

"Stop. I am not propositioning you. I'm explaining."

Her hands were on my shoulders, holding me. I cleared my throat. "What the hell are you talking about?"

"Listen. What if we made love?"

I sighed. "Okay. What if we did? I think the matron would come in. Maybe a few female guards. I can't satisfy more than half a dozen at a time."

She looked at me with sorrow, and I felt ashamed.

"What if we made love. Not here. At home. Not once. Many times. What if you liked me. What if I then asked you to. . . ." She gritted her teeth and shook her head from side to side, then spoke in a rush of words so fast that it took me many long seconds to sort out what she had said. "What if I then asked you to fuck other women I knew, asked you to fuck them for pay, and we could split the money, half and half, half to you for doing it, half to me for finding you the women? What would you feel like then? *What would you feel like then?*" She was shaking me back and forth.

Like I said, the words came out so fast, it took
me a while to sort them out. When I did, I didn't
think; I simply wrapped my arms around her.

"No!" She pushed away from me, breaking the
encirclement. Walking over to a corner, she stood
there, her back to me, her shoulders shaking.

Now I had done it. I had asked the question and
gotten the answer.

An awful answer. Certainly not one I had been
expecting. Clenching one hand into a fist, I ground
it into the palm of the other hand. I wished Blasingame were alive. I wouldn't push him into the
press. I'd make him wish I had, though. To him,
Suzanne was a whore. Maybe all women were,
even his wife. It was a sure bet he gave them all
scarves. Maybe identical ones.

And now I had to do something worse than I had
already done: ask more questions. I sat there and
tried to find a way out of it but couldn't. "I'm
sorry," I said softly, walking up to her, hoping the
words would cover the multitude of sins and sor-
rows involved.

Her arms lifted, elbows bent, and she moved her
hands across her face, wiping her eyes. She said
something so thickly that I couldn't catch what it
was. I asked her to repeat it.

"I said I didn't want you to know."

I touched my hand to her back. "Hey, it's okay."
Through the gaudy orange uniform I felt her
warmth. Of their own volition, my fingers spread
out, capturing more of the sensation. I turned her
around.

"It wasn't that I didn't want to tell you," she
sniffed, wiping her nose with her hand. I didn't
even have the traditional handkerchief to offer
her. "It was that I didn't want you to know."

I understood the difference quite clearly. I started to speak, but my throat was dry. I tried again. "It's okay. What you told me . . . helps."

Her eyes widened. "How could it? It didn't have anything to do with Ralph's death." She backed away suddenly. Under my hand I felt the muscles of her back, and the totally uncalled for thought that gymnasts have strong back muscles entered my head. My fingers must have had some kind of telepathic power, because Suzanne reacted. "Unless you think I pushed him over the railings because of that!"

My hand forced her back toward me. Well, not exactly toward me, but at least it prevented her from backing into the wall. The truth was that I didn't know what to think. All I knew what to do was ask more questions. "Suzanne, please understand. I have to ask you to tell me about it."

"I just did."

Ignoring that, I proceeded. "When Blasingame asked you . . . to . . . have sex with other men . . . did he go into detail?"

Horror, disgust, and hatred seemed to flash across her face in quick succession. For one wild second I thought she was going to slap me, or punch me. But she swallowed whatever she had been going to say or do and replied, through gritted teeth. "No. What do you mean?" Shrugging my hand off her back, she walked over to the table. Pulling out a chair, she sat in it, elbows on the table, head in her hands.

I leaned against the table again. "Did he give you names of men? Did he tell you how it would work? Where it would take place? How often? That sort of thing." *That sort of thing. Bože moj.*

She shook her head. "You think this did have

something to do with his death. You think it was murder." They were statements, not questions.

"Yes."

Suzanne traced a carving of initials on the table with her thumbnail. "I was so mad, once I realized he was serious. He had brought it up once before, but I thought it was just one of the stupid things men think are funny. I didn't like it, but I let it go. Then he brought it up the very next day." She glanced up at me, then returned her attention to the initials on the table. "Somehow, I don't know how, but somehow I realized he meant it. That was when I lost my temper. I don't remember what I said, but I told him to leave—that he was the lowest scum on earth, that I never wanted to see him again. Things like that."

Agitated, she jumped up from the table and walked around it. "He tried to . . . to, I don't know what you'd call it—pacify me? ingratiate himself with me? reason with me? He wouldn't leave. He acted as if all I needed was more explanations and I would agree! So, I pulled out the gun and told him if he didn't leave by the time I had counted to ten, I'd kill him. I opened the apartment door, threw out his jacket and shoes, and counted. I guess there was somebody in the hall. I hardly remember." Standing close to me, she said quietly, "That was the last I saw of him. Except when he'd come down to the composing room on business, of course. But I never spoke to him again."

She returned to the chair with a thump. "He never mentioned names. Or places. Or how. Or anything. I never gave him a chance to. All I gave him a chance to do was show how incredibly stupid I was. I don't know why I didn't understand it before. He used to buy me presents—the things you saw in the closet: nightgowns, lingerie. They were . . . flimsy. Not sexy, just . . . I don't know; they weren't me. I never wore them. He wanted to take pictures of me wearing them. That should have told me, but it didn't. I thought it was just . . . dumb. I wouldn't let him take the pictures." She looked at me. "I was ashamed of myself for weeks. I blamed myself. I couldn't admit to myself how much I hated Ralph. That would have been admitting I hated myself. I couldn't separate the two."

"I understand," I replied. And I did understand, though simply saying so sounded inadequate. I reached out a hand to touch her hair but pulled back. "Suzanne, did . . . Blasingame . . . how well did Blasingame know Ruby Good?"

Startled, she looked up. "Ruby?" she asked. "Ralph?" She stared at me. "I don't think he did. He never said so."

"Okay. Then who at the *Truth*, uh, 'stood in line' for Ruby, as you put it."

She blushed. "That was just an expression. I was mad. I don't know if they did or not. Stand in line, I mean. Ruby was always saying things to different men like 'My place tonight?' I don't know if it was kidding or not."

I nodded.

The door in front of me opened, and a guard stepped in, motioning her head and rattling her ring of keys.

"Is that my exit line?" Suzanne stood up and gave a weak smile.

"You'll be back for another act," I responded.

"Not here, I hope." She walked to the guard, then turned back to me. "Will you let me know how you're doing? On the case, I mean."

I nodded. She walked through the doorway and the door closed behind her.

Chapter Twenty

NEEDING THE TRUTH of familiar objects around me, I went home to think. There I sat in my favorite chair—a corduroy lounger—and leaned back, staring at the blank wall without seeing it.

What Suzanne had told me shed a fuzzy spotlight on things. If Blasingame wanted to be a pimp for Suzanne, then chances were, since his name was already in Ruby Good's book, he had wanted to be the same for Ruby Good. I now had procuring (and maybe blackmail) as a motive for murder. And if Blasingame had been procuring for Ruby Good, might she have resented his butting into her business and skimming off the profits? Maybe. The problem with a fuzzy spotlight is that it leaves things . . . fuzzy. Dragan would say that this spotlight shed as much light on Suzanne's motives as on anyone's.

As the thoughts spun round and round in my head, over and over, I realized that something was missing: *pivo*.

From the refrigerator I pulled a six-pack of Augsburger. Back in the chair, I lifted a bottle and saluted the wall. This one was for Dragan. Dragan thought Suzanne killed Ruby Good. And, working backwards from that, he thought she probably killed Blasingame, although he had no evidence. And yet—yet, Dragan wasn't quite sure, was he?

Neither was I. Suzanne did everything so innocent-like and so guilty-like at the same time that she could be innocent. Somebody was probably framing her—starting with the dirty proof and silk scarf and culminating with the gun and the red hairs. That's what I told myself as I hoisted a second bottle of *pivo* to toast Suzanne.

Blasingame, Morton, and Hubbard. The three highest-paid *Truth* employees in Ruby Good's little black book. Had it been black? I had forgotten to ask Dragan. And he had never said. They bore thinking about, and even though Gallant disapproved, I hoisted a third bottle of beer to Blasingame. Goofus then pointed out that fair was fair: Hubbard and Morton deserved equal treatment.

By the time I had given fair treatment to everybody even tangentially involved with the case, Saturday was shot and so was I. I was in no shape to go around detecting anything. In fact, I was damned lucky to detect the way to the bedroom.

A few minutes short of noon on Sunday, I awoke with a rotten feeling like I hadn't had since staying up all night playing poker with Dragan—and that had been back in college. My mind told me I should exercise and get the rotten feeling out of my system: run, swim, or lift weights. My body told my mind there was a bad connection, and it would have to call back later—much later.

After a long shower and a short breakfast that I

forced myself to eat, I went out and walked through Lincoln Park for a couple of hours, stopping at the Lincoln Park Zoo and feeding peanuts to Brick and Kup, the small brown bears named after the announcers for the Chicago Bears. By three o'clock, I felt, if not fully human, at least on the level of Australopithecus. It was time to see somebody and ask some questions.

Who? Who would be available at three on a Sunday afternoon, I asked myself.

The news never stops, suggested Gallant.

Right. I would go to the *Truth-Examiner* to see Morton and Hubbard.

Wrong, I learned when I got there. The news may never stop, but foremen did. Morton wouldn't be in because Sunday was his day off, and Hubbard wouldn't be in until the nine o'clock shift started. Stumped for somebody to question, I asked whether Adrian Venable had a hire. No. Whiffing on three out of three, I thought maybe I should go home and watch the playoffs on television.

One out does not retire the side, suggested Gallant. So I got three addresses from Jeff, who always seemed to be around. I wondered if Jeff would snap up peanuts the way Brick and Kup did. I decided against throwing him any.

Morton and Hubbard lived in the suburbs. Venable lived in a hotel, just a hop, skip, and jump from the *Truth-Examiner.* I opted for the easy choice.

Venable wasn't in. "Leaves here most afternoons around 1:00," the desk clerk informed me.

"Where does he go?" I asked.

When the clerk looked up at the ceiling and

down at the register, I pulled out my wallet and slipped a five across the desk.

"Goes for his afternoon workout at the gym. Three blocks west."

The gym was in an old building I had not paid much attention to before: one of those structures that surprises you when it looms up at you from the middle of the city, like the Medinah Temple, whose Byzantine domes seem out of place whenever I spy them. Especially so when the Shriners meet there, fezzes and all. Once through the doors of the building, I managed to find my way to the gym by smell. It exists even in new gyms: the smell of sweat, often mixed with chlorine from a nearby pool, perhaps accented with the smell of leather from the bags. In old gyms, the smell permeates the entire building.

Adrian Venable wasn't in the weight room. Nor was he by the bags. I lingered a moment, watching a thin man in gray sweats work out on the speed bag. He was good. The motion of the bag, however, made me dizzy. Turning away, I continued my search.

What I saw in the next room made me blink. It wasn't Venable, but rather Jack Morton. He was whipping around a high bar—the kind they have in men's Olympic competition—so fast that my stomach lurched. He didn't look bad, either, not for somebody approaching fifty years.

Since I knew next to nothing about gymnastics, I stood around and watched. I even walked the perimeter of the gym floor. Thanks to televised Olympic gymnastics competition, I was able to recognize equipment such as the horse, the rings, and the uneven parallel bars.

After I tired of walking and observing the equipment, I found a comfortable spot on some bleachers at the side of the gym, took off my sport jacket, folded it neatly, draped it over the bleachers, and leaned against them, watching. Morton hadn't spotted me yet or, if he had, had succeeded admirably in paying me no attention whatsoever.

A guy came up to me. He was maybe five-ten. His powerful-looking chest and shoulders were enhanced by high-waisted white pants that were held up by suspenders of sorts. He wore a sleeveless dark T-shirt.

"Hello," he said, looking me over. "I noticed you looking. Are you interested in joining the club?"

"No," I replied.

"Interested in gymnastics?"

"Sort of."

"My name's Bruno," he offered, sticking out a big hand. "Maybe I can help." He had a very strong grip.

"Frank Dragovic," I said, putting some extra strength into my handshake. I didn't want him to feel he was shaking hands with a wimp.

"Dragovic," he repeated. "Russian, huh?"

"No. I have all the time in the world."

He thought about it. "Ha. Ha, ha! That's a good one. Guess you get tired of being asked if you're Russian, huh?"

"About that help," I began.

"Yeah, sure."

Pulling out my wallet, I showed him my license. He looked at it, back at me, back at it, then at me. "What's this all about? I don't want to get anybody in trouble."

"No trouble. I just want to know some things about gymnastics."

"Like what?" He was suspicious.

"Oh, for starters, what's that guy doing on the high bar over there?" I nodded in Morton's direction.

"That's Jack. He's on the horizontal bar," Bruno corrected. "Well, he's doing a back uprise now . . . now a three-quarter back giant . . . that was a good one. That's a backward giant with a cross change . . . there's a kip. . . ."

My head was spinning about as fast as Morton was. "Listen," I suggested, "If we can't talk in English, maybe we can try Croatian. *Šta znači* kip?"

Hooking his thumbs into the front of his suspenders, Bruno stared at me and tried to sort it all out. He did, finally. "You didn't understand what I was saying, huh?"

I nodded, and he asked me what I wanted to know.

"That high bar," I said, indicating Jack Morton and the bar.

"Horizontal bar," corrected Bruno.

I glared at him. "How high is that horizontal bar?" I asked, judging it to be about eight feet off the ground.

"Eight feet, two-and-a-half inches," he answered promptly. "Say one hundred inches," he explained.

Maybe he thought he was translating it into Croatian. I didn't ask.

"Now, when you come down off that bar," I began.

"Dismount," the ever-helpful Bruno offered.

"When you *dismount,*" I said wearily, "what height are you landing from? I mean, I've seen gymnasts—" I waited for a correction, fearing I may have used the wrong word; when there was none, I continued— "on television sail way up into the air before they come—before they dismount."

My guide nodded. "Oh, yes. You can easily come down from twelve feet. Easily. Now, that's what a lot of people don't appreciate. Work on the horizontal bar is one of the most spectacular gymnastic events. It builds shoulder and chest strength." Bruno flexed his shoulders, just in case I missed the point, then hitched his thumbs into his suspenders once more. "It builds courage and daring. Believe you me, it's daring to come down from a height of twelve, even fourteen feet. But, you see," he said, unhitching a thumb long enough to scratch his crotch briefly, "what most people don't realize is the tremendous agility the horizontal bar helps develop. It's those dismounts, see? You come down from twelve feet, flying all the way, you've got to have a tremendous amount of leg strength. In the thighs," he added, slapping one of his own muscular thighs. "You've got to know how to land right in the legs. You've got to be agile."

"How about women?" I asked.

Bruno shook his head as he looked me over. I felt as if I should be wearing my nonexistent DON'T LOOK AT ME, MAN T-shirt.

"Nope," he said. "Women don't have the chest and arm strength to work out like that on the horizontal bar. They used to perform on the parallel bars," he said, pointing them out to me, just in case I had missed them, "but even that required too much chest and shoulder strength. So, let's see, maybe fifty years ago, some smart babe lowered one of the parallel bars, see? That way, women could use what shoulder and arm strength they had, but they could supplement it with their hip and leg strength."

Bruno would have probably continued, but I interrupted. "How high's the higher of the two uneven parallel bars?"

"Oh, not quite eight feet." He was a little less exact when it came to the women's equipment. "I think seven-and-a-half feet. Yeah, that sounds about right. We could go measure if you want," he offered.

"No, thanks." I was silent a moment, thinking. Bruno's white-shod feet did a pitty-pat on the floor. He was no doubt eager to offer more help. Reaching over for my jacket, I pulled out a notebook and pen, flipped open the notebook, and drew a sketch. Moving to stand behind me, Bruno watched from over my shoulder.

"Look," I said, showing him the sketch of the catwalk. "This is a catwalk. These are the railings; these are the approximate dimensions." I wrote in the figures, estimating that the bottom of the catwalk was fourteen feet from the floor of the press room.

"Yeah?" He was interested.

I handed him the pad, and he looked at it more closely, then up at me. "What about it?" he asked.

"Do you think somebody walking on that catwalk could get down to the floor quickly and safely, without getting hurt?"

"Piece 'a cake."

"Yeah?"

"Sure. You mean can somebody dismount, right?"

"Right."

"Well, it's a piece 'a cake. This wall here is six feet away?"

"About that."

"Well, things would be safer if it was ten feet;

but, sure, somebody who knew what he was doing could do a stem rise here, holding the upper rail, slipping through the lower one, and simply dismount, all in one trick."

"English, please."

"Here," said Bruno, handing me the notebook and pen. "I'll show you. Watch me from the waist down. Watch what I do with my legs. You'll see."

He went over to a second horizontal bar, and I watched him hold himself up on the bar, his body against it, the bar hitting him at thigh level. Slipping his legs under the bar, he followed them with the rest of his body, his legs already on the other side, pointing up. Next thing I knew, he had already switched handholds, turned over, and dismounted. It was slick. I told him so when he came back.

"Okay," I said. "That helped. But I have one more question."

"Sure. What is it?"

"Could a woman do it?"

Bruno nodded. "If she worked out on the uneven parallel bars she could. Make no mistake about it, these babes ain't weak. The bars require more strength than any other women's event."

There it was. Whatever Jack Morton or Lee Hubbard could have done, Suzanne could have done.

Thanking Bruno for his help, I wandered over to Jack Morton, who was still flying around the horizontal bar, developing his shoulders and arms, his courage and daring, but not, as far as I could tell, his eyesight.

Thrusting two fingers into my mouth, I let out a sharp whistle. Morton stopped in mid-air, looked at me from his upsidedown perch, and then, still gripping the bar, let himself swing down into an upright position. He dropped off the bar and landed about eighteen inches from where I stood, unintentionally spraying me with flecks of sweat.

"Thanks for noticing me. I have a few more questions."

"Sorry, Dragovic, I'm in the middle of a workout. Besides, I told you all you can possibly want to know about the procedures in the composing room. Why don't you drop by the *Truth* again tomorrow if you have to go over it again?" Morton turned to go.

"Just a minute," I said.

He turned back to me. "Yeah?"

"The questions I have aren't about composing room procedures."

He studied me a moment, then shrugged. "Regardless. I'm in the middle of a workout."

"My questions concern gambling. Gambling and other vices. Gambling and other vices and *Truth* employees."

That made him study me longer, his facial expression somewhere between a sneer and a scowl. "I thought we paid cops to ask your kind of questions."

"Suzanne Quering is paying me to ask them."

Morton turned slowly and walked back to the horizontal bars.

"I'll be here when your workout is through," I warned.

"Too bad. After my workout I spend time with my family. Sunday afternoon we always visit relatives."

"I'll be there when you get home Sunday night."

"Sunday night I read a book. Look," he said, turning toward me, "I'll make this easy on you. I'll be home Monday. Why don't you come see me at noon?"

"I'll be there," I answered, watching him mount the horizontal bar and dissolve into a blur of motion.

Chapter Twenty-one

WATCHING JACK MORTON spin, twist, turn, and fall was too much for somebody who had drunk so much *pivo* the night before. I turned to leave . . . and saw Adrian Venable standing outside the doorway.

"Detective Dragovic," he greeted with a smile and a twinkle. "What are you doing here?"

"The usual. Asking questions. What about you?"

Venable flexed his biceps. "The usual. Weight room."

He stood there and appraised me. I stood there and appraised him.

"Tell me about Frederick Douglass Williams," I said, not even knowing how the thought came into my head.

"Why?" demanded Venable.

"Because he's gone," I explained reasonably, "and I can't ask him directly, that's why."

"What kind of things would you ask him?" countered Venable.

"Did you know that Suzanne has been arrested?"
I asked, watching him closely.

His lips tightened. "Yes," he answered after a
moment's hesitation. "Chandra Robinson called
Jeff to tell him Suzanne couldn't show up for
work. Union regulation, you know. If subs can't
show up, they have to call in. I heard it from Jeff."

"Word travels fast," I commented.

Venable shrugged.

"So what about it? Suzanne has been arrested: I
need all the information I can get. What do you
know about Williams?"

With a sigh of reluctance, Venable gave in, recit-
ing the information. "He's been at the *Truth* three
or four years. Originally he's from Baltimore, I believe. Worked for an Afro-American newspaper of
some kind there. Frederick is a craftsman: he sets
excellent type. Very meticulous. Not fast, but not
slow, either."

"Married?"

"No."

"Physically fit, I take it?"

"Look, Dragovic," lectured Venable, "you can't
build a case on being physically fit. What are you
getting at?"

Good question. I wasn't sure, but I plowed ahead
anyway. "He's athletic. I saw him walking on his
hands across a plank table the other night."

Pooh-poohing any implications of my observation, Venable shook his head. "He's a fan of Walter
Payton's, that's all. It means nothing. Look,
Dragovic. Buy me a beer, and I'll answer more
questions."

A beer was the last thing I needed, but I nodded.
"You've got a deal."

I waited while Venable got out of his sweats and

into his street clothes. We walked out of the gym and down the street. "Your limp seems a lot better," I observed.

"It comes and goes. Been that way for ten years. I hardly notice it, except on very damp days."

We found a bar nearby and slipped into a booth. Venable ordered ale. Wondering whether barroom coffee was drinkable and deciding it wasn't, I asked for orange juice.

"I don't believe that Suzanne is guilty," argued Venable. "If Jack couldn't help you, I'm sure I can. Shoot."

"Umm. My questions aren't about Suzanne; they're about Hubbard and Morton."

The drinks came. Venable took his ale, gripping the mug silently.

"Cheers," I toasted, lifting my glass of orange juice.

Venable's mug of ale remained on the table; his eyes avoided me.

"What's wrong?"

"Jack and Lee are my friends. I'm loyal to my friends."

"I thought Suzanne was your friend, too," I reasoned.

"Of course she's my friend. But Jack and Lee and I go back a long way. It's different."

"Jack and Lee aren't suspected of murder. Suzanne is."

Venable swallowed some ale. "Right. Then why ask questions about Jack and Lee? They had nothing to do with it."

"Probably not," I assured him, "but I've still got to ask the questions. For instance: Morton was there at the time Blasingame went into the presses. He was gambling, I'm told."

"That's no crime. Half the pressmen and composing room gamble after hours."

"So it wasn't unusual that Morton was there at two, three o'clock in the morning?"

Venable drank more ale, then shook his head. "No. Jack's there until that time most nights when there's a game."

"What about you? Did you leave at 1:00 that night?"

"I left, but not with the shift. I had a cup of coffee, sat around, and watched the poker game. I left around 2:00."

"Morton was still there when you left?" I asked, finishing my orange juice.

Venable nodded, then added, "Jack barely knew Blasingame. What you're thinking is impossible."

"Don't guess at what I'm thinking," I said in irritation. "Morton knows Suzanne. Could he have set that dirty proof and put her slug on it?"

The question angered Venable. He drained his ale, slammed the mug on the counter, and signaled to the waitress for another order.

We sat in silence until the second round came.

"Detective Dragovic. I don't think Jack *could* have set that dirty proof. When would he have done it? The travel stories don't come down until after midnight, usually. Actually, they're often down for a few days or weeks before that. But they're accumulated behind the foreman's desk, see? So how—"

I suppose Venable figured it out at the same time I did: any foreman or copy cutter with premeditated murder on his mind could have selected a travel story and set it dirty at any time. The only catch was the tape had to be handed in the early morning of Blasingame's fall.

There was no use in belaboring the point with Venable, so I changed direction slightly. "Did the police show you the scarf that was found in the presses?"

He nodded, then brightened considerably. "It couldn't have been Jack's now, could it? Or Lee's?"

Some friend of Suzanne's he was turning out to be. "Did you recognize it as Suzanne's?"

Tipping the mug back, he swallowed a considerable amount of ale. "Nobody could recognize it as anything other than a mess. It *could* have been Suzanne's. But I told you: I don't believe Suzanne would murder anybody."

"Could the scarf have been Ruby Good's?"

"Sure. I suppose Ruby wore an occasional scarf. Poor Ruby."

"Why do you say 'poor Ruby?'"

He shrugged. "She's dead. I set the article. I was shocked. Everybody knows about it now. Except for the funeral. Nobody knows when that will be."

"She was shot. Twice."

He winced and swallowed more dark and sudsy ale.

"Got any idea why she was killed?" I asked him.

Putting down the mug with a thump, Venable looked at me. I could swear that I saw the muscles in his forearms twitch. Inwardly, I groaned, being in no shape to take on anybody at the moment, let alone an ale-drinking Englishman with muscular forearms and a red-headed temper. "What do you mean by that remark?" he demanded.

"My intentions are pure. You know a lot about what goes on in the composing room," I said, proud that I had remembered the name of the room they set type in. "I thought if anybody would know, you would."

"If I knew anything, I'd tell the police," he replied in a hostile tone.

I looked at him. "I don't think you'd tell the police about this."

His eyes slid away, to the other side of the room, then back to his ale. Although I waited, he remained silent.

"Ruby Good was a prostitute," I told him.

"She wasn't," he denied hotly. "She was a typesetter."

I shook my head. "That was just a convenient way to solicit. She was a prostitute. Of the worst kind."

He waited.

"She blackmailed the men afterwards."

Finishing his ale, he signaled the waitress for a third. I shook my head: two orange juices were plenty. The ale came and I continued. "Her most ready source of customers was at the *Truth*. It's likely somebody you know killed her."

"No! Nobody I know would do that."

I stared into my orange juice, took a swallow, and looked at him. "Were you one of Ruby's customers?"

He jumped up. "Wait a minute, Dragovic! Are you saying—"

I leaned over and pushed him back into the booth. "Don't get uptight. I'm asking a simple question. Were you?"

It seemed to take him a long time to come up with the answer. Finally, he spoke. "No. I wasn't, and that's the truth."

"But you knew what Ruby was doing, didn't you?"

He sighed and took to his ale once again. "Yes. All right. I knew."

"Right." I swallowed the remains of my orange juice and settled the glass gently on the table. "How did you know?"

"I'm not going to tell you that."

"The cops have Ruby's list of names."

"Ruby kept a list?" he asked, nearly choking on his drink. "I don't believe it! She wasn't the methodical sort. Why would she keep a list?"

I shrugged. "Fond memories, maybe."

Venable frowned at me in disapproval.

Sweeping my forearm across the table, I shoved my empty glass and his not-empty mug to one end. "Regardless of the reasons, she kept one. And I think you have a damned good idea of some of the names in it. And if you don't tell me, Venable, you could end up talking to the police a long, long time."

He didn't like it at all. But he named me names. Maybe ten of them. The names included Morton's. One name was conspicuously absent.

I was in no mood for evasions. "Come on, Venable. Tell me the one that's sticking in your throat."

He pulled his mug back and hung onto it. When he spoke, I thought he was talking to the glass. "I don't like this, Dragovic. I gave you Jack's name because . . . well, I assumed you knew it was in the book. Why else would you have been asking all those questions about him? I'm sure Jack has an alibi. Why don't you talk to the men he played poker with?"

"I'm not asking you about Morton now. We're talking about your other friend."

"Look, hell yes, he told me about him and Ruby, and how much money she asked for afterwards. She took pictures, he said. But you've got to understand. Ruby invited him over. He'd have never thought of it himself. That's the kind of person Ruby was—she always knew when somebody was ripe. But Lee wouldn't have killed her. Neither would Jack. I'd stake my life on that."

"I wouldn't if I were you," I replied.

Venable looked acutely uncomfortable. "Look. Lee's only one of many. You question them all, and then you'll see that Lee would never have killed Ruby. Lee's as innocent as . . . as Suzanne Quering. You'll see."

"As you say, I'll see." I stood up, dropped money on the table, and left Adrian Venable there to think about lust, or friendship, or deadlifts, or setting tomorrow's news. With luck, the answers to today's problems would be in it, already solved.

Stepping out into the October air, I realized that I had recovered enough from my beer hangover to feel hungry. I walked north, toward home, wondering where to eat. What I really wanted was some *vruća jagnjetina* (hot lamb to you), preferably roasted over an open spit. But in October, it was weeks past the last of the Croatian picnics where I could have bought *vruća jagnjetina*. And up here on State and Illinois, it was miles away, too.

"Come home," my mother would have said, "and I'll give you good Croatian cooking." "Try a Greek restaurant in an emergency," my father would have advised. "Greeks can cook as good as your mother can." "They can *not!*" my mother would have insisted. But there were no Greek restaurants on State Street either.

There being neither Croatian nor Greek food nearby, I walked into the Hamburger Hamlet on Walton and Rush. The wait was twenty minutes, so

I sat at the bar, sipped a drink, and ate guacamole. While I waited, I thought about Ruby Good's business.

Over the chili-burger and fries, I considered all the possible names in Ruby Good's book, wishing I had insisted on more names from Dragan. There were plenty of people at the *Truth-Examiner* with motive to kill Ruby Good. But why would somebody—presumably the same person—want to kill Blasingame? Wouldn't it solve everything, I thought, if Ruby Good had pushed Ralph Blasingame over the rails because he wouldn't pay her blackmail fee, then turned Suzanne's gun on herself and shot herself.

Twice? asked Gallant.

Before or after she returned the gun to Suzanne's locker? sneered Goofus.

Things were getting bad when they teamed up on me like that.

Dragan thinks Suzanne did it, Gallant reminded me unnecessarily.

She was jealous of Ruby Good, added Goofus, *so she bumped off the john, then wasted the jane.*

"Don't talk in that television jargon," I admonished him. "I won't listen to it."

Dinner stretched out to seven-thirty, leaving me plenty of time to walk back to the *Truth* and catch Lee Hubbard before his 9:00 P.M. shift.

My plans suffered a setback: I learned that even foremen could hire subs to replace them. Well, not exactly. They couldn't hire subs to be foremen for the evening, but they could hire subs to work the keyboard while a regular with seniority was appointed foreman for the evening. Lee Hubbard, in other words, did not show up for the nine o'clock shift.

Had Adrian Venable called and told his good
friend Lee Hubbard that I would be waiting to ask
him questions? Well, Hubbard couldn't stay away
from work forever. Besides, I had his home address and could pay him a visit Monday, after talking to Jack Morton.

There was nothing to do but call it a day and go
home.

As I turned the key in the lock, thankful to be
home, my phone began to ring. I caught it on the
fourth ring. "Hello?"

"Let me speak to Dragovic," a deep masculine
voice demanded.

If the voice didn't belong to Ted Haapala, then
the *Truth-Examiner* wasn't black and white and
read all over. "If you want to schedule another
round, I've got Monday morning free."

There was a moment of silence on the other end.
Finally, Haapala spoke. "I don't want to schedule
another round, Dragovic. I'm sorry about the first
one. I . . . damn it, you were on the wrong track,
asking me those questions! In fact, that's why I
called."

It was his dime, his time. I waited silently.

He cleared his throat. "I've got a tip for you, and
if you're worth your salt as a detective, you'll follow up on it."

"What is it that I'll follow up on?"

"Be at the *Truth-Examiner* tomorrow night.
That's Monday. Be there late, say, about midnight.
No, get there sooner—maybe eleven. Wait outside,
by the lower-level entrance. You got that so far?"

"Keep talking," I replied.

"Wait for some reporters to come out. You can
recognize the difference between a reporter and a
pressman, I hope? There might be some women

reporters. Ignore them. Choose one of the men. Follow him. If you don't botch the job, you'll find out what story Gayle Blasingame is working on."

"Why can't you just tell me?"

"You've got to earn it, Dragovic."

The click on the other end of the line told me that Haapala had hung up.

I did the same, turned out the light, and went to bed. Monday was going to be one hell of a long day.

Chapter Twenty-two

MONDAY MORNING I called Aaron, asking what progress he was making in getting Suzanne out of jail. When he said it would be a while yet, I thought I'd better visit her. Since I didn't want to press Aaron to get me permission to see her in private again, I spoke to her through the visitor's phone system, which separated us by thick walls of glass.

Suzanne asked me what the punishment was for jailbreaking. She had asked Aaron the same question, making me assume she was quite depressed. I guess I associate a repeated joke with depression. *I* was certainly depressed. Even so, I tried leaving on an optimistic note, telling her I was on my way to talk to some people about Ruby's death. The news didn't seem to cheer her up.

Jack Morton lived in Elmhurst: I took the Eisenhower west to his house. Morton himself answered the door, looked at me, then said, "You're early. We'll talk in the basement."

Down the stairs I followed him, into a paneled room. Bits of wire and metal and sheets of paper were scattered over a table. He saw me glance at his materials. "A computer," he explained. "Something called an Apple I."

I stood over the table where a green circuit board was mounted on a large sheet of plywood. Morton was connecting it to a keyboard encased in green metal. If a floppy disk was flopping around in the mess, I didn't recognize it. "I was under the impression you didn't like automation— the evils of Full Page Makeup and all that."

"You've got a good memory," Morton grunted, "but you missed the point. FPM is inevitable. I intend to be prepared for it when it comes. I'll know so much about computers and floppy disks and data processing that the *Truth* will think they can't run the place without me."

Staring at the wires and keyboard, I somehow doubted it.

"Look, make yourself at home for a couple of minutes: I'm right in the middle of this thing." Picking up a sheet of instructions, he frowned, then pulled up a chair and went to work.

For a few minutes I watched him. Eventually, I turned to look around his basement room. One of the paneled walls was full of framed photographs: several of a younger Jack Morton swinging on the trapeze bar; one of Lee Hubbard doing the same; one of Morton catching Hubbard; one of Adrian Venable in a pair of tight white pants holding a standing Morton on one shoulder, a standing Hubbard on the other. I'd have to remember to never tangle with Venable. There was another of him bound in iron chains: did he break them by flexing his muscles? One photo showed Hubbard and Morton both kissing another trapeze artist. She was a blonde who reminded me a bit of Ruby Good. Several photos showed Hubbard and Venable in street clothes. The wall contained no photos of Hubbard, Venable, or Morton doing newspaper work.

The opposite wall, however, was hung with molded press plates. Wandering over to them, I noticed that most were front pages of the *Truth-Examiner;* some were front pages of sections, mainly sports.

"What did you come here for, Dragovic?"

Turning, I looked at Morton, who had pushed aside his sheet of instructions and was now sitting at his computer worktable staring at me.

Acknowledging his challenge, I answered. "I think you know. I think from the way you act, the cops have already been here. About Ruby Good's little black book."

"So you know that, too." He shook his head. "Well, I'll tell you the same thing I told them. Sure, I screwed Ruby. Why not? Sure, I paid for it. But it was worth it. Sure, she blackmailed me, and I paid —a hundred bucks a week. But you see, it wasn't any big deal. For that hundred bucks, I got to screw Ruby without paying for it." He waited, then continued. "Don't you get it? Can't you see—I would have had to pay her every time I wanted to screw. And some things cost more than others. This way, everything was free."

"Right. Free. Five thousand two hundred a year. How much do you make, Morton?"

"None of your damned business! What I make is mine, and I can spend it any way I want to, and I don't have to report it to any dick! And I'm not ashamed of it, either. I'm not ashamed of anything."

"Did you tell the cops about the gambling that goes on in the *Truth* after hours?" I asked, concluding from his expression that he hadn't. "Lieutenant Brdar would be very interested in that information."

Morton stood and walked to the wall of photographs. Running a finger across the top of one of the frames, he inspected it.

"You don't have to look for dirt that hard, Morton. We were talking about gambling."

"Yeah. Okay. But so what? The fact is, I win. I win seventy, eighty, a hundred bucks a week easily. So you see, that paid for Ruby. I had no reason to kill her."

The rest of the conversation went pretty much the same way. Jack Morton did not feel guilty about using Ruby Good's "services," to use his terminology. He admitted no motive for murder, but he was glad, I noticed, to give me the names of other composing room employees who "went home with Ruby." (He, too, left out Hubbard's name.) More reluctantly, he gave me the names of his fellow gamblers.

Leaving Morton, I stopped at a McDonald's for a quick lunch, then drove northwest to Schaumburg, where Lee Hubbard lived. A green Chevy Impala was parked in Hubbard's driveway. A woman answered the door—one kid tagging along behind her, the other in her arms. She told me that Lee wasn't home, and she didn't know when he would return.

That left me with a lot of time until eleven o'clock in the evening, when I would "earn" whatever it was that Haapala wanted me to know. Taking the Northwest Tollway and the Kennedy, I drove back into the city. Near the lower levels of the *Truth-Examiner*, I found a parking space. Then I entered the *Truth*—to talk to a few other employees in the composing room, and to verify that Lee Hubbard would show up at 9:00 P.M.

Jeff, the man in the cage, stopped me at the door.

"Hey, Dragovic. Nothing doing."

I stared at him.

"You can't go in there."

"What do you mean?" I demanded. "You said I could ask questions for Suzanne. Remember?"

He nodded. "Sure, I remember. But I've got my orders. You can't go in there."

Walking up to the tiny room, I leaned across the counter of the half-door. "Who gave you those orders?"

Jeff shrugged. "Jack Morton. There's nothing I can do about it."

"Right." There was no sense in getting angry at Jeff. "Will Hubbard be in tonight?"

Jeff looked at the board. "He doesn't have a hire, so, yeah, he should be in."

I felt grimy, my mind full of cobwebs. I could also feel my temper getting the better of me.

Careful, Frank, warned Gallant.

Let's slug someone, suggested Goofus.

Let's cross Michigan Avenue and work out at the Downtown Court Club, advised Gallant.

Gallant's advice seeming sounder than Goofus's, I walked out of the *Truth* and into the Downtown Court Club, where I had a membership. I swam for a mile, just managing to avoid the five o'clock incoming crowd. Ah, the joys and advantages of flexible work hours.

After my swim I felt a lot better. Crossing Michigan Avenue again, I parked my well-exercised body outside the lower doors of the *Truth* and waited. When I recognized one of the in-coming five o'clock typesetters, I stopped him. He was co-operative enough to answer my questions about Morton's gambling. So was the next one I stopped. Ditto for the third. The two who gambled confirmed that Morton was a steady winner at cards and that neither Hubbard nor Venable gambled. Nor had Blasingame or Haapala ever sat in on the games—the typesetters were horrified at the thought of it. Venable came by and stopped to chat, but I sent him on his way.

There was nothing much to do at the *Truth* until the witching hour, so I walked east, then north along the lake. By six my footsteps had taken me to the Bastille, where I had an early dinner, topped by coffee and flourless chocolate cake. Even my mother loved flourless chocolate cake, so you know it had to be good.

Returning to the *Truth-Examiner,* I once again waited outside, near the loading dock. Lee Hubbard would be in sometime after eight, but before nine, I theorized. By nine on the dot, though, I concluded that I'd missed him. Maybe he came in through the upper-level entrance. It didn't make sense, but it made more sense than a third door that I didn't know about.

I ran up the stairs to the composing room, where Jeff was still in his cubbyhole.

"I told you—" he began.

"Just tell Lee Hubbard I want a word with him. I'll wait here."

"Can't," replied Jeff.

I pointed at the phone on the counter. "For chrissake, just pick up the phone, call the composing room, and ask him to see me for a minute."

Jeff shook his head. "I can't, because he's not here. He hired a sub."

"When?" I demanded of Jeff. "He didn't have one earlier."

"Yeah, well, he has one now. Lee wouldn't let his job go dark."

I left there feeling I had been made a chump of. The problem was, I wasn't sure how, or why.

There was nothing to do but sit in my car and wait until eleven or twelve, whenever the reporters I was supposed to watch for would materialize.

Close to midnight, they came out in groups of two and three: four men dressed in business suits, three women dressed in dresses. Marcia was one of the women. Starting the motor, I pulled out of my parking place and drove slowly down the street. Stopping alongside the parking lot, my lights off, I waited for one of the men to come out.

He did, driving a new Buick. He took Grand to Rush, turning north. Maybe, I thought sleepily, he was going to visit my office? No: we passed it and continued north to Walton. And that was when he began cruising. With a jolt, I straightened behind the wheel. He was looking for a pickup. And he got one.

A few seconds of negotiations at the window of his car, and she climbed in. The whole thing took a matter of minutes. The reporter turned west on Division, south on Clark, east on Pearson, and north on Dearborn. Then he parked the car. I double-parked, lights off, and watched. They got out of the car and went into an apartment building.

I drove home slowly, thinking: Gayle Blasingame had reporters working on a story on prostitution. What did it mean? And why did Haapala want me to know about it? Come Tuesday, I'd have to think about it. Except, I realized wearily, it already was Tuesday.

About eight hours later, when Tuesday was bright and sunny, I woke up and decided that Lee Hubbard had to be home. So I cut myself a grapefruit, cooked myself some oatmeal, followed it with a cup of coffee and some *gibanica*, and drove back to Schaumburg.

The green Chevy was still parked in the driveway. The door was answered by the same woman. When I said I wanted to see Lee, she asked me in. "Lee, there's somebody here to see you," she called down to the lower level.

He came up the stairs. His eyes flickered when he saw me, but other than that he didn't express any emotion. Reaching his hand for the doorknob, he gave a long speech: "We'll talk outside."

Outside, he walked away from the front door, around the car, and toward the corner of the chain-link fence that surrounded the backyard. The fence was coated with black vinyl and made me think of funerals. Hubbard stopped and turned and looked at me. He wasn't one for beginning conversations, I could see that. Possibly because it's very difficult to begin one with no.

"How much a week were you paying Ruby Good in blackmail money?"

I could see him sizing me up. We were the same height and roughly the same build. He had the intense look that many unsatisfied people have. He probably thought I was going to threaten him physically, and he looked ready to take me up on it. "No. I told the cops."

"Lee, listen very carefully. I don't want to hear the word 'No' from you the rest of the day. If I hear even the beginning of a 'No,' I'm going to get an irresistible urge to walk into your house and tell your wife about Ruby Good."

I watched in satisfaction at the myriad of looks that passed over his face. I didn't know what Hubbard had told the cops, but I'm sure they wouldn't have pulled this one on him.

"What was the question?" he asked at last.

"How much were you paying Ruby Good a week?"

"Fifty."

Throwing him a look of contempt, I straightened the lapels of my jacket and turned toward the house.

"No, wait!" Hubbard grabbed my sleeve.

"I'm going to forget you said that, Lee. I'm going to pretend I heard only 'Wait.'"

"It's true. Fifty dollars. That's the truth." He gripped the black fence with his fingertips.

"That's hard to believe," I said, shaking my head. "She was charging others at least twice that."

"I know, I know. But Ruby knew I had a wife and two kids. That's why she made it fifty."

"Sure. She had a heart of gold. She charged according to ability to pay, didn't she? Just think, if you had four kids, you could have gotten in free."

Hubbard nodded.

I grabbed him by his shirt and pulled him away from the fence. "Listen, Lee. I don't believe that shit. Tell me how much you paid right now or I'm going to end this funny game."

"Fifty! It was fifty!"

I pushed him away from me and turned toward the house. I was halfway there before he caught up to me, pulling me back toward the fence.

"It was fifty," he whispered, as if somebody might hear us. "But that wasn't the reason it was fifty."

"What was the reason it was fifty?" If he told me it was because he was good in bed, I was going to land him a right hook followed by a left cross, pick him up, and impale him on his black vinyl chain-link fence.

He licked his lips and looked around.

"There's nobody hiding behind the fence, Lee. And I'm not wearing a bug. Why was it fifty?"

"Business. I made a deal."

"Come on. What kind of deal?" I was ready for him to tell me he'd give Ruby easy copy to set. My fingers twitched, getting ready.

"More business. I'd send more business Ruby's way."

I stared at Lee Hubbard.

"In other words," I said after I had grasped the situation, "you were a pimp."

The fist came, his left. Blocking it, I threw three sharp jabs that sent him up against the fence. He conceded suddenly, crossing his arms in front of himself. I stepped back, recognizing I hadn't won any battle, but feeling better nonetheless. "Don't get upset when people use the right words, Hubbard. If there's something you don't like, change your behavior, not the word that names it."

"Get out of here. I've told you all I'm going to."

"I don't think you have." I stared at the back

door of the house, then at the kitchen windows, just so he'd get the point. There are a lot of things private detectives can do that the cops would never think of doing. Some cops wouldn't, at any rate. "Whose idea was it?"

"What?"

"Whose idea was it for you to round up more customers for Ruby?"

He thought about it a while, then answered. "Mine. I couldn't afford the hundred a week she wanted to keep from telling . . . I couldn't afford the hundred a week."

"When did Ruby start her prostitution business?"

"A year ago. Maybe a year-and-a-half."

"And the blackmail?"

Hubbard thought about it. "About six, seven months ago."

"How many men did you send her way?"

"Four."

"Four. You'd think she'd have given you a break —seeing you have two kids and a wife and all— and cut you down twenty-five dollars a customer."

Hubbard said nothing.

"Why didn't she? What was the bargain?"

Licking his lips, he looked at the back of his house. His fingers clutched the links of the black vinyl fence. "The fifty included visits. I could afford fifty a week. All I'd have to do is get the over-time Thursday and Friday nights. I'm not hurting for money."

Staring out across the neighboring lawns, I did some mental calculating. "How many customers would you say Ruby had?"

"I can't give you names. I won't. I don't know."

"I'm not asking for names. Ruby left the names in a book. I'm asking for numbers. How many?"

"I don't know. Maybe . . . maybe fifteen. Maybe twenty. It could have been higher: thirty, maybe. We used to talk about it at first . . . before she started the . . ."

"Blackmail," I supplied.

He nodded. Apparently the word yes was too much for his mouth to form. "After that, we didn't talk about it."

I understood that. One was bragging; the other was being caught. I filed away the numbers in my mind, to think about later. Meanwhile, I wasn't done with Lee Hubbard. The next question I asked him was why he had missed two nights work. At first he resisted. Finally, he said he had been sick. Sure: sick at the thought of being asked questions about Ruby Good. I asked him again about the dirty proof of Suzanne's that he had pointed out to the cops. I accused him of knowing that Ruby Good had set the proof and of changing the code on it to get Suzanne in trouble. For good measure, I also accused him of setting the paper tape he found on the pegboard.

Lee Hubbard had an answer to these accusations. His eyes didn't even flicker. "No."

We were back at Square No, and since I didn't really feel like telling his wife anything, I left Schaumburg with a lot of big information but no small pieces to fit it together with—sort of like trying to build a house with only boards and blocks: no nails, no mortar.

Chapter Twenty-three

IT WOULD BE wrong to say that by the time I had finished talking to Lee Hubbard I was depressed. I was not depressed. Morose, perhaps. Without hope, maybe. But not merely depressed.

Here it was, Tuesday afternoon, and I was stuck in a traffic jam on the Kennedy, heading back into the city. I had now spent one full week trying to prove whether Blasingame had been murdered and, if so, who did it. Since taking on the case, I had discovered a second corpse, had helped land my client in jail, had hurt and insulted my best friend by hiding evidence, had drunk myself into a beer stupor, had been knocked on my ass by a sucker punch from a suspect, and had in return punched (not once, but three times) another suspect.

Keep it up, Frank, cheered Goofus.

The case isn't over yet, Gallant rallied.

"The case isn't anywhere, that's the problem," I said aloud in my Chevrolet, rolling down the window to let in some fresh air.

By the time I got to my office, my morose mood had metamorphosed into mad—mad at myself, mad at Blasingame, mad at Dragan, mad at the *Truth-Examiner,* mad at the accumulated hangups on my telephone answering machine, and mad at the bills that had collected in my absence.

The phone rang. It was probably Haapala, and I was prepared to be equally mad at him. However, I checked myself and answered the phone.

"This is Frank Dragovic speaking. How can I help you?"

At the other end of the line I heard silence.

"Frank, are you all right?" It was my mother.

"Yeah, sure. Why?"

"That's a funny way to answer the telephone."

"It lets people know they're consulting a professional."

"It sounds strange. And, Frank, I've been thinking about Galina."

"Who?" I asked.

"You know. Galina."

"I don't know any Galina."

"Yes you do, Frank. You told me about her. Galina and Teddy."

I thumped my fist on the desk, causing the phone to ring.

"Are you still there?" my mother asked. "Hello, Frank?"

"I'm here. Galina and Teddy. Right. Sorry. What about Galina?" Some day I would have to stop making up stories—say in about sixty years.

"Well, I've been thinking why she might have said what she did. You know, about Teddy not coming over to see her when she heard about her husband's accident, and Teddy saying he did."

"Yeah?"

"Well, you said they're in business together. Maybe Galina wants to have the business to herself. Maybe she wants people to think that Teddy can't run the business. That he can't do the right thing by coming to pay his respects."

"That's probably true," I confessed. "I forgot to tell you that the police know that Teddy did come by. So it was Galina who was lying, like you said."

My mother made a sound of disapproval. "See! You just can't trust some people. Galina probably feels a great rivalry with Teddy. For all you know,

Frank, she felt the same rivalry toward her husband. Maybe she wants the business to herself—
maybe she had something to do with her husband's death."

I was silent a while, mulling it over.

"What do you think?" prodded my mother.

"Maybe," I answered. "I suppose it's possible."

"See! I thought so."

"But what about Teddy's limp? It doesn't explain that," I argued, scratching my chin and wincing at my sore jaw. Teddy could really throw a punch.

There was silence on the other end of the line.

"Mom?"

"What limp? I don't remember you saying anything about Teddy having a limp. What does that have to do with anything?"

Oops. Now I was obligated to explain about the limp, building a loading dock onto the hardware store that Teddy and Galina ran, just so Teddy could stumble and fall and sprain his ankle.

By the time that conversation was over, I was convinced that I had neglected Ted Haapala and Gayle Blasingame (also known as Teddy and Galina) for too long. I kept thinking of Suzanne in jail, and kept thinking that she must feel that I had failed. And on top of that, I kept thinking that I should be one hundred percent convinced she was innocent: only ninety percent of me had made it that far.

Nine out of ten ain't bad, Frank.

Refusing to play Goofus's number game, I decided to walk to the *Truth-Examiner*. Ted Haapala and Gayle Blasingame. Haapala's name had not been in Ruby Good's black book. If it had, Dragan would have told me, for Haapala surely made more money (much more) than either Morton or

Hubbard. The absence of his name from the book
more or less left Haapala out of consideration for
Ruby Good's murder. Besides, he would have had
to have some connection to Suzanne to use her
gun, and as far as I could tell, he didn't. But I
wasn't convinced that Haapala was out of consideration for Blasingame's death. On the other hand,
I *was* convinced that the two deaths were related,
so that kept me going around in circles.

Then there was Gayle Blasingame. Her name
was not in Ruby Good's little black book. Naturally. That, however, didn't mean she had no connection to Ruby. In fact, she did indirectly, since
her husband did. The question was, did she know
about Ruby's business?

I stopped in my tracks on Rush Street. Gayle
Blasingame. Ralph Blasingame. Ruby Good. Sarah
Bellam. Dragan had believed Gayle Blasingame
when she said Suzanne had threatened to kill
Ralph. He had believed her because Sarah Bellam,
a private detective who Gayle Blasingame had
hired to follow her husband, swore to it. Sarah
wouldn't lie and wouldn't misconstrue. And Sarah's office was just a few blocks away, on Grand
Avenue. Turning west on Grand, I walked there,
hoping she would be in.

Like me, Sarah had no secretary. Couldn't afford
one. Trying the doorknob, I found the door unlocked and walked in.

Thwack! Thwing!

From the outer room, I peered around the corner of the inner office door. Sarah was kneeling on
the floor, throwing darts at the far wall.

Thwack!

"Oh, Frank. It's you." She threw another dart,

then rose, walked to the far wall, and pulled five darts out of the notecards they had penetrated.

"That's a hell of a way to decide what case to take," I commented. "And why were you kneeling?"

"Professional secret, Frank. What's up?" Sarah turned over the penetrated cards, frowned, then filed them back in her green card file.

Pointing at her card file, I predicted, "One of these days, all our cases will be on floppy disks. Did you know that?"

"Not mine. That stuff would bend the hell out of my darts."

I made myself uncomfortable in one of Sarah's low-slung canvas chairs. She claimed the chairs prevented clients from jumping up and taking a swing at her. "Remember the time you tailed Ralph Blasingame for his wife?"

Sitting on the edge of her desk, she dangled a foot clad in a hiking boot in front of me. Running two fingers down the crease of her corduroy pants, she thought about it. "Sure. He's dead. The papers say it was an accident."

"Did you ever tail him out to Leavitt Avenue, to a house owned—or probably rented—by Ruby Good?"

"Yeah, I did," Sarah answered, tracing the lacings of her hiking boots with one finger. "She's dead, too," she added. "And Suzanne Quering's under arrest. What's the connection?"

"I wish I knew," I answered, shrugging my shoulders. "So you told Gayle Blasingame about Ruby Good."

"Of course."

"Did you check out the inside of the house?"

"No. That wasn't my job. What was in it?"

"Ummph." With a grunt I struggled out of the chair. "Video cameras. Blackmail. Anyway, if you didn't know, then neither did Gayle Blasingame."

"Good luck, Frank." Sarah pulled another stack of cards out of her file and tacked them to the wall. As I left, I heard the soft whistle and thwang of another dart penetrating the cards.

It was a short walk from Sarah's office to the *Truth-Examiner*. I nodded to the guard behind the circular desk; he nodded back. I wondered if I could get my newspapers at a discount, me being almost a regular at the *Truth*.

Upstairs, Gayle Blasingame was in her office. Her louvres were not drawn. She was sitting at her desk, holding the telephone receiver. She saw me pass the window, and by the time I had entered her office, she had the receiver in the cradle.

"I have no appointment with you, Mr. Dragovic," she announced, pulling her appointment calendar toward her and running the ever-present pencil down it, as if looking for the appointment. She probably learned that kind of behavior in assertiveness training class. I was not intimidated. A copyboy might have been. There are only two approaches to behavior such as Gayle Blasingame had just displayed. One: pick up the calendar and throw it through the window. Two: ignore it.

"I have some news for you. Editors are supposed to be interested in news."

"I doubt that I would be interested in anything you consider news, Mr. Dragovic."

Closing the door behind me, I twirled the louvred blinds closed, feeling like a wimp with a baton as I did it. Then I sat in the chair opposite Gayle Blasingame's desk. She reached for the phone, just as before. I yanked it away from her, wishing she would surprise me instead of bore me. Suzanne always surprised me.

Having stolen her prop, I watched her. She glared hatred at me, then pulled open her desk drawer and fumbled around for a cigarette. For a minute, I thought she was going to lean over and expect me to light it, but she didn't. She lit it herself with a desktop lighter made out of old wooden type—two capital letters: *G* and *B*.

Inhaling, she blew the smoke into the air, leaned back in her chair, crossed her legs, and looked at me through unsquinted eyes. "What is your 'news'?"

"My news is that I know why Suzanne Quering threatened to kill your husband."

After another drag on the cigarette (and more time to think), she told me that she didn't think such information could be considered news, but she would deign to listen to it. Those weren't her exact words, of course, but the gist of what she said.

"He was procuring," I told her.

I watched the expressions cross her face as she took the obvious meaning, then rejected it, looked for another, and settled on an approach. "Procuring solutions? Was there a problem in the composing room?" She blew more smoke—of the cigarette variety—in my direction.

Not bad, I thought. Not bad at all.

But I couldn't let her get away with it. I shrugged. "Maybe you aren't familiar with the word. Your husband was pimping."

Her cool evaporated instantly: she was on her feet, the cigarette discarded. "That's a lie! How

dare you!" She reached for the phone and again I
pulled it out of her reach.

"Nope. It's the truth. He wanted women to serve
as prostitutes for him, with him supplying the clients."

"*No!*" she screamed. "It's not true! What reason
would Ralph have to do that?"

"Money," I suggested.

Gayle Blasingame sat in her chair and put her
head in her hands. I waited. After a few minutes,
she looked up. "You can't prove that. It's her word
against his, and he's dead and she's in jail. Nobody
would believe it." By the time she finished the
speech, she had regained most of her composure.

I nodded. "True. I don't think it is a lie, but let's
suppose it is a lie that he was pimping. Consider
what we say in Croatian: *Laž ide na kratkim
nogam.* Literal translation: 'A lie travels on short
feet'—which is a way of saying that the truth will
out. Of course," I offered with a flourish of my
hand, "consider all the damage that will have been
done by the short-legged little lie before the truth
wins the race."

The implications were pretty clear. She went
very stiff. Clearing her throat, she warned, "You
. . . you could be sued for slander if you tried to
spread something like that. I have the best lawyers
in the city. I'd call them the minute you left this
office."

Not even a worthy bluff. "It won't work," I informed her. "My sister and brother-in-law are both
lawyers. Their kids will probably be lawyers.
Maybe carpenters," I amended. "The fact is, the
news about your husband would spread from one
floor of the *Truth* to another in a matter of min-

utes—seconds, probably, since telephones were invented."

"What do you want?"

That was more like it. Settling into a comfortable chair, I pulled out my notebook and began. "You're working with reporters on an exposé. Judging from the reporter I followed the other night, the exposé is on prostitution."

Stubbing out her cigarette, she crossed her hands on the desk. "Perhaps."

"Perhaps nothing," I responded. "If I have to follow more reporters to confirm the story, I will, but I won't be very happy about it, if you get my drift."

She got it. "Yes. The story—a series of articles, actually—will be on prostitution: the prostitutes, the customers, the atmosphere, sex, venereal disease, the vice squad, the protest from neighborhood residents, everything."

Suddenly the door to the office opened, and Ted Haapala stepped in—that is, he started to step in—but when he saw me, he stepped out again. Gayle Blasingame smirked after he closed the door.

"When did you begin work on the story? Before or after your husband's death?"

"Before. It's been going on for about six weeks now."

"What did you know about Ruby Good?"

She lit another cigarette and slowly inhaled. "She worked in the composing room too. I don't know what he saw in her."

"He was seeing her at the same time he saw Suzanne Quering?"

"Yes."

"He stopped seeing Suzanne Quering about three months ago."

"Yes, after she threatened him with a gun! Ralph wasn't stupid."

"What about Ruby Good?" I asked.

Gayle Blasingame tensed. "What do you mean?"

"Did he stop seeing her?"

She didn't answer immediately. When she did, it was a simple yes.

"When?"

"About the same time."

"Why?"

"I don't see what good all these questions are doing. I don't see what you're getting at," she protested.

"Why did he stop seeing Ruby Good?"

"I made him. I told him it was Ruby Good—and everybody else!—or me. He chose me. A divorce would have been messy."

"Did you know that your husband was procuring for Ruby Good?" I asked.

Seething with anger, she snuffed out the half-smoked cigarette. "No! I told you, I don't believe it! Why would he do something like that?"

"I told you: money." Leaning back in my chair, I folded the notebook and tucked it away. "It's possible that your reporters stumbled onto the prostitution in the composing room. That might have led them to your husband. It's possible that you killed your husband so that word would never get out about his pimping."

"*No!*" Her protest was vehement. It even sounded genuine. "You're wrong." She straightened herself in her chair, placed a palm on her desktop, and looked directly at me. Assertiveness training again. "I think, Mr. Dragovic, that even you realize the flaw in your thinking. If I had known that Ralph was procuring for Ruby Good—

and I still don't believe it—then the motive ran the other way. Ralph would have a motive to murder *me*. I would have no motive to murder *him*."

She was shrewd, all right. She had grudgingly answered all my questions because she didn't want any rumors spread about her now-dead husband—not that she gave two puffs about Ralph Blasingame. It was her own reputation, and her own chances of filling his position, that she was worried about. Being shrewd, however, didn't necessarily make her a murderer. What she said bore thinking about, and so I stood up, ready to depart. "By the way, did your husband buy you that green scarf I saw the other day?"

Gayle Blasingame stood, too. "Yes. When Ralph couldn't think of an appropriate gift, he ended up buying a silk scarf." She walked around her desk and approached me. "Wait," she said.

I waited.

"About the story I'm working on."

"Yeah?"

"I'd appreciate it if you kept the information to yourself. I wouldn't want Ted Haapala to know about it."

"He won't hear about it from me," I promised, closing the door behind me.

Across the space of the newsroom, Haapala's office was dark. When I asked where he was, I was told he had gone to a meeting.

I hung around for a few hours, waiting for Haapala, but had no luck. When I wandered into the test kitchen, the rich aroma of food made me realize how hungry I was. Marcia fed me a late lunch of chicken breast stuffed with raisins and carrots. In quiet voices, so we wouldn't be overheard, we talked about the prostitution story. Marcia knew nothing about Ruby Good or the composing room.

When four o'clock passed, I decided that Haapala wasn't going to be back from his meeting, so I walked out to the loading dock. After about thirty minutes, I saw Adrian Venable walking along the street toward the *Truth-Examiner*, his limp only slightly noticeable. I walked toward him.

"Hello, Detective Dragovic," he greeted when our paths crossed.

"Hubbard says he took two days off work because he was sick," I said, skipping the greeting. "But I don't believe it."

"Blimey," he sighed in an exaggerated accent.

"Why did your good friend Lee Hubbard take off?" I asked.

Venable squared off, facing me. "Because I told him to."

"Why?"

He sighed. "Because Lee has a terrible temper. I wanted to tell him what questions you would be asking, and I wanted him to be prepared for them. If I hadn't done it, Lee would have knocked your block off after your first question about Ruby. Then you'd have thought he was guilty. This way, you don't."

"Don't I?" I asked—and left Venable standing there as I walked back to my office.

Chapter Twenty-four

■

WHAT REMAINED OF Tuesday evening I spent in my office, catching up on bills and billing, correspondence and telephoning. Stefanie called and reminded me that I had to appear in court for her in the morning, for Aaron in the afternoon. Taking the appropriate case file cards out of my desk drawer, I noted the court date facts on them, then tossed them back into the drawer. At 10:30, I called it quits and went home.

Early Wednesday morning I lifted weights; late Wednesday morning I appeared in court; early Wednesday afternoon I likewise appeared in court; later Wednesday afternoon I went back to my office. By the time the rush hour started, I was in it, driving to the Southeast Side. The fact that it was Wednesday and that I was driving to the Southeast Side served to remind me of last Wednesday, when I had done the same thing—the same thing, *sans* Ruby Good, Suzanne's gun, Suzanne in jail, and other such niceties.

Stefanie, Aaron, Peter, and the twins were also at my folks' for dinner. We sat and talked and set the table and ate the salad, ham, buttered green beans, and cold potato salad made with oil, vinegar, and onions, following it all with a wide assortment of pastries and cookies. My mother announced to the whole dinner table that I was seeing two women: one with brown hair, one with red.

"Oh, yeah?" Aaron commented before I could warn him. "I'm seeing a redhead too. She's in jail."

Everybody made the connection.

"Frank!" my mother protested, wanting an explanation.

I refused to comment.

After dinner we washed the dishes, and after Stefanie and Aaron and the kids had gone, and after I had resisted all inquiries about "the redhead," I found myself driving home, still thinking.

As I stepped into my apartment, an overpowering wave of fatigue washed over me. Stumbling into bed, I succumbed to sleep.

Sometime in the middle of the night I became aware that the wind was picking up. Probably a storm on its way, I thought muzzily, rolling over and succumbing to sleep once again. Then, I don't know how much later, I woke again, aware that the rattling and knocking may have been a storm brewing, but it was also something else. I sat up and listened. There it was, a muffled knocking. *Rat tat tat.* Then silence. *Tap tap tap tap.* I looked at the clock radio, whose digital face offered no help except to tell me it was 3:23 A.M. Who the hell, I thought, getting out of bed and angrily tying a robe around myself, was knocking on my door at this hour of the night? Or morning.

Switching on the bedroom light, I stomped through the hall and the combination dining and living room. I was almost to the door—more than halfway, certainly, for I had already switched on the dining room light—when I realized that the knocking was *not* coming from the door.

Instinctively, I stopped, turning out the light. Then I stared at the balcony door, hidden behind the pulled drapes. Shaking my head to clear it of any sleep-induced notions, I listened. *Rat tat tat.* Somebody was knocking on my balcony door. My balcony door is three floors above ground level.

There are no stairs leading from it to the ground. It was isolated, I had thought, as are the other forty-two balconies just like it (forty of them above mine, two below), and therefore inviolate. Who, or what, was out there?

Tying my robe more tightly, I advanced toward the door, half expecting to see Poe's raven when I carefully pulled aside the drapes.

What I saw was a figure dressed all in black from head to toe, pressed close to the screen. As I stared, I was aware that it was a woman. And then, when she saw me and smiled, I realized that it was Suzanne.

Unlocking the glass door, I slid it across the track, pulled aside the screen door, and yanked Suzanne into the dining room. Speechless, I simply stared at her. Stepping out on the balcony, I looked over the bright red railing. There were no ladders to be seen. No ropes. No pulleys or winches. No springboard either. From where I stood, it was a drop of, say, thirty feet to the ground—if you could accept the solid concrete of the patio around the swimming pool as "ground."

Back inside, I locked up, adjusted the drape, and took a deep breath. "How the hell did you get on my balcony?" I demanded.

"It wasn't hard," she answered, removing a black watch cap into which she had tucked her hair. As she shook her hair loose, I saw that her outfit consisted of a black turtleneck sweater, black corduroy pants, even black gym shoes. "I took a running jump to the railing of the first balcony," she explained, "pulled myself up to the second balcony, stood on its railing, and pulled myself up here. Anybody could do it. I thought maybe

you weren't home. It took you forever to come to
the door."

"Suzanne," I said, suddenly aware that my teeth
had been clenched so hard that my jaw now ached.
I opened my mouth wide, rubbing my jaw. "Suzanne," I repeated, "what are you doing here?"

"I thought I could stay here until you found out
who killed Ralph and Ruby."

"No!" I exploded. "That is not what I mean. Goddamn it, Suzanne—are you out of jail?"

"Well," she hesitated. "Sure. Here I am."

My jaw hurt again and I rubbed it. It was difficult to talk. "What I meant was, have you been
released from jail?"

She crossed her arms across her chest, grabbed
the bottom of her sweater, and pulled it off over
her head. I can't even begin to tell you the thoughts
that ran through my head in those few seconds.
One of them, at least, was that she didn't have anything on underneath the sweater. But she did: a
flesh colored tank top. Thank god.

I cleared my throat. "Well?"

"No. I . . . I . . . uh . . . escaped."

I leaned back against the dining room table,
thrusting my hands into the pockets of my robe.
"You escaped. Just like that."

She nodded.

"How, Suzanne? How did you escape?"

She looked away. "There's lots of ways of escaping from jail. People do it all the time. I read about
it in the paper."

Sure. Lots of ways.

For starters, I could think of two: Money. Sex.

Something of what I was thinking must have
shown on my face, for she reacted angrily. "With a

rope! I tied a rope around the fifth floor water pipes. Then I let myself down."

"Uh-huh," I replied, suppressing a shudder. "And where'd you get the rope?"

She clasped her hands together, rubbing them. "I . . . I . . ."

I waited, watching her silently.

"I promised I wouldn't tell, Frank. I had to promise."

"Somebody helped you."

"Yes. But . . . but the person who helped made me promise not to tell. The person wouldn't want to get in trouble."

"No," I agreed, "the person wouldn't."

She nodded, still clasping her hands. I reached over and pulled them apart, placing them at her sides.

"The person . . . I'll tell you what, we'll just call the person 'he,' even though we will accept that the person might be a she—"

"Let's call the person shehe, like in a movie, I forget which. Mr. Shehe."

I rubbed my knuckles across my eyes. *Bože moj.*

"Okay," I relented. "Right. Shehe helped you, and you promised not to tell on himher." To myself, I thought that perhaps Shehe could also be Youyou, but I wasn't about to bring up the possibility of her guilt again—not to her.

Again she nodded earnestly, making me feel like a villain of the lowest order.

"At least I'm glad to see you were dressed . . . safely." I nodded toward the clothes she was wearing, and at those she had already discarded. "Good clothes for climbing. Good color for the dark."

"Thank you," she said, pleased. "I thought so."

I think I came closer to giving in and taking her

to bed—willingly or unwillingly—at that moment than at any other.

Control, warned Gallant.

Do it, cheered Goofus.

This is the 1970s, Frank—haven't you heard of women's liberation? You can't go around imposing your desires on women. Doesn't it matter what she thinks? asked Gallant.

No! shouted Goofus.

"It pays to own practical clothes," I commented.

"Yes," agreed Suzanne, more at ease. "Especially if they're black."

So Shehe had been in Suzanne's apartment. I stared at the wall opposite me. Clothes. Apartment. Suddenly something clicked: something I had observed before but misinterpreted. I thought about it for a while.

"Did Shehe tell you to come here?"

She shook her head vigorously, like an earnest child. "No. I was supposed to go to Canada."

"Why Canada?" I asked, wondering whether Frederick Douglass Williams had reached Halifax yet on his two-week vacation.

She cleared her throat. "I think . . . Shehe thinks I killed Ruby. So Shehe thinks I should leave the country."

"How were you supposed to get to Canada?"

"The person who helped me got me a car."

"Where is it?" I asked, convinced already that it was a stolen car.

"I parked it near my place. Then I ran down here. I didn't want the car near your apartment. Not after . . . not after the gun."

I wondered how many cops in their patrol cars might have seen her run down to my place. "What kind of car is it?"

She furrowed her brow. "Green. An American car. Four doors. I don't know," she shrugged.

A green, four-door American car. Where had I seen . . . oh, yes. Lee Hubbard's driveway.

"Okay." I held out my hand. "Give me the keys."

Reaching into a pocket, she pulled out a key—a shiny new key. Shehe was a smooth operator.

"I'm going to move your car. Where did you park it?"

She told me.

Back in the bedroom, I pulled on some clothes. When I came out, Suzanne was walking around the living room, studying the furnishings.

"I don't know how long I'll be," I told her. "You may as well get some sleep." I nodded back toward the bedroom.

"No!" She stiffened. "I'll sleep on the couch."

"The bed."

"The couch. You slept on the couch. I don't want to sl—" She stammered. "I mean, I shouldn't take your bed. I'll sleep on the couch."

"Suzanne," I explained, placing my hands on her shoulders, "I am not going to be in my bed. I will sleep on the couch."

She started to protest, but I held up a hand. "There's a very good reason for this. If anybody comes to the door—or, possibly, to the balcony window," I said, although I think she missed the sarcasm, "—the person they see should be me, not you."

"It doesn't seem right, though. You should have the bed. It's more comfortable."

I turned her toward the hall and walked behind her to the bedroom. "Bed," I ordered, pointing to the bed. "Sleep," I suggested.

She turned to me. "Frank."

"What?"

"Thank you for letting me stay. I didn't want to go to Canada."

I turned off the bedroom light, strongly tempted to stay and make a liar out of myself. "Good night," I said.

Less than half an hour later, I had walked up Clark and found her car. It was possible, I told myself as I fit the key into the lock, that it wasn't the car from Lee Hubbard's driveway. After all, there must have been fifty such cars in the city. In another ten minutes I was on the Dan Ryan, heading south. *Shehe indeed,* I muttered, concentrating my thoughts on clothes and apartments and jail breaks. I didn't have to concentrate on the traffic because at this hour of the morning what little traffic there was was coming into the city, not driving out of it.

Just past 95th Street, I-94 swung left to Hammond, Indiana and Chicago Heights, Illinois; a right swing poured into I-57 for Memphis and points south. Taking the right swing, I drove as far south as Vollmer Road. Pulling over to the side of the highway, I got out, leaving the car unlocked but pocketing the key. From my pocket I pulled a siphon; in a few minutes the gas that had been in the tank lay on the ground. Then I put the car in neutral and pushed it about one hundred yards down the road, away from the gas. If the car was ever tied to Suzanne, both Shehe and the police would assume she was flying south.

Then I walked, heading east on Vollmer Road until I got to the Illinois Central Gulf station. Within ten minutes I caught an early morning train. By 5:45 in the morning, I was back home, turning the key in my lock and wondering whether Suzanne would still be there.

The apartment seemed abnormally still, but that may have been because I seldom found myself coming in at 5:45 A.M. The gray light of dawn was visible where the drapes failed to cover the windows completely. I walked through the hall and into the bedroom.

Suzanne was sleeping in my bed. She was curled facing the door, one hand in a fist under her face, the other spread out across the blankets. Her clothes were in a heap on the floor. I wondered what she was wearing. Silently, I stepped closer. I couldn't tell for certain without waking her, but if she wasn't wearing one of my undershirts, I couldn't find my way home from the south suburbs. I wondered whether she had helped herself to my jockey shorts as well, but I didn't dare check.

Closing the door softly behind me, I walked aimlessly into the front of the apartment and sat on the couch. And thought. And thought. After a while, I paced and thought. After more than an hour of this, I walked back into the bedroom and placed a hand on Suzanne's shoulder.

"Hey, Suzie Q." I rocked her back and forth. "Time to wake up."

"Hmm?" She opened her eyes slowly, then sat up suddenly. "What?!"

"It's okay, Suzie Q. Everything's under control. But you've got to get out of bed. I'm going to shower. Be ready to leave in half an hour."

"Where? Why? I don't want to leave. And don't call me Suzie Q!"

"It's okay. You'll be safer where I'm taking you.

Come on." I turned, gathered up some fresh clothes, and stepped into the bathroom.

When I stepped out, more or less dressed, Suzanne was standing there, fully dressed and sullen-looking. I smiled.

She frowned. "I don't see why I have to go. I let you stay at my place."

Shaking a can of shaving lather, I shook my head. "Don't argue. We don't have time. Who do you think will probably be knocking at the door early this afternoon looking for you?" I spread the lather thickly across my cheeks, less thickly around the edges of my mustache, which, I noticed, needed a trim. Later. In the mirror, I glanced at Suzanne.

The look of recognition came into her eyes. "The cops?"

"Right." Positioning the razor at the top right of my cheek, I stroked downward.

A loud pounding on the door caused Suzanne to jump and me to cut myself.

Chapter Twenty-five

I GRABBED SUZANNE'S arm, looked quickly around the bedroom to make certain she had left no telltale signs, and moved with her to the balcony door. Thank god the drapes were still pulled. "Stay here," I whispered, pushing her out to the balcony. She nodded. I locked the screen, then the sliding glass door.

By the time I got to the door, the knocking had increased—so had the blood trickling down my face and neck. Here goes nothing, I thought, pulling open the door.

"Dragan. I thought it was the navy reserve." I tried to sound surprised and slightly annoyed but didn't know if I succeeded.

Dragan stood there and stared at me. So did his buddy, Joe Flynn.

"Well, come in for chrissake!" I stepped aside, making an exaggerated motion that he should enter. Then, stopping the pantomime, I asked with concern, "Is something wrong?"

"You cut yourself shaving," he commented.

"Thanks to you," I retaliated. "Do you always knock like that at, what, eight o'clock in the morning?" Walking into the kitchen, I yanked a section of paper towel off the roll. Holding it against my cut, I walked back toward the bedroom and bathroom—away from the balcony. "Do you mind if I finish slicing at my face?" I asked, picking up the razor and shaving gingerly around the cut. Damn it. I had chopped off a corner of my mustache. "What's up?" I asked, deciding to even up the 'stache by shaving off part of the other corner.

"Seen your client lately?"

"Yeah," I replied, catching his eye in the mirror. "Tuesday morning, I think. No, Monday. I saw her Monday. And the previous Saturday. Why? It was all on the level. Aaron arranged the first visit." Maybe I was offering too much innocent information. I'd have to tone it down.

"She's missing."

Straightening, I examined my face in the mirror. "Missing?" I intoned, bending to splash my face with water. The cut was still bleeding.

"Jail break." Dragan watched me, but whether he was commiserating with my inability to staunch the blood or whether he was examining my performance for flaws, I didn't know.

"There was a jail break? You're trying to tell me Suzanne Quering busted out of jail?"

"Looks that way."

"Jesus!" I dried my face on a towel and threw the towel across the room to the bed. "Why would she do something so stupid?" I asked, not having to feign my annoyance one bit. "Aaron would have gotten her out."

Dragan said nothing.

"Anybody else get out?" I asked.

"We think she was alone."

"Alone? How the hell did she get out?"

Dragan shrugged. "A rope. We think she must have had outside help."

I looked hard at Dragan, as if to say, *You'd better not be thinking I helped her, Dragan.*

He got the message. "So, she hasn't showed up here," he observed to the mirror.

"Hey! Hey, what the hell—what's he doing!" I shouted, following Joe Flynn, who was checking out the closets. In my concentration on Dragan, I hadn't even noticed what Flynn was doing. "God-damn it, Dragan, do you think I took her out of your crummy jail and brought her here?!" My volume increased. Grabbing Flynn by the shoulder, I spun him around. "Let's see your search warrant, buddy."

"I'm no buddy of yours, Dragovic."

"Not with your manners you aren't."

"Frankie, calm down." Dragan came up and pulled me back. "Don't take this the wrong way. We . . . uh, we just have to search the most likely places."

"You think if she came here I wouldn't try to convince her to give herself up? You think I'd help in a jail break? She probably doesn't even know where I live!" I shouted.

Dragan loosened his collar, then straightened his tie, tightening the collar again. "She probably doesn't, Frank, but I have to be able to report that I searched, see. Like now Joe can say he looked, see. He can say he looked with your full cooperation, because we didn't have a search warrant." Dragan looked around. He wandered into the hall. His eyes stopped on the balcony door. He looked at me. "I'll just open your curtains for you, Frank."

"Leave them alone," I ordered.

"No, Frank, I'll get them." He moved toward the door.

"Get away from that balcony, Dragan," I warned.

Dragan stopped.

"That's a goddamn *insult*, Dragan! You think she's out there. You think I have her hidden on my goddamn balcony. That's why you want to open the drapes."

Dragan turned and walked to the other end of

the combination living and dining room. "No, Frank, that's not so," he said calmly. "I just want to open your drapes." He began to pull the far drapes open, one by one. "That way, see, you won't cut yourself when you shave."

Standing with my back to the balcony door, I implored him. "Don't do this, Dragan."

Reaching around me, he pulled open the drape.

I closed my eyes.

He went to the next window and pulled that drape. Then I heard him go to the kitchen and pull those drapes.

I opened my eyes.

"Nice day," said Dragan, standing next to me and looking out over the balcony.

I turned and faced the balcony. Except for five large clay pots of marigolds, one lounge chair, and one Weber grill, it was empty. I took a deep breath. "Not bad. I think I'll go for a run this afternoon."

He nodded. "Where you going now?"

"I was going to see Stefanie. Now I'd better talk business with Aaron."

Dragan nodded.

"Have you told Aaron yet?" I asked, trying to breathe evenly.

"No. We were on our way there next."

"Jesus, Dragan! She's hardly likely to go there! And you couldn't get away with pulling Stefanie's drapes open, let me tell you! She'd slap a lawsuit on you faster than you could think!"

"You're bleeding into your collar," Dragan observed. "Better change your shirt."

"Right."

"Uh, Frank."

"Yeah?"

"Sometimes people want to pull drapes open for

their friends. Sort of to help them out. Let them see the light." Dragan rocked back and forth on his feet, looking out through the balcony window toward the Loop to the south. "Friends shouldn't hold any hard feelings."

"Right."

Dragan patted me on the back and left.

I waited to make certain they had really left, threw the deadbolt for double certainty, and sprinted to the balcony door. Out on the balcony, I looked around. I stood at the rail and looked up; I looked down.

"Suzanne!" I whispered.

"Is it okay?" her whisper came from below.

"Where the hell are you?" I demanded.

"Here." Suiting action to words, she appeared below me, standing on the balcony railing. From there, she easily pulled herself up to my level. Afraid that somebody might be looking, I pushed her inside.

"Was it the cops?" she asked nonchalantly.

"Yes." I wiped my brow.

"Then I don't have to leave," she announced, walking into the kitchen. "I'm starving. Let's have some breakfast."

I stared at her. Now that Dragan had searched my apartment, she probably was safe here. I watched her open cabinet drawers and pull a box of oatmeal from a shelf. I moved forward to help her. What the hell—if she stayed here, she'd stay out of trouble. Maybe.

It was nearly ten o'clock when I left home, warning Suzanne that I might not return until late evening.

I spent the day in dogged footwork, trying to learn who had done what Wednesday night, when

Suzanne had been breaking out of jail. First I
spoke to Gayle Blasingame, who appeared unhappy to see me, but who answered my questions
nonetheless. She had, she said, been home all evening. Later in the evening, I checked with the
doorman at her apartment. He said he had not
seen her leave. I tried to speak to Haapala, but
once again he managed to be in a meeting. Marcia
saw me and once again fed me lunch, pumping me
for information on the case.

Chandra Robinson had been at work Wednesday
evening, along with Jack Morton and Adrian Venable. All three had worked the five o'clock shift.
Morton and Venable, however, had both worked
two hours overtime, punching out at 3:00 A.M. Lee
Hubbard had worked his 9:00 P.M. shift, getting off
at 5:00. Lee's car, I learned, had been stolen from
the empty lot under the S-curve where he had
parked it. He had gone out to his car at lunch time
(midnight), but the car wasn't there. So he spent
the rest of his evening reporting it to the police.

Wednesday had been a busy night, people upstairs and down coming and going, lots of news
coming in, including follow-ups on the World Series that the Yankees had won Tuesday evening,
scoring 8 runs to the Dodgers' 4, taking the Series
four games to two. I remembered that I owed Dragan ten dollars, since I had bet on the Dodgers.
Advertising was up, I learned, with all kinds of ads
coming in for the Sunday papers for early-bird
Christmas shoppers. Travel, too, was big in October. So was cooking. And recreation. In short, the
whole *Truth-Examiner* had been a beehive of activity Wednesday evening while Suzanne had been
breaking out of jail with Shehe's help.

By 8:00 P.M., I decided it was safe to go home: I

was so tired and so hungry that being alone with Suzanne in my own apartment would probably not be a temptation. On the way, I stopped at the Kamehachi restaurant, picking up an order of negamaki and another of chicken teriyaki to go. I shared it with Suzanne, who was standing in front of the refrigerator with a hungry look when I walked in.

After dinner, I kicked her out of the living room and into the bedroom. "I'm tired," I announced. "I need the sleep to think." Opening the couch, I threw some sheets across it, pulled a blanket out of the closet, dropped my clothes on the floor, and crawled under the covers. The last thought I remember having was that I was picking up bad habits from Suzanne.

When the phone woke me, I was a million miles away. God knows how long it was ringing before I dragged myself out of the deepest of sleep cycles. I was aware of the ringing before I was aware of a white apparition standing over me.

The apparition shook my shoulder. "Frank. Wake up. Your phone is ringing."

Rubbing my eyes, I sat up slowly. The apparition was wearing my undershirt and my Jockey shorts.

"Get me my robe, will you?" I asked it.

It trotted off, red hair bouncing, and returned with my robe.

"Turn around, will you?" I asked it.

It turned.

The phone stopped ringing.

I stood there in my robe and shrugged. "That's that," I mumbled. "Let's go back to sleep."

"No," said Suzanne. "It stopped before. It'll start again." She sat on the edge of the couch, now a bed, her hands on her knees.

I sighed and sat down beside her. "What time is it?"

"A little after midnight."

"Umm. Not as inconsiderate as some callers," I said, thinking that my underwear had never looked so good before.

"People call you after midnight?!" she asked indignantly, missing the point.

"People—" I stopped because the phone started to ring again.

"Yeah?" I answered it in the kitchen.

"Frank? I'm in trouble." Marcia's voice trembled.

The first thought that flashed through my mind was that she was pregnant. The second was that she would hardly call me at midnight to report it. "What's wrong?" I asked.

"I can't tell you over the phone. Could you come down here?"

"Where are you?"

"At the *Truth.* Will you come? Please say you will, Frank. I don't know what to do. It isn't my fault. I was just—"

"Marcia?"

"It's okay. I just can't tell you. Will you come?"

"Yes. Are you in the kitchen?"

"No. I'm . . . I'm in Ted's office. Ted Haapala."

Now it was my turn to be silent.

"Frank? Are you still there?"

"Yeah, Marcia. I'll be down as soon as I put some clothes on."

I hung up and turned around, nearly colliding with Suzanne, who was standing right behind me. "Who's Marcia?" she asked. "Where are you going?"

"Marcia Paxton," I explained as I walked to the

bedroom. "A friend. She's a feature writer at the
Truth." I started to pull clothes out of my drawers.
"I've got to get dressed, Suzanne."

When I left, Suzanne was standing at the apartment door. She grabbed the lapel of my jacket.
"Frank. Will you be . . . careful?"

A lock of hair had fallen across her eyes. I
brushed it back with a finger. "Sure," I answered.
"I'll be careful."

Chapter Twenty-six

■

FROM THE FRONT desk of the *Truth,* the guard
called Ted Haapala's office to confirm that
Haapala was indeed there and that I should indeed
be sent up. As I took the stairs two at a time, I
reflected that I was getting pretty sick of the *Truth.*
And whatever it was that Marcia Paxton was in
trouble about, I wasn't going to like it.

Turning down the by now too-familiar corridors, I ended up in the large, now-dark newsroom.
The only light came from Haapala's office; inside,
Marcia and Haapala sat, not speaking. I entered
without knocking.

"Frank!" Jumping up, Marcia threw herself at
me, more or less.

I could see that she was distraught, with traces
of tears on her face. Holding her with one arm, I
kept an eye on Haapala. "What's wrong?" I asked.

"She said you took them," he growled. "I should have known. All your questions . . . you're a common thief, Dragovic, and I'm telling you right now that I won't play your game."

I bridled, but my anger was secondary to another problem. The man was talking to me in English, but I didn't understand a word he was saying. Gently, I separated myself from Marcia, who was recovering. Once I had her at arm's length, I asked her what Haapala was talking about.

"I told him, Frank. I had to tell him. I was afraid. I'm sorry."

Bože moj. (My god.) Now there were two of them talking gibberish.

"Marcia, start at the beginning. What did you tell him?"

"That you broke into my office and took the package, Dragovic!" shouted Haapala, leaping to his feet and pounding the desk.

Keeping one eye on his ashtray (in case he decided to heft it at me again) and another on his fists (in case he had a very long reach), I stepped back toward the door—not to run, but to better assess the situation.

"I told him you took it, Frank. He found me here. He . . . he threatened me. He said I had to give him the package or . . . or he'd call the police."

"You scum," growled Haapala. "Marcia's a nice person. Why'd you get her involved in your dirty work? What'd you expect—more of them?"

"I see," I said, and for a certain distance I did. Marcia had been in Ted's office. What for, I had no idea. To deliver some midnight cookies, perhaps? In any case, Haapala came and found her and bullied her, and Marcia, not understanding what he was talking about, but sensing he was talking about something pretty serious, told him I was the guilty party.

Not bad, when you think about it. It got me down here, and that's what Marcia wanted.

"Okay," I agreed, nodding at Haapala. "We'll talk."

"Damn right we'll talk."

"Marcia," I asked, "what were you doing in his office?"

"Cut the crap!" snapped Haapala. "Forget it! If you have a score to settle with her, do it later."

"Shutup," I told him. "You sound like a two-bit gangster from a one-bit movie." Directing an angry look (one I didn't have to fake in the least) at Haapala, I waited until he retreated. Glaring at me, he finally sat down.

Marcia looked at Haapala, then at me.

"Come on," I coaxed. "Whatever it is, you may as well tell it all right here."

"Don't be angry with me, Frank."

"I'm not, Marcia. But if somebody doesn't tell me what's going on here, I will become *very* angry."

"Well, I was down here late for a . . . uh, I was down here late."

"Marcia," Haapala announced, waving a hand magnanimously in the air, "I know why you were here. I know all about Gayle's night-time meetings and the exposé she's working on. I even tried to help Dragovic out by telling him about it," he growled. "There are no secrets. Get to the point."

Marcia frowned disapprovingly at Haapala. "Well, okay, yes, I was down here for Gayle's meeting. It let out late, and everybody left as soon as the meeting was over. All of a sudden, I was alone.

The newsroom was dark. I thought . . . well, I thought . . ." Marcia looked at Haapala, then at me, imploringly.

"You thought you'd help me out?" I offered.

She nodded eagerly. "Yes. That's it. I thought . . . I mean, here you were everyday, seeing Gayle or Ted, and not getting anywhere. And then you kept trying to see Ted, and he was always at a meeting. I thought he was avoiding you."

Haapala lit a cigar, puffed on it, and growled. "Cut the crap. Get to the point."

"So—so tonight I thought I'd look around in Ted's office. There wasn't anybody here who would notice."

"Except me," Haapala said. "I've been waiting for a repeat visit, and this was it. I caught her red-handed going through my desk."

"You did not, Ted" retorted Marcia. "Most of the drawers were locked."

He blew a puff of smoke her way. "That's a technicality. You were trying to open them, and if I hadn't caught you, you would have."

"I see," I said. "He came in and caught you. He accused you of having broken in before and taken something."

"Yes. And whatever it was, Frank, it was pretty important. He was very upset about it."

"Not 'was,' " corrected Haapala. "Is."

"Right. I've got the picture. And then you told him I broke into his office earlier and had the package."

Marcia nodded. "I'm sorry, Frank, but I—"

"It's okay," I interrupted. "It had to come out sooner or later."

"But, Frank—"

"Marcia," I interrupted again, "I want you to go sit outside, in the newsroom, and wait for me."

From behind his desk, Haapala made motions of protest. "Nothing doing!" he shouted. "The two of you are in this together."

"Only one of us knows what was in the package," I said. "Do you want both of us to know?"

Stubbing out his cigar, he stood. "Sit where I can keep an eye on you," he ordered Marcia.

Marcia protested, but I insisted. She went out, but not before telling Haapala she was disappointed that he had spied on Gayle.

We waited until she got settled at a desk.

Pulling a comfortable chair away from Haapala's desk, I sat, crossing one leg over the other, ankle resting on kneecap. Casual. "So. How much are the tapes worth to you?"

"*Worth to me?*" roared Haapala, pacing the area behind his desk. "It's worth your ass staying out of jail for you to return them! Those were private! I won't be blackmailed!" he shouted, pounding the desk.

I observed this performance with a jaundiced eye. "Very good," I commented. "If I didn't already know who the tapes belonged to, I'd believe you. Not, of course, that I would return them. But I would believe they were your property from that performance."

He stopped the ape-man pounding and looked at me. On his desk was a long yellow wooden box with bright flowers painted on it. Scandinavian, I would bet. Haapala slid the wooden lid off the box, took out a cigar, and closed the lid. Then he cut the cigar on both ends, lit it, and puffed.

"I don't know what you're talking about, Dragovic. You broke into my office and took private tapes from my desk drawer. That's theft. If you don't return them—now—I'm going to call the cops."

Heaving myself out of the chair, I grabbed his phone and handed it to him. "Call. Lieutenant Brdar's in charge of the case."

He turned pale. I don't think it was the taste of the cigar. "Case? What case?"

"The Blasingame case. Also the Good case. You remember Ruby Good, don't you? I described her to you."

The information seemed to stun him. He dropped into his chair. "I don't know what you're talking about," he repeated, but his bluff had lost most of the wind that had filled its sails.

"Sure you do. The videocassettes show Ruby Good and various composing room employees in what the delicate call 'compromising positions.' Ruby Good used the film to blackmail the men. Only, Ruby Good didn't have the brains or organizational talent to come up with that scheme. You know and I know that Blasingame was the brains behind it." I returned to my chair, sat, and crossed my legs the other way. I noticed that I had put on mismatched blue socks in my haste. Quickly, I went back to my original position. "You took the tapes from Blasingame. That's bad, Haapala—very bad. Once the cops know who has the tapes, they'll assume that person is the killer."

"No!"

"Unfortunately, yes. It stands to reason, you see. Blasingame was blackmailing people. The cops will assume that's the reason he was murdered. Naturally they'll assume that whoever has the tapes committed the murder."

Haapala managed to look both frightened and confused. "What do you want? Money?"

I shook my head. "The truth—and if you tell me it's down in the lobby, fifteen cents, you won't ever have to speak to me again. Lieutenant Brdar will take over."

Removing the cigar from his mouth, he twirled it in his fingers. He studied the glowing tip. He studied the stub. He studied me.

I sat there and tried to look like a man who had broken into his office and stolen his dirty pictures.

"What are you going to do with the truth if I tell it to you?" he asked hoarsely.

"Use it to free an innocent person. And to trap a guilty one."

"Innocent and guilty in what way?"

"The same way. Innocent and guilty of murder."

"They say," said Haapala, watching me, "that private detectives have a public rivalry with the cops. Is that true?"

I knew what he wanted; I just wasn't sure that I could provide it. "If I'm satisfied you're telling me the truth, I won't tell the cops." The cops, after all, might think that Suzanne broke into his office and took the tapes.

"Mmm." He blew smoke out of his mouth. "And what about you? I want to be satisfied that you won't use the tapes for blackmail."

"I'm the one who has to be satisfied, Haapala. Satisfied that *you* weren't using them for blackmail. Satisfied that you didn't push Blasingame into the presses."

"You just said Ralph was doing the blackmailing! I wasn't! You know I wasn't."

"I don't know. I want you to tell me. Quit the dancing around, Haapala. Give it to me straight or give it to the cops." I shifted forward in my chair as if to reach for the phone.

"Okay, okay." He ground his cigar into the ashtray. "It wasn't blackmail. Blackmail is when you blackmail somebody."

His definition left much to be desired. I waited.

"It's when you take money for keeping something secret!" he said in exasperation.

"Keep talking."

Placing his hands on the desk, he leaned forward. "I used to be a reporter," he said proudly. "Ralph didn't know a thing about reporting. He didn't know much about newspapers period. I wanted his job. No, I *deserved* his job. He was making a mess of it. He just wasn't trying hard. He collected his paycheck, but he wasn't really a newspaper man." Clearing his throat, Haapala settled back in his chair, as if before an audience. "Well, after a while, I did more than brood about Ralph. I studied him. You might say I was doing some investigating on my own."

I might. But I didn't.

"I thought he was up to something. He was into making money elsewhere, that's what I mean. I didn't know how or when or where. So, I tailed him." Haapala looked at me as if asking for admiration.

"When did this investigation of yours start?"

"A little over two months ago. I started tailing him maybe five weeks before . . . before his accident."

"And?" I prodded.

"Well, I couldn't find much. He went to a house on Leavitt Street maybe once or twice a week. Occasionally he came back to the office late at night, one or two in the morning, spent about an hour or so there, with the door locked and the blinds pulled, then went home."

The picture was getting clearer: Blasingame kept the tapes locked in his desk drawer; Haapala broke in and took them.

"So, I broke into Ralph's office and took what he kept locked up. Hell, I've gotten into desks before. Ralph was stupid." He glowered at me. "So was I, damn it, leaving those tapes here!"

"Don't jump ahead of the story," I advised.

"Yeah, you're right. Okay. I took the tapes from Ralph's desk, then took them home. As soon as I got home and saw what they were, I figured Ralph's game was blackmail. I knew I had him by the short hairs then. Only—" Haapala stopped and looked at me, then cleared his throat again. "Well, I don't know if you appreciate my position, Dragovic."

He meant that I operated in such lowly surroundings, with such trash for clients, that I couldn't begin to understand what a head honcho of a newspaper like the *Truth-Examiner* had to suffer. "Forget the appreciation. Just tell me what you did."

But telling me what he did wasn't good enough for Haapala. He had to justify his actions. "You've got to appreciate my position," he reiterated. "I had the evidence I needed to show that Ralph should be fired. But what could I do with it? Suppose I had gone to the board and told them? They'd have had a meeting, and Ralph would have been asked to resign. There's no doubt about that," he assured me, leaning forward again. "You can't be doing investigative exposés on everyone under the sun and have mud in your own house."

"But you didn't do that, did you?"

"No."

"Why not?"

He sighed. "I wanted respect. If I were still a reporter and had dug that up and gone to the top, I'd have respect. But I wasn't, and the Old Man at the top, he'd know I dug it up to get rid of Ralph. He knew I was smarting, that Blasingame was a thorn in my side. And I wouldn't get any respect for it. It wouldn't be playing by the rules. Sure, they'd have gotten rid of Ralph, but it's for sure I wouldn't have gotten his job. They'd have imported somebody from Philadelphia or Los Angeles."

"So you confronted Blasingame with the tapes."

Haapala nodded. "That Monday, I went home for dinner, then left wearing . . . uh, a disguise." His face reddened. "I wore one while I was tailing Ralph. Anyway," he hurried on, "I was outside the building here, waiting for Ralph. When I saw him come in the building, I followed. I knocked on his door and made him let me in. That's when I told him I knew about his blackmailing racket. I told him I had the tapes and that I wanted him to resign the next morning—Tuesday morning."

I waited.

Fiddling with the bright yellow box, Haapala continued, but the telling of the story came more slowly, as if he were no longer proud of himself. "He said we had to talk. He said I wouldn't be worth shit as a reporter if I didn't give him a chance to explain things. I think he was going to try to tell me it was a scam. Regardless, he was right: I owed him a chance to explain." Haapala paused, as if retracing his steps. "Anyway, Ralph wanted to talk up on the catwalk. He seemed . . . paranoid. He said that if I had found the stuff, he wasn't safe, and he wouldn't discuss it anywhere but there, where we couldn't be heard." Haapala shrugged. "So we went up the catwalk."

"At two in the morning?"

"I know it sounds crazy now, but there was nothing wrong with it then."

"What happened on the catwalk?"

He winced. "I think now that Ralph . . . Ralph . . ." He stopped.

"Go on."

Haapala licked his lips. "We stood there on the catwalk. I began to tell Ralph what I knew and what I wanted: his resignation by 10:00 A.M. Tuesday. He motioned me to be silent, said he didn't want to talk until the presses started. So we waited a while and they started. Nobody saw us. Ralph kept back in the shadows. Thank god." Reaching into a desk drawer, Haapala pulled out a handful of paper tissue and wiped his brow.

"It . . ." he seemed to choke on his words. Clearing his throat, he tried again. "It was the most frightening experience of my life." He gave a nervous laugh and looked at me. "I don't scare easily, Dragovic. But I nearly shit my pants up on that catwalk."

"Heights bother you?" I asked.

"No! You idiot!" He slapped the desk with both hands. "Ralph tried to push me off!"

I stared at Haapala. He was sweating as if we were in a sauna. "Blasingame tried to push you off?" I asked, not sure I had heard right.

He pulled himself together and answered with a nod. "I fell sideways, though. Then I felt myself slipping through the rails. My ankle twisted under me. And then I gripped the railing above me with both hands and pulled myself up."

I stared at him—at his bowling-ball head, his thick, strong hands, his bulk, his fear. "He didn't try to push you again?"

He shook his head. "No. We just stood there, staring at each other. Then I backed away. After I got a certain distance, I turned and ran down the catwalk. There's a door underneath the rails. It leads into the back hallway. I ran through the hallway and out the back. I was still in my, uh, disguise. Nobody saw me, or, if they did, they didn't recognize me. I went home and to bed. I didn't even realize how badly my ankle hurt until I got up to answer the phone—the call that told me what happened to Ralph."

Telling the story had shaken up Haapala badly. I waited while he recovered.

"I faked the fall on the loading dock. Thank god. After that I didn't have to hide the pain. I . . . I took care of things here in the newsroom that morning, and then, sometime in the afternoon, I decided I should destroy the tapes." Now he glared at me. "But they weren't here. You had already broken into my desk and taken them—or Marcia Paxton had."

"So you let the police arrest Suzanne Quering," I said, not bothering to conceal my contempt.

"Oh, no! Nothing doing, Dragovic! If they'd have arrested her—or anybody!—for murdering Ralph, I'd have come forward and told what I knew. She's under arrest for killing Ruby Good." Righteous and unintimidated, Haapala glared at me.

Scratching the stubble on my chin, I wondered if I would ever again get an uninterrupted night's sleep. Probably not, I thought, realizing I had to ask Haapala more questions now, while his defenses were down. So I spent the next two hours asking the questions, over and over, until I was satisfied.

"I wish," sighed Haapala as I was standing up to leave, "there was some way I could let the cops know without telling them . . . everything."

"Know what?" I asked.

"Know that Ralph committed suicide!" he answered indignantly. "If they knew, they'd stop this investigation."

"Suicide?" I repeated, realizing that I must have sounded in a stupor.

"It's obvious," he snapped, back to his impatient self. "He didn't want to resign. He didn't want to give up the blackmail. He didn't succeed in killing me. It's obvious he threw himself over the railing." Haapala shuddered.

Groggily, I stared at Haapala. "Did Blasingame have a silk scarf on him when the two of you were up on that walk?" I asked.

Groggily, he stared back at me. "No. Not that I noticed."

I shuddered, too. Then I opened the door and looked for Marcia. She wasn't there.

"Where the hell—?" asked Haapala.

We both looked toward the light coming from the glassed-in test kitchens. We could see Marcia working at one of the stoves, probably cooking up an early morning snack.

Shaking his head, Haapala left. I checked in on Marcia, who insisted on feeding me an omelet made with broccoli, cheese, and mushrooms as she pumped me for information. I accepted the food but retained the information.

Then we, too, left the *Truth*.

Chapter Twenty-seven

BY THE TIME I dropped Marcia off, reassuring her that she wasn't in serious trouble with Haapala, drove back home, parked the car, and walked up to my apartment, it was nearly 5:30 A.M. Lately I had begun to feel like a vampire, returning to sleep the sleep of the dead just as dawn began to stir the living.

Unlike a vampire, though, I welcomed the light —the light that had dawned, the idea that had clicked in my brain. After my talk with Haapala, I was more convinced than ever that I was on the right track. Turning the key in the lock quietly, I stepped into my apartment.

There was my sofa bed, as rumpled as I had left it five hours ago, except that Suzanne was now sleeping in it. She certainly didn't take instructions well, I thought. I gazed at her a while, then scribbled a note and left it on the dining room table: WAKE ME IF I'M NOT UP BY 1:00 P.M. Back in the bedroom, I hung up my clothes, threw the mismatched blue socks into the laundry bag, and crawled into bed.

The next thing I remember, somebody was shaking me. Sensing no danger, I came to groggily.

"It's one o'clock."

"Umm. Right." Rolling over and twisting the covers with me, I sought more sleep on the other side of the bed.

I heard the patter of feet, and the shaking continued on the refuge side of the bed.

"Wake up. It's one o'clock. You have to go to work."

I opened my eyes and looked at Suzanne, noticing that she was dressed in her black jail-breaking outfit. Perhaps I should offer her one of my suits and shirts and ties, I thought.

Don't bother. She'll take them if she wants them, said Goofus.

"Right," I said, sitting up. "Work."

"How about some food? I made us sort of a brunch and some orange juice and coffee."

I could smell the coffee brewing. "Give me five minutes."

As I washed up and brushed my teeth, I realized that, despite Marcia's omelet, I was starving. What, I wondered, would we have for brunch? An omelet, probably. An egg, cheese, and mushroom omelet with whole wheat muffins and butter and jam. Maybe I was out of mushrooms: I couldn't remember.

In the kitchen, I stopped dead in my tracks. "What's this?!" I demanded, looking at the table.

Suzanne looked at me in surprise. "Can't you see? It's tuna fish salad on a bagel."

"Tuna fish," I mumbled numbly. "On a bagel." Sliding into a chair, I prodded the bagel-cum-tuna with my knife. "Where, uh, did you get the idea to put tuna fish on a bagel?" I asked after a swallow or two of orange juice.

Suzanne stood there, a knife in her hand. She pointed the knife at me. "Are you trying to say you don't like tuna fish and bagels? You have tuna fish, so you must eat it. You have bagels, so you must eat them."

"No, no," I protested, "I wasn't trying to say anything like that." As evidence, I took a huge bite of tuna and bagel and chewed. "It's just," I explained, my mouth still full, "that I was looking forward to pizza."

She smiled as she poured the coffee. "Me, too, but you didn't have any, and I'm not supposed to go out. I didn't think I could call for delivery either."

"You did the right thing," I assured her, polishing off my half bagel heaped with tuna. "Is there more of this stuff?" I asked.

There was, and I ended up having two more bagel halves with tuna mixture on top.

This is not Croatian eating, pouted Goofus, but I ignored him.

You have an ulterior motive for eating like this, chastised Gallant.

Motive. I didn't like the thought of it. I didn't like the thought of what I had to do. Risky. Very risky. After my second cup of coffee, I piled the dishes in the sink and told Suzanne that we had to talk.

She sat on the couch, her feet together, knees pressed tight, hands on knees. It was as if she sensed something she wouldn't like.

I sat in my favorite chair, across the coffee table from her. Not knowing quite how to begin, I simply said, "Suzanne, I've solved your case."

She stared at me in such silence that I wasn't sure she had comprehended.

"Blasingame and Ruby Good," I explained. "The dirty proof with your slug on it. Your gun. I know what happened."

Her face was white and her hands were clenched. "You don't seem happy about it."

Realizing that I had expected her to ask for the details, I was surprised by her comment. "No," I replied, looking at her and realizing that she, too, seemed unhappy about it. "I'm not happy about it."

"Why not?"

It seemed to me that the tables had been turned, with Suzanne asking the questions that made me uncomfortable. *Tell her,* said Gallant.

"It's complex," I said, leaning forward in my chair and spreading out my hands, palms down. Interlocking my fingers, I cracked my knuckles: a nervous habit. "Sometimes you know things, but they aren't easy to prove." I waited for her to say something, but she didn't, so I continued. "So sometimes you have to . . . take risks. Sometimes you have to ask other people to do the same."

"Me?"

I nodded.

She came over to my end of the room and sat down on the coffee table, facing me. She took one of my hands in hers. We sat there, face to face, knee to knee, caught in circumstances that made us neither lovers nor friends, but, like trapeze artists, spinning in the air between the landing places.

"I'll help you, Frank. I'm not afraid. I trust you."

"Good." Sandwiching both her hands between mine, I felt their warmth. "I want you to hear me out. Do you promise to do that?"

"I promise," she answered solemnly.

So far, so good. "Tonight, we've got to set a trap." I looked at her, but she didn't say anything. "You and I are going to the *Truth-Examiner* tonight. You're going to type a phony story."

"No!" she objected, trying to pull away. "I'll be arrested!"

Shaking my head, I held on to her hands firmly. "No, you won't be. Not if we play our cards right."

"No! Why do I have to go with you?"

"Because you have to type a story."

She chewed on her lower lip. "Why can't Chandra do it? She'll help, I know she will."

"I don't want Chandra to do it," I replied. "Nobody from the composing room will see you, Suzanne. We're going up to the newsroom."

"Why? Who . . . was Ralph murdered?"

I nodded.

She swallowed hard. "Who . . . did it? Who killed him?"

I shook my head. "You've got to earn it, Suzanne."

She glared at me. "You mean I've got to do what you want, that's what you mean!"

I didn't say anything.

"Why can't the police just arrest—arrest whoever did it?"

"I don't have any proof. If you help me, we can change that."

She swallowed and her eyes widened. In the afternoon light, they were clear gray outlined in a smoky gray. "They'll recognize me."

"There's that risk. But I think it's slight." Since she didn't look convinced, I tried another tact. "Consider the alternatives. You can't stay here forever. You don't want to leave the country. We've got to set the trap. They'd never expect you to go to the *Truth.*"

"I've got to think about it."

Letting her pull away from my grasp, I watched as she walked back to the couch, where she sat with her feet propped up on my coffee table. She sat that way for a maybe a quarter of an hour, then she got up, walked to my chair, and announced her decision.

"Okay," she said. "But it had better work."

That's what I thought, too.

I spent the rest of the afternoon preparing us for our late-night trip to the *Truth.* From Aaron and Stefanie I borrowed a couple of cameras with carrying straps. They would serve a twofold purpose: wearing them over her black jail-breaking outfit, Suzanne would look like a newspaper photographer and would probably arouse no suspicion; in addition, we could use them to take pictures. From a video rental house, I rented a video camera and recording unit, and spent nearly an hour getting it set up in my apartment, hiding the camera behind a bushy philodendron. At the Walgreen's drugstore I purchased some black eye mascara and lots of pins for Suzanne's hair.

I also made a trip to the *Truth-Examiner,* checking up on people and their schedules, letting it be known that I was around asking questions. I told Marcia that I wanted to use the test kitchens for a couple of hours in the early morning. She didn't like it, but she finally agreed to leave a note with the guard at the front desk, giving me permission to enter the building, in case I had any trouble.

Finally, around eight o'clock, almost everything was ready. By that time I was hungry as hell. Since it was going to be a long night, I decided we should eat well. From the Treasure Island store next door, I bought French rolls, salad fixings, Idaho potatoes, two thick steaks, and ice cream. Suzanne and I fixed dinner.

While we waited for the food to cook, I worked on the article that I wanted Suzanne to type. In essence, it said that thanks to the help of Chicago Private Detective Frank Dragovic, police had sufficient evidence to make an arrest in the Blasingame and Good cases. It also said that Suzanne Quering, *Truth* employee, was not guilty of the crimes as previously suspected, but that another *Truth* employee, name not yet released by the police, was.

The article and dinner finished in a dead heat. Setting the writing aside, I dished out the food: the first normal meal I'd had in days.

Suzanne picked at her food.

"What's wrong?" I asked, devouring my steak.

"Nothing," she answered.

But I could tell that she was nervous. "Eat," I admonished. "It's going to be a long evening."

We left my apartment close to midnight. Suzanne (dressed in black, with her red eyebrows now blackened, her red hair pinned and tucked firmly beneath her black watchcap) looked nervously around her as I parked my car in one of the lots by the *Truth-Examiner*.

"Don't worry," I assured her. "You look like a photographer."

The note that Marcia had left assured our passage into the building. Once up the stairs, we walked into the test kitchens, which were already dark. From there, I made certain the coast was clear. When the newsroom was empty, except for Ted Haapala sitting in his office, we walked toward one of the reporter's desks. "Here," I said.

"No," said Suzanne, walking toward another desk.

"What the hell's the difference?" I whispered, following her.

"We'll give it Bob McCarthy's byline. He covers police reports. We'll use his typewriter. We've got to do it right." As she spoke, she settled in at his desk. Working quickly, she pulled a sheet of yellow newsprint paper from the stack on his desk, inserted it deftly into the typewriter, placed my story alongside it, and began to type.

I watched over her shoulder.

"You're making too many mistakes," I whispered.

"I'm doing that on *purpose*. Bob McCarthy makes lots of typos."

"But you're adding words—and sentences!—that I don't have!" What was she doing to my story?

"I'm going to cross them out. Don't interrupt me."

I didn't like it; but I didn't stop it.

Suzanne inserted a second sheet of paper and finished the story. Then she sat at the desk with both sheets of paper, found a pencil in the desk drawer, and edited the copy, crossing out the sentences that weren't mine. "This makes it look authentic," she explained.

I reached for the story, but she pulled it away from me. As I watched, she pulled the wastebasket out from under the desk. "I thought so," she mumbled. Pulling a Styrofoam coffee cup out of the wastebasket, she dumped its remaining liquid on the paper, then spread the stains into a ring with the bottom of the cup. "There!" she exclaimed. "That looks real."

It looked dirty to me, but maybe dirty was real. I snapped the light off and motioned Suzanne back to the kitchen. Then I walked into Haapala's office and handed him the copy—story, I mean.

Chewing on a cigar, Haapala read it: twice. Inhaling, he looked at me. "Not bad. With a little training, you could be a good reporter. With your connections and your investigative skills . . . hell, you and I would make quite a team,

Dragovic. We'd put Gayle Blasingame's teams to shame. You interested?"

"Later," I answered, looking at my watch. "Remember to leave the minute you hand in the story."

"Yeah, yeah." Raising his bowling-ball rotundness from the chair, Haapala walked out of his office, switching off the light. In the darkness, I found my way back to the kitchen. In the dark, Suzanne was waiting.

For about fifteen minutes, we waited alone. Then the door to the newsroom swung open. We heard the click-click of high heels: a woman walked across the floor. The light in Gayle Blasingame's office went on. Through the glass windows of the dark test kitchen, I snapped a couple of pictures. Suzanne looked at me, her eyebrows raised. Ignoring the silent questions she was asking, I concentrated on staring into the newsroom.

The light in Gayle Blasingame's office stayed on. In another fifteen minutes, we heard somebody striding across the newsroom floor. The lights in the newsroom flooded on, and Jack Morton stood there. Suzanne and I shrank back toward the ovens, but I crept forward again to take some pictures. Looking all around, Morton walked to Haapala's office, looked in, walked to Gayle Blasingame's office, asked her something, shrugged again, and walked back toward the light switch.

"Looks like we had the same idea, Jack." Chandra Robinson stood there, her hand over the light switch, preventing Morton from turning it off. I snapped another couple of pictures.

"What do you mean?" demanded Morton. "You aren't permitted up here."

Chandra laughed. "Neither are you, Jack. I could report you to the union."

"I had to see about some copy, that's all," blustered Morton.

"Oh yeah. McCarthy's copy. You wanted to ask him who did it, didn't you? I'll bet you're disappointed it wasn't Suzanne. But I knew all along she didn't do it."

"How did you know?" asked Morton, turning off the light as the two of them walked away.

Three minutes didn't pass before another figure crept into the newsroom: Adrian Venable. He walked through the dark newsroom, looking at nameplates, until he got to Bob McCarthy's desk. Fiddling nervously at the desk, Venable touched the lamp, the typewriter, the sheets of yellow newsprint. Then he walked away, but not in the direction from which he had entered the newsroom.

As I snapped pictures, I caught Venable suddenly dropping behind a desk. Again I could sense Suzanne looking up at me. Again I ignored her plea for confirmation or denial. Lee Hubbard was walking through the newsroom. I snapped more pictures. Like Venable, Hubbard walked along in the dark, looking at nameplates. When he got to McCarthy's desk, he stopped. Like Venable, he looked around. Then he, too, left, walking out of the dark newsroom by the back door. When Hubbard left, Adrian Venable rose from behind the desk and followed the path that Hubbard had taken.

I waited until they were gone. Then I picked up the phone in the *Truth*'s test kitchens and dialed Dragan's home number.

"Hallo?!" roared Dragan at the other end.

I told him what to do and hung up before he could protest.

Then Suzanne and I carefully but quickly made our way out of the *Truth* and back to my car. I drove home faster than the law allowed.

Chapter Twenty-eight

■

LOCKING MY APARTMENT door behind us, I looked around. Empty. Turning on a few lights here and there, I sat and listened. Everything was quiet. Then I stood and walked with Suzanne toward the bedroom.

"Stay here and listen," I said. "Don't come out unless I call you. Understood?"

She nodded in agreement: I had my doubts. Reaching out, I removed the black watchcap from her head; her hair was beginning to tumble down from its various pins and clips. Handing her the watchcap, I walked into my combination dining room–living room. I tested the sliding glass balcony door. Locked. Then I walked to the main door—the door that regular visitors use—and unlatched the deadbolt. I didn't want to make things too difficult for our caller. Finally, I turned on the video recording unit and settled back on the couch with the Friday evening edition of the *Truth-Examiner*.

After what seemed like the remainder of the

night but was actually less than thirty minutes, I heard a faint knocking at the door. Ignoring it, I slid down on the couch, letting the paper fall over my face.

The light knocking repeated itself twice. It was followed by a soft clicking sound, after which I felt the draft from the hallway. The hairs on my arms felt prickly and tense: I could sense somebody standing there, probably surprised to find the lights on—even more surprised to find me asleep on the couch. Then I heard a soft click as the door was closed and the latch-bolt caught. I swear that the fine hair on my ears stood on end as I sensed somebody walking across the carpet toward me.

I sat up, the newspaper sliding off me onto the floor. "Hello, Venable."

It was gratifying to see the looks that passed over his face: first shock, then suspicion, then anger. They disappeared quickly, replaced by his friendly, charming look.

"How long have you known?" he asked, standing behind the couch.

I remained seated but ready to move. "Not long. A day or two."

"There are police at my apartment," he offered. "I presume you told them the tapes were there."

"I did."

Pursing his lips, he whistled a tune softly. "Not a very smart place to keep them, I agree," he said amiably. "But I didn't want them in my locker—just in case the cops searched the *Truth.*"

I nodded in understanding. "Not necessarily a dumb place. Blasingame had, after all, kept them in his desk for, what—half a year?—and look where it got him."

"More like nine, ten months, I think," clarified

Venable, as if we were carrying on a civilized conversation.

Shuffling slightly across the carpet, he moved closer to my end of the couch. I lifted my arms behind my head as if waking up. Flexing my shoulders, I moved forward on the couch, ready to rise if necessary.

"How'd you tumble to me?" he asked.

"I saw pictures of you and Hubbard and Morton in Morton's basement room. You were wearing white pants and suspenders. It didn't dawn on me until days later: you were a flyer, too, weren't you?"

He nodded. "Catcher, mainly. But flyer, too. An amateur, really. Just something to do during the winter months."

"Is that how you got the limp?" I asked.

A pained look crossed his face. "Yes. We were on the bars one day. Lee dropped me. I missed the net. Didn't fly after that. Lee and Jack, they didn't talk about it either. I was certain they wouldn't tell anybody I had worked on the trapeze."

"So you told me you had been a strongman during your circus days. That wasn't all you had been, though, was it?"

Venable smiled tightly. "What else did you get out of the pictures?"

"The chains wrapped around you. You didn't use your muscles to get out of them, did you? It was part of an escape artist's act."

"Righto," he answered casually, moving closer.

I stood and faced him. "It hit me a few days after I saw the pictures. Whoever gave Suzanne those black clothes had been in her apartment. So who had the key to do that? Not a lover. Not a friend. Not a cop. It had to be somebody who could break into her apartment without any difficulty. Did you use the window or the door?" I asked.

"Ahh! I see. That's what made you tumble to it. She didn't go to Canada after all, did she?"

"No," I said, "she didn't."

Venable shook his head. "I should have known. I wish she had, though."

"I'll bet you do. How'd you get into her apartment?"

"The door. It wasn't hard."

"No," I agreed, "it probably wasn't. I see you handled my door without any problems." Thrusting my hands into my pockets, I stared at Venable. "It turned out to be a big mistake, though, trying to frame Suzanne."

Flexing his fingers, he shrugged. Loosening his arms, I thought. Getting ready.

"The way I see it," I said, "is this. You're the one who knew everything that went on in the composing room. Lee, your good friend, probably told you that he was being blackmailed. You probably figured out the same about Morton. You all assumed that there was somebody behind Ruby Good—somebody doing the blackmailing. Had to. In fact, for her own protection, Ruby needed that known."

"For her own protection, she did," he agreed.

"How did you figure out it was Blasingame? Did Ruby tell you?"

He shook his head. "No. I watched her place every night for a couple of weeks. I recognized Blasingame immediately. I followed him there, then back to the office. I just figured that he was the brains behind the scheme."

"So you planned to kill him."

"Absolutely not!" protested Venable.

"Uh-uh," I disagreed. "You planned it. You took Suzanne's scarf. Either you broke into her apartment and took it, or you lifted it from her chair at work one evening. You had it ready to use, didn't you?"

"You've got that part wrong," he answered smugly. Indignantly, almost. "Blasingame was holding the scarf in his hand. I think he had it when he pushed Haapala. Anyway, he was definitely holding it in his hand as Haapala walked away."

"Is that the truth?" I asked.

"Absolutely."

I believed him. So Blasingame, too, had planned to frame somebody. The bastard deserved what he got.

"Okay, so you didn't plan to kill him."

"Righto. It was an accident."

"Not quite," I argued, shaking my head. "I said you didn't *plan* to kill him. The way I figure it, you watched him. That was easy for you to do. The two evening-shift foremen were your friends. In addition, you set good type behind the pillar. So you were able to wander around a lot: coffee breaks, doughnut breaks, lunch breaks. You were watching Blasingame the night he and Haapala met. You saw Blasingame try to push Haapala into the presses, then you saw Haapala walk away. That gave you the idea, Venable. You swung up on the rails and pushed—maybe with your feet—Blasingame to his death. You used your acrobatic skills to flip over the rails. Then you walked out the back door like Haapala had." Quickly, I glanced at his leg. "But you landed hard, didn't you?"

He nodded, watching me. "Twisted the hell out

of my leg. Luckily it was the game one. Who would notice?"

I had noticed that his limp had been getting better—but it wasn't until I saw Jack Morton's hanging photographs that it all came together. "Still," I said, "you were scared. You must have decided almost immediately to frame Suzanne. Didn't you?"

"I didn't want to," protested Venable, as if frameup were worse than murder. "But I had to protect myself."

"So you set a dirty copy with her code on it."

"Dirty proof," he corrected automatically. "It was the best I could do on short notice."

"That isn't all you did. You set the story twice. The second tape—the one that Lee Hubbard found hanging on the pegboard—that went to the cops."

"Insurance," explained Venable.

"Uh-huh. Why Suzanne? Why not Hubbard or Morton?"

Venable looked horrified. "I told you, Dragovic! I'm loyal to my friends."

"Right. So the only other person who qualified was Suzanne—because she's a gymnast."

With an absentminded nod of agreement, he took a step back from the couch.

"Don't jump me yet," I cautioned.

His eyebrows shot up into his hairline. He must have thought I was a real chump.

"I want to know the whole story. What did you do after you pushed Blasingame?"

"I went straight to Haapala's office. His desk was a snap to get into. I scooped up the package of tapes and put them in my locker. Then I set the dirty proof on the Colorado travel story."

"When did you kill Ruby?" I asked.

"It was an accident."

"That won't wash. She was shot twice."

Flexing his hands again, Venable kept his eyes on me. "The next morning I called her up, told her not to come to work, that somebody had found out about the blackmail."

"Go on," I prodded. Behind me, I imagined that I heard the video recorder running.

"I went to Ruby's. I told her I had the tapes and that I would be her new partner."

"Ruby objected," I guessed.

"She said she could do it herself. I didn't like that she said that to me. She'd go in with Blasingame but not with me."

I could sense his renewed anger at Ruby Good. "Why not?" I asked.

He was silent, considering. "I see no need to tell you."

"Let me guess. She taunted you. Maybe because you weren't one of her customers. Maybe," I said, watching him closely, "she said that you preferred men to women."

His hands clenched into fists. "She laughed," was all he said. "She laughed at me."

"Still, you brought the gun from Suzanne's locker with you—that's premeditation, Venable."

He laughed harshly. "No. I didn't have the gun with me that night—never thought of it. I told Ruby to stay home from work the next night, that I'd make her a better offer. Then I took Suzanne's gun from her locker—and a few red hairs from her chair. *That's* premeditation, Dragovic."

"Why did you steal Hubbard's car to help Suzanne escape?"

"You. I didn't trust you. You didn't believe Suzanne was guilty. You were always around, asking questions. So I figured she'd dig herself a deeper hole by escaping."

"Um-hmm. Why Hubbard's car?"

"It would complicate things more, in case she was found. Lee wouldn't get in any trouble—he was clean."

Maybe. And maybe Venable subconsciously wanted Hubbard, too, to fall under suspicion. I stared at him, waiting for his next move.

He seemed to be gazing at the wall opposite my head. When he spoke, it was as if he were coming back from a far distance. "You figured it out. That's why the cops were at my apartment, looking for the tapes. You told them. Damn you, Dragovic! I had intended to make a one-shot haul with those tapes: five thousand dollars per customer. That would have been close to two hundred thousand dollars." I could sense his anger mounting as he thought about the money. "Lucky for me I read about my impending arrest, Dragovic. Unlucky for you."

"The story didn't give your name."

"How—" He stammered. "How—the story isn't out yet. How . . . it . . . you . . ."

"Uh-huh. It was a trap, Venable. I wrote the story, then I watched the newsroom and saw you come up. I was certain you wouldn't believe the story unless you could check it out."

First in surprise, then in fury, he studied me. "So you did this to drag a confession out of me."

"I wouldn't say 'drag.' You've spoken quite freely. And by the way," I added, watching him rise on the balls of his feet, "the whole thing has been taped—video, that is. And the cops are downstairs, waiting for my call."

That was when he vaulted the couch and flew at

me, feet first. Since I'd been expecting it, I dodged out of his way. But the coffee table behind me blocked me, and Venable's flying feet hit my shoulder. The impact was so hard that I thought he had dislocated it. We fell across the table—books and plants flying everywhere, Venable on top of me, his hands grabbing for my throat. Rolling over, I took him with me. We landed on the floor and both sprang to our feet. Venable ran at me like a ram, butting me backward. Crashing against my bookcase, we bounced away from it. The bookcase began to sway: I thought we'd both be buried under an avalanche of books. It toppled and we jumped apart.

The next thing I knew, Suzanne was there, and before I could even blink at that fact, she had jumped on Venable, straddling him from behind. Bending, he flipped her off and threw her against me. I stumbled backward over the fallen bookcase, Suzanne with me.

That gave Venable time to reach the balcony door. Unlocking it, he jerked it open and was out on the balcony and over the railing as Suzanne and I disentangled and ran after him.

"Jesus!" I breathed, watching him scramble down the railings. "Watch where he goes," I ordered Suzanne, turning to run out the apartment door and down the stairs.

"Frank, no! There's no time!"

And before I could stop her, she was over the railing, following Venable.

I looked at the door to the hallway and stairs. I looked down at the swimming pool, thirty feet below me. I looked at Venable, who had landed on the concrete patio with a slight jarring of his body, and at Suzanne, who was close behind him. Stepping over the railing, I cautiously lowered myself to the balcony below me.

By the time I reached the third-floor balcony, Venable was vaulting over the poolside fence, heading west. Beyond him lay the Treasure Island parking lot, Treasure Island, and Wells Street. By the time I reached the second floor balcony, Suzanne was following him.

"Dragan!" I shouted at the top of my lungs. "Dragan!" Landing on the concrete floor of the pool deck, I discovered to my surprise that I was still in one piece.

Compared to descending the balconies, vaulting the fence was a breeze. Suzanne was turning the corner at Treasure Island, heading south on Wells. I looked behind me, back toward the back door of the apartment building, and saw the cop stationed there. "Follow them, for chrissake!" I shouted, motioning with my hand. Increasing my speed, I glanced back: the cop was following me.

Turning south on Wells, I spotted a commotion across the street. Venable had apparently bumped into some Friday evening strollers, who had grabbed him in anger. He broke free just as Suzanne got there. As she ran after him, I shortened the distance by taking the diagonal across the street, dodging a slow-moving car looking for a late-night parking place.

"Go, Red!" somebody shouted after Suzanne.

Venable ran south, dodging cars as he crossed North Avenue. The short-legged lie was running a hell of a lot faster than I thought it could. By putting on a burst of speed, I narrowed the gap between Suzanne and myself, just as she narrowed the gap between herself and Venable. And then, on the east side of Wells Avenue, I noticed another running figure: Dragan. I glanced over my shoulder. The other cop was still behind me. There was no doubt, I thought, but that one of us would catch Venable. I wanted it to be me.

Ahead of me, Venable took a sharp right into a narrow gap between two four-flats. Suzanne followed him, and I was practically on top of her heels. "Let me by," I huffed.

Naturally she didn't.

Venable looked back once, then jumped high, grabbing the bottom of a fire escape on one of the buildings. Shouldering Suzanne aside, I leaped forward, catching Venable's short but powerful legs as he tried to hoist himself onto the fire escape. Together we hung there—me pulling downward, Venable pulling upward.

Suzanne jumped and caught the bottom of the railing beside me. Unencumbered, she pulled herself up to the fire escape. I looked up just in time to watch her jump hard on Venable's hands.

The two of us fell, but this time I managed to get out of his way. He landed on his side, his elbow catching the impact of the fall. I heard it crack.

Dragan huffed to a stop behind us. "What?" he breathed.

Joe Flynn came running and stopped alongside Dragan.

"Okay, Frank. Where'd he come from?" demanded Dragan, breathing hard and pointing at Venable, who sat holding his elbow, his head bent into his knees.

"You found the tapes in his apartment?" I asked, trying hard to breathe evenly.

"Yeah. They radioed in that they found them. Where'd he come from?" he repeated, pointing at Venable. "Did you have him in your apartment?

What the hell were you doing? And why the hell did we have to run half-way to the South side?"

I patted Dragan's slight gut. "Good for the gut, Dragan."

He glared at me.

"Okay, okay." I briefly told him what I had done with the fake story, and with the videotape.

Dragan listened, then gave a flick of his head to Joe Flynn. Flynn cuffed Venable, then radioed for a patrol car.

We waited in silence for the car. When it came, Dragan sent Flynn back to the station with Venable. Then he looked up at the fire escape above us. There was nobody in sight.

"You can come down now," he said.

Only silence greeted him.

"Come on, I know you're up there," he said impatiently. "I could hardly miss you running down the street."

"Suzanne," I said. "Come on."

She stepped forward so we both could see her. I motioned for her to come down. She dropped from the fire escape to the alleyway, landing in front of Dragan, her red hair bouncing.

Dragan looked at her. Then he looked at me. He grasped the part of his nose just between his eyes and breathed deeply. Finally, he spoke. "You helped her escape from jail."

I protested. "I did not!"

"He didn't!" Suzanne said earnestly. "Adrian did."

Again Dragan pinched his nose and breathed deeply. "Okay. But she was in your apartment."

"Dragan," I implored. "You searched my apartment."

"You're playing games," said Dragan. "I'm going

to figure it out. I'm going to figure it out, Frank, and then I'm going to be pissed!"

"No, you aren't," I said—leaving unclear what he wasn't going to do: figure it out or be pissed off about it. "Don't you want to see the videotape?" I asked.

"What videotape?" he demanded.

"The videotape with Venable's confession. He broke into my apartment: I confronted him and got the whole thing on tape."

"A setup," he grumbled.

"You've never staged a setup, Dragan?" I demanded.

He looked at Suzanne; he looked at me. He looked at the fire escape, then back at Suzanne, then back at me.

I put my arm around his shoulder. "C'mon. I think you want the tape as evidence."

We walked back to my apartment in silence.

Dragan looked at my living room. The bookcase lay across the couch. Books were strewn over the floor, couch, and coffee table. A cactus plant had been knocked off the table and out of its pot. Wet potting soil was scattered over the floor. I stooped to pack the soil back into the planter. As he stood there, looking around, I could almost hear his brain whirring. Then he walked over to the philodendron, parted its leaves, and pulled out the video camera. "Let's see the tape," he demanded.

Shoving some books aside, he made himself comfortable on the couch. Then he looked at Suzanne. Clearing aside more books, he motioned that she should sit beside him. She did. Maybe I should offer them buttered popcorn.

I got the tape set up and turned on the television.

Dragan and Suzanne sat and watched. I stood and watched.

When the tape got to the part where Venable jumped me, I turned off the television. "Well?" I asked Dragan.

For reply, he stood up, pushed me aside, and turned the television back on.

"Hey!" I protested, reaching for the knob.

But he brushed me aside and stood there and watched until he saw the picture of Suzanne coming out of the hallway and jumping Venable. He watched the rest of the scuffling, then saw us run out the balcony door. After that, the camera showed only my broken and battered living room.

"She was here all along," he said.

"No!" Suzanne protested. "I was in the bedroom, but I had just come in tonight. From the *Truth*—after I typed the story for Frank."

"Right," said Dragan, pinching his nose and breathing deeply. He stood that way for maybe three, four minutes. Finally, he removed the video cassette from the recorder on top of the unit, stepped over my bookcase and walked toward the door.

I followed him. Suzanne followed me.

Dragan turned. *"Laku noć,"* he said to me. "Good night."

"Laku noć," I replied.

He opened the door, then turned around and pointed a finger at Suzanne. "You. Be at headquarters tomorrow morning. Eight sharp."

"What for?" she demanded.

"So I can let you out of jail, damn it!" Turning, he stalked out of the apartment, leaving the door open behind him.

I stared at Suzanne. She stared back solemnly, then gave a tentative smile. I smiled back.

Stepping closer, she wrapped her arms around my waist and hugged me—hard, of course, with enough force to crack a rib or two. But that was Suzanne. "Thank you," she said.

I smiled and walked to the balcony. I slid the door closed and locked it. Then I walked back to the foyer and closed the door softly. The case was closed.

Reading—
For The
Fun Of It

Ask a teacher to define the most important skill for success and inevitably she will reply, "the ability to read."

But millions of young people never acquire that skill for the simple reason that they've never discovered the pleasures books bring.

That's why there's RIF—Reading is Fundamental. The nation's largest reading motivation program, RIF works with community groups to get youngsters into books and reading. RIF makes it possible for young people to have books that interest them, books they can choose and keep. And RIF involves young people in activities that make them want to read—**for the fun of it.**

The more children read, the more they learn, and the more they **want** to learn.

There are children in your community—maybe in your own home—who need RIF. For more information, write to:

RIF
Dept. BK-3
Box 23444
Washington, D.C.
20026

Founded in 1966, RIF is a national, nonprofit organization with local projects run by volunteers in every state of the union.

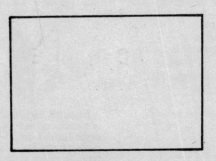